Dark Garden Days

*For my family, here and remembered,
and friends who have shared joys, sorrows,
love and laughter with luminous generosity*

…for hope is always born at the same time as love…

– MIQUEL DE CERVANTES, *DON QUIXOTE*

Chapter 1

Gabrielle and Jonathan

Shadows of bare tree limbs grew long and menacing in the last light of evening and crawled over parched flower stems with blossoms bent and withered as the heads of dozing ancients. The shade crept silently upward, along Gabrielle's back, encircling her neck as if choking her. She didn't seem to notice though, even when fingers of darkness clutched her palette and brush, and she continued painting at an old easel in the garden.

From the kitchen window, Jonathan could see Gabrielle's canvas held harsh colors and dark silhouettes so he didn't call to her but began preparing dinner instead. Though he was no artist, he had always believed there weren't any hues which couldn't be placed together in a work of art. But, whenever he noticed her painting in the autumn garden, as he had several times recently and at the same time last year, the colors appearing on her canvas were always inexplicably incompatible.

He rubbed a beef tenderloin with Dijon mustard mixed with chopped basil and parsley and placed it under the broiler then glanced out into the garden, unaware of how long he remained there, watching her, until the timer went off. It was nearly dark but Jonathan's eyes had adjusted to it and he could still see her. He continued to move about the kitchen in the illumination of the stove's clock, not wanting to switch on a light just yet, not wanting the perception of an imperative.

Hunger stormed through him in thunderous rumblings so he cut up fontal cheese and placed honey in a condiment bowl next to it. Dipping a piece, he pictured the café in Piazza del Campo, in Sienna, where he and friends had tasted this combination for the first time. After a second piece, too tempted, he carried the cheese board to the dining room table and left it there with a bottle of wine to avoid eating the entire thing himself.

Next, he poured a blend of scallions sautéed in wine and butter over a split loaf of country bread and placed it in the oven, removing the tenderloin to a platter to rest, and returned to the sink to wash romaine for a salad. A check of the garden brought a feeling of relief, since Gabrielle was gathering her things to come in. Jonathan put the romaine on salad plates, adding sliced almonds, mandarin oranges and a little of the uncooked scallions and began making a light French dressing. Each task and detail of preparation was a pleasant distraction.

The metallic sound of sharpening his knife to slice the tenderloin was just beginning to cause a nails-on-blackboard jaw tightening when the door between Gabrielle's studio and the back entrance hall opened with a piercing creak, painful duet of knife and hinge. He had been meaning to oil it for months now and made a mental note, for at least the third time, to do it right after dinner. Whistling to alert her of his presence, a thoughtful but wasted gesture since the house was filled with inviting aromas and a little smoke from the broiler, he switched on the kitchen light.

Gabrielle stepped into the dining room so quietly Jonathan wasn't sure, at first, if the sound he heard was her voice calling his name softly or the draft entering with her. Her gaze was far away and she almost whispered, "Hello, Jonathan."

"Hi Brie," a gentle reply from the kitchen so there was no immediate demand for conversation. Just as he anticipated, she said nothing else and began setting the table, three place settings, and decanted the wine. Jonathan was always fascinated by the way Gabrielle placed the dishes, napkins and every piece of silverware with almost a caress to each one. No matter the mood, there seemed to be something pleasing to her about the rare occasions when their schedules allowed her and Jonathan and Jesse to have a meal together, at home. Even on the days when she seemed distracted and didn't contribute as much to the conversation, there was a noticeable contentment and she would listen and smile, glancing from one to the other as they talked.

Gabrielle dipped a piece of cheese in the honey and closed her eyes to appreciate the unfamiliar and tantalizing pairing, touching a forefinger and middle finger to her lips and smiling.

Jonathan removed the bread from the oven as Jesse arrived home just in time for dinner, always an event. He was a gifted pediatric dentist, whose fingers could work miracles in the tiniest of mouths, but coming through the door and negotiating the path to the closet to hang his coat, without crashing and breakage, was always an insurmountable challenge. Perhaps it was his size, just five feet nine inches but with a broad, muscular build making him seem considerably larger when entering a room or fitting into smaller spaces. Or, maybe it was because he usually had an armful of charts, keys, bags of new CD's and videos he was always buying to amuse his young patients along with his ever-present iced tea bottle.

Between them, Gabrielle and Jonathan had purchased what was now an impressive collection of brief cases and back packs for him, as gifts, but Jesse never seemed to be comfortable utilizing any of them. In response to the curiosity of a friend who opened the closet in his bedroom and discovered the leathery herd, he'd answered honestly, "I admire people who can carry them well but, for me, briefcases feel like pretension in a way and backpacks are something to become entangled in or to forget somewhere."

As Jesse entered the kitchen, his shoulder hit the edge of the calendar they all used as a way to communicate about their schedules, popping the push pins from the cork board that held it. Bending to pick them up, the tip of his Eeyore umbrella caught the basket of bread Jonathan had just placed on the counter and flipped it off the edge into Jonathan's ready hands. Jesse yelped and stood up suddenly, from the surprise of sticking himself with one of the pushpins he was trying to retrieve from the floor just under the refrigerator. While he sucked on his injured finger, his empty iced tea bottle rolled across the room as he unknowingly dropped his keys onto the swinging top of the garbage can.

Jonathan glanced at Gabrielle, who was standing in the doorway between the kitchen and dining room. Smiling at each other, they watched the keys slide slowly into the trash, as Jesse continued to the closet unaware of the bread basket, iced tea bottle or the keys.

Now Jesse called out, "Hi, you two!" then turned around and stepped on the empty bottle, producing a loud "crack" and an amusing look of confusion.

Fond memories of their college days came back to Jonathan. He shook his head and laughed, recalling Jesse's books always spilling from his arms and papers scattering across the campus in some personal Jesse turbulence. Add to this the numerous injuries, from looking in one direction, usually related to the female gender, while walking in another and colliding with inconsiderate trees and architecture. He was an unexpected wind gust and pleasant breeze all at once.

They sat down to eat and, as the conversation began, so did the choreography of keeping things away from Jesse's expressive and enthusiastic gestures, like moving a child's milk glass slightly out of reach. Both Jonathan and Gabrielle participated in this little table dance without even being aware of it.

The conversation jumped from one subject to another as they discussed some of what had happened in the world since they last sat down together for a meal. It began lightly with Dan Marino setting the NFL touchdown passing record and the Dow Jones closing over five thousand for the first time. But then it took a bleak turn as they talked about the assassination of Yitzhak Rabin, Prime Minister of Israel, and the death of sixteen people in a suicide bombing of the Egyptian Embassy in Islamabad, as they noted seven months had passed since the Oklahoma City bombing.

"It's so unspeakably sad to learn of the atrocities committed in the name of some misguided concept or belief or out of an unconscionable desire for money and power in every part of this world," Gabrielle uttered and then they ate in silence for a while.

"I saw her…last night…walking a little white dog," Jesse opened the conversation again, feeling he wanted to lighten the subject and mood of this dinnertime together they so seldom got to enjoy.

"Who?" Gabrielle responded politely, already knowing the answer but not quite ready for this discussion again. As she asked the question, she moved his wine goblet back a bit further in anticipation of an animated response.

"She looks so much like her and has this great smile and a kind of bouncy, ambling walk. I know. I know! Please don't look at me with that 'poor pathetic Jesse' expression! I promise myself I'm going to try to be attracted to some other type of woman but it just doesn't happen."

Jesse was twenty-nine years old, successful, sweet, funny and really good looking, with brown eyes flecked with gold and laughter. His one flaw, which left him single and dateless, was his hopeless obsession with Meg Ryan, not thinking he could have her but obsessed with finding someone just like her.

Until 1989, when he saw her for the first time in "*When Harry Met Sally,*" his dating life could be described as relatively limited, since he was always extremely shy and painfully awkward when trying to meet someone new. Jonathan understood this was because Jesse had attended all-male private academies for both his elementary and high school education. Jesse often referred to this fact as his dad's 'Sins of the father' syndrome – no way his son was going to be the wild child he had been. Many hilarious and a few nearly disastrous adventures occurred during his college years, whenever Jonathan and Jesse's other friends decided to do interventions to help him overcome his intensive fear of meeting women. Falling "in love" with Meg Ryan placed even greater negative odds on his dating probabilities.

For a while, Jonathan thought Jesse had outgrown his infatuation but, in 1994, Ryan starred in "*When a Man Loves a Woman,*" won the Harvard Hasty Pudding award as Woman of the Year, was nominated for a Golden Globe for "*Sleepless *in Seattle*" so it all started again. Then, last May, Gabrielle agreed to go to the movies with Jesse to see "*French Kiss*" and he was, once again, hopelessly smitten by the time the opening airplane scene was over. Only half joking, Jonathan called Gabrielle an enabler.

Since then, when not caring for his little patients, playing his guitar or one of the sports he loved, Jesse's life was this unending and, thus far, futile quest to find his own Meg Ryan. If you didn't know him, this might seem scary or strange but it was really just like him to devote himself so completely and clumsily to it.

"Jesse," Gabrielle began gently, "maybe, if you actually dated one of the women you've been attracted to, you might find you don't really care whether or not she's exactly like Meg." They all called the star 'Meg' now, casually, as if she were an old friend. "You could be missing someone absolutely perfect for you. And, anyway, unless you intend to hire a live-in script writer, director and make-up artist, any woman, including Meg herself, is destined to disappoint you. Eventually she is going to do something…"

"Like speak!" Jonathan interjected a little louder and more sarcastically than he intended.

Gabrielle shot a look at Jonathan and continued. "Why don't you just walk right up to this new person, introduce yourself and invite her to dinner or, if that seems too long a time for the first meeting, then for coffee, or ice cream or something?"

"Okay, I'll think about it. I'm sorry I brought it up! I see her in the town green all the time and just keep hoping proximity will bring some coincidental reason to start a conversation. Now, can we change the subject, please? This meat is delicious and so is the bread. Who cooked?"

Jonathan raised an eyebrow, tipped his head and smirked and Jesse said, "Well, it could happen…someday." And they all laughed because Gabrielle knew nothing about the kitchen or cooking, although, she was always a willing participant in the cleaning up afterward.

"Oh, before I forget, I spoke with Sean today and he scheduled a driver for us for the December clinics but it's going to cost between eighteen-hundred and two-thousand dollars for the liability insurance on the truck and the December and July clinics if we cover them together – much more if we do it separately," Jesse groaned a little as he spoke. "It seems like a lot of money for just four weeks of coverage in total but I gave him the go ahead because we really don't have a choice."

Every year, for a week in December and three weeks in July, they went on the road to bring medical and dental care to underprivileged and uninsured children in inner cities and rural areas of the New England states and New York where they both maintained professional licenses. Sometimes, this involved medical care for children whose parents were uninsured or unable to negotiate the paperwork needed to acquire coverage under existing programs. For those families they provided assistance with forms and information for the future along with the treatment. But often the problem was parents with immigration issues who needed to remain anonymous. At the clinics, there were no questions asked, just compassionate care for the children. Word travelled quickly and there had been a marked increase in patients coming from other states as well.

An old tandem trailer truck Jesse and Jonathan converted to a dental and medical clinic on wheels, and the driver were provided by Erin and Sean Mulligan, who owned a moving company called "On the Road Again." The Mulligan's four children became patients of Jesse's when he opened his pediatric dental practice and the entire family had just become patients in Jonathan's family practice within the last year. The couple's limitless generosity contributed enormously to the creation of the clinic on wheels.

Except for the truck, driver and occasional contributions from family and friends, Jesse and Jonathan paid for everything themselves. They didn't wish it to turn into a charitable foundation limited by unreasonable administrative costs and soliciting of funds. Jonathan loathed receiving mailings from the ones which waste money and trees on address labels and other enclosures and constantly harass the people who have already given. Every penny went directly toward the cost of medical supplies and transportation. The only salaries paid were to Jesse's dental hygienist, who did teeth cleanings and initial screenings, and Jonathan's nurse assistant, who did triage. Jesse and Jonathan felt they had to do something and this was, simply, a private way to give back.

While they admired their professional colleagues who travelled to Third World countries to bring medical care, Jesse and Jonathan felt they couldn't overlook the underprivileged who existed all around them, nearly invisible behind the façade of wealth and advantage that defines the United States to so many.

During the December clinics, they took a week off from their own practices but, for the three weeks in July, Jesse and Jonathan would fly or drive between the location of the clinic and their own practices seeing patients for sixteen to eighteen hours a day, bringing more serious cases back to their offices.

Gabrielle had accompanied them the previous July, assisting with paperwork and errands and helped them paint and redecorate the trailers to be more appealing to the children. She also surprised them by bringing art supplies, drinks and snacks, followed by toothbrushes, and setting up an activity area outside. The distraction helped time pass unnoticed, encouraging people to stay who might have become impatient with the long wait and left without receiving treatment. In addition, she collected food, toiletries, jackets and sneakers, which were distributed to the parents and children once they finished their care, another incentive to stay or come back if work couldn't be completed in one visit.

Because she might not be available for the December clinics, Gabrielle had already collected art supplies, snacks, small gifts and items of clothing and food. She also arranged with local colleges and high schools, along the scheduled route, to provide students as volunteers to aid Jonathan and Jesse in the clinics, while helping them fulfill their community service requirements. Jesse and Jonathan were surprised and very grateful, when they learned about Gabrielle's thoughtful arrangements.

"Have I ever heard the story of how you two met and became friends?" Gabrielle asked, immediately embarrassed by her own abrupt and obvious change of subject, but more uncomfortable with the praise. She was also trying to make a conscious effort to appear less distracted and really interested in the personal details of their lives before she knew them. She only learned about them during these infrequent dinner conversations and always looked forward to the next revelation.

She sat back slightly, sipping the last of her wine and savoring the flavors of blackberry and red currant she discovered in it. When the glass was empty, she held it up toward the chandelier, admiring how the light danced along the delicate crystal. Colors - prisms - white light interpreted by retinal cones and nesting in quiet places in the brain to be reprised and shared, paintbrush on canvas. Realizing she was distracted again, she started to put the wine glass down and attempted to refocus on the conversation. "I don't remember hearing you talk about it before." When she took hold of the rim to place it carefully on the table, the wine glass sang as her fingers let go of it and just as she finished her question, turning it into a musical accompaniment.

Charmed by the gift of the beautiful sound and her smile, Jonathan finished his wine and tried to duplicate the song on his own glass and Jesse did the same. The mood was light and happier as Jesse poured more wine for them all.

Jonathan was distracted by Gabrielle's delight and couldn't remember what her question had been before they started playing with the wine glasses. "What did you ask me? Oh, yes, about how Jesse and I met and became friends." He ate a few quick bites, drank some wine and then went on to explain, "We met while we were in college and, even when Jesse went off to Tuft's dental school, in Massachusetts, and I went to medical school in Maine, Jesse spent many holidays, vacations and summers with my family."

Jonathan was one of five children in a wild, wonderful household. They were a family who struggled financially at times but there was always joy, kindness and generosity in his home. Jonathan recalled some moments he hadn't appreciated as a child. "One vivid memory I have is of my father, a hardworking machinist, watching me and my siblings finish, too quickly, our sometimes, meager dinner and suddenly declaring he was full. His chair scraped loudly on the linoleum floor as he rose to his great height to serve little portions of his remaining dinner onto each of our plates."

Jonathan had been an only child until his sixth birthday. His mother was pregnant and confined to bed so they settled for a small party at home. She went into labor during the celebration, although she hadn't realized, at first, the discomfort she felt was significant. After the birthday cake and presents, discomfort became contractions and she was rushed to the hospital by ambulance giving birth, prematurely, to quadruplets, two sets of identical twins, Caleb and Colin, Cassy and Carly, only one hour after arriving on the maternity floor.

In another home, five children sharing the same birthday and four of them sharing the same first letter for their names might have been cause for jealousy and resentment but Jonathan's mother and father presented the tiny babies as precious gifts who chose to be born on their big brother's birthday. So, as they began arriving home, one at a time, Jonathan came to cherish them as much as his parents did. However, once they began crawling and then walking, Jonathan would occasionally hide in his room with the door locked just to get away from the intrusion of four little bodies trying to climb on him, forty curious fingers grabbing and touching his games or projects.

Although he wouldn't admit it out loud, Jonathan's favorite was Cassy, the tiniest of the babies and last to come home. Even at six, he sensed her frailty and watched over her. Although she was quite precocious and began speaking at ten months, long before her siblings, physically she had a poor appetite and was unable to crawl or sit up by herself.

Physical therapy hadn't helped and there was no definitive diagnosis, except for a vague and frustrating "failure to thrive." Their parents, who were constantly searching for answers and help, were told about an osteopathic physician who worked with children with low muscle tone and related problems and they immediately scheduled an evaluation.

Until learning of this doctor they were unaware that there were two distinct kinds of full physicians in the United States, M.D.s and D.O.s. Cassy was eleven months old by the time they took her for the initial appointment with the doctor. Jonathan had insisted on going with them for the visit, a touching sign of his devotion to her.

From the first osteopathic manual medicine treatment and cranial work, combined with a home exercise program and a diet created by a nutritionist the doctor referred them to, Jonathan's parents began to see an improvement, a toning and strengthening. Within two months she began sitting by herself and crawling. By nineteen months old, though still very small compared to her siblings, Cassy caught up with her brothers and sister in walking and climbing and remained far ahead of them in talking, a chatty and very funny toddler who understood her power to enchant, especially her older brother.

The experience of witnessing Cassy's progress shaped Jonathan's desire to be an osteopathic physician at a very young age. He became fascinated with the combination of allopathic, osteopathic, and natural medicine applied by their doctor to help Cassy. He also observed how thorough, yet kind, the doctor had been as he questioned his parents about Cassy, listening carefully to their answers and concerns. Every symptom and occurrence, even seemingly insignificant ones, were important components of the doctor's diagnoses and recommendations for treatment, the osteopathic philosophy of whole-body health. Jonathan's solo family practice had grown beyond his expectations, in the last year and a half, and he was very content with the choice he'd made.

"When Jesse came to stay for the first time," Jonathan explained to Gabrielle, "my sisters and brothers were just turning thirteen and it was a household of adolescent moodiness, homework, comings and goings for various sports events and music and dance lessons, in short..."

"...a madhouse but a wonderfully amusing and loving one," Jesse interrupted, "I think I spent the entire first weekend just sitting with my mouth open, not at all sure how to participate in the constant activity and, for me, confusion. It was so much to take in but a great deal of fun and I loved watching and listening to the interactions and teasing. I have no siblings so I never experienced anything like it."

Gabrielle sighed and nodded slightly, seeming to second his thought, then sipped the last bit of her wine and encouraged them to continue. She was genuinely absorbed now in learning the stories and memories that shaped the close and, often, comical friendship Jesse and Jonathan shared.

Jonathan tried to focus on finishing his story as he watched Gabrielle tilt her head revealing her lovely neck and just a touch of cleavage above her loosely buttoned tunic shirt, "In the years that followed, Jesse became like a member of our family" Jonathan finally managed to say.

Gabrielle turned to Jesse, "What was your growing up like?"

Jesse, the only child of divorced parents, began to speak about his own childhood and, as Gabrielle listened, Jonathan tried to focus his attention on Jesse. He was distracted though, as he recalled the disturbing mood of her painting, before coming into the house for dinner, sure it was a harbinger of dark days ahead. There was a chilling aspect to her sitting for hours in the shadows and biting air staring at the canvas with uncharacteristic cheerlessness which caused a profound worry and sadness in him. And sometimes, when a despondent mist joined the shadows and dead flowers, he imagined the Headless Horseman appearing out of the melancholy and carrying her away. Coming out of his own thoughts, Jonathan realized Jesse had been speaking for some time and tried to catch up with the conversation.

"I grew up splitting my life, per a custody agreement, between my parents, six months with each. I stayed with the house and they moved in and out, so it was always me and one adult.

After six months with one parent, the other would move in and immediately begin to reorganize everything, rules, schedules, contents of drawers and closets and even the arrangement of the lawn furniture. I lost track, long ago, of how the house was arranged originally and who had actually started it. Even though this seemed to offset the supposed benefit of not changing me from one house to another, at some point, it became a great source of amusement to me. I would move things around too, even hanging pictures upside down, delighting in the added disorder and trying very hard, I think, to be a part of the illusive mystery of my parent's relationship.

My mother, Tessa, an orthodontist and my father, Michael, a general dentist shared a practice until the divorce. Afterward, they continued their individual practices several towns away from each other, still referring patients once in a while. When I decided to pursue dentistry as a career, influenced, I'm certain, by hanging out in my parent's offices and playing with dental instruments, I made it very clear I wouldn't be joining either of them because it was time to separate myself a bit and, anyway, a choice would have been impossible."

He would sometimes detect, in his parent's interactions, a sense of playfulness and flirting and, since neither had ever remarried and he never understood why they had divorced in the first place, he continued, even into adulthood, to believe they would someday be a couple again.

Jesse added to Jonathan's earlier story about his visits with the Blake family. "With each stay at Jonathan's home, I became more acquainted with the dynamic of tormenting him in collusion with his sisters and brothers and it was great fun and a bit of payback for Jonathan joining my friends in harassing me about meeting women all through college…"

"…and, so, he introduced my family to *The Waltons* and taught my brothers and sisters the exaggerated and sugary 'Goodnight Jon Boy' for bedtime. Even now, when I leave a family gathering, sleep over or end a conversation with one of my siblings on the phone, it continues."

Gabrielle laughed in response, enjoying both the stories and the way they finished each other's sentences, as if they were twins too.

"So, enough about Jonathan and me, what's up with you? Any new commissions?" Jesse felt they had talked about themselves far too long and wanted to bring Gabrielle into the conversation, not understanding, as Jonathan did, today she was more comfortable just listening.

She sipped slowly from her water glass, giving herself time to decide how to reply, "Well, I'm going away for a bit…leaving tomorrow morning, actually…"

Whenever Gabrielle spent time in the dead garden, her painting changed and sometimes occasioned a going off somewhere. Unlike her usual travel for her work when they always knew her destination and when to expect her return, these trips were abrupt and as incomprehensible as the colors on her canvas. Jonathan wished he could encourage her not to go but said nothing.

"And, then, I do have a new commission to paint another ceiling and some wall murals for Emory," Gabrielle continued.

With that, they all laughed heartily and raised their water glasses in a mock toast. "To Emory and his endless supply of ceilings and walls."

On this late-November evening in 1995, as the three enjoyed their dinner together and raised their glasses to Emory, Gabrielle had the pleasure of telling Jonathan and Jesse, "The new murals I'll be painting are not commissioned because Emory and Cara are moving again. It's because they're expecting a baby, in the Spring, a girl at last!" Gabrielle smiled, gratified by the look of obvious shock, followed by delight on their faces and happy Cara finally gave her permission to share the news she kept to herself for so long. Apparently, they had no idea, while Gabrielle guessed only weeks after Cara knew and shared the secret until Cara felt confident the pregnancy was going well. Because of several miscarriages in the last few years, she didn't even want to tell Emory until completing her first trimester, wanting to avoid the sadness of yet another disappointment.

Emory, who was forty-nine, and Cara, who was twelve years younger, began to lose hope of ever having a daughter and so, in honor of her surprising and happily-anticipated arrival, they decided they wanted Gabrielle to paint murals on the walls and ceiling of the nursery.

The night was an endless one for Jonathan, who slept very little. He telephoned his secretary and asked her to move his patients to a later start so he would still be home when Gabrielle left. He needn't have changed his schedule, though, because she rose at dawn and was loading her car when he came downstairs at six. By the time she came back into the kitchen, Jonathan had hot chocolate in a travel mug and bottled water ready for her.

She loved the way he looked in the early morning, his straight brown hair, streaked with natural blond highlights, messy and standing in spikes and his jade green eyes, half opened like a sleepy child – a tall sleepy child since he was six-feet-three-inches with the exquisite build of a gymnast. His wire-framed glasses made him appear more like a college professor than an athlete though.

How funny it was, she had no idea what made her think of it just now, *that Jonathan had no nickname. He was always Jonathan to everyone, just Jonathan, a soft and gentle name, even when shouted, and so fitting.*

She started to say something but simply accepted the travel mug and water with a quiet, "Thank you, Jonathan...see you soon" and left. He stepped out onto the porch and watched her drive away.

Suddenly, Gabrielle stopped, placed the car in reverse and travelled, rather recklessly, down the road and back into the driveway. She jumped out of the still-running car, leaving the door wide open, ran to Jonathan and began in a rapid whisper, "If...if ever I don't return, read 'Don Quixote' and come for me on Marginal Way. Please don't tell anyone, not even Jesse. I'll find a way to meet you there someday...if I can...I love you, Jonathan." And, with that, she threw herself at him, kissing his neck, then, was gone before he had a chance to respond.

Jonathan stood, frozen, his heart pounding, trying to sort out her words as her car disappeared, the tightness in his chest he felt when they first met now a dreadful ache. Never, in spite of nearly six months of painful longing on his part, had they ever discussed having feelings for each other or touched for anything more than a hug. Why hadn't he grabbed hold of her and taken her in his arms? Why didn't he tell her what was in his heart? Or, try to persuade her not to leave?

After a moment, only slightly more clear-headed, he ran into the kitchen, grabbed his keys and jumped into his car, not remembering he was in slippers and dressed only in the sweat pants and tank top he'd thrown on to come downstairs. He didn't notice the November chill either and sped off in the direction she headed.

For almost three hours he searched for her everywhere, wishing he'd had been more persuasive when he tried to convince her she needed to carry a cell phone. He returned home with just enough time to take a shower and get to his office, so angry at himself he could barely function. Her ominous words "...if ever I don't return..." lodged somewhere between his brain and heart, a quiet, gentle man raged and smashed whatever came into reach then collapsed into a chair, with his face in his hands, and wept.

Chapter 2

Cara and Emory

Jonathan was the engaged and caring physician he always was while treating patients all day but, when evening came and he returned home, he was consumed with the mystery of Gabrielle's departure. Tonight, he was recalling their first meeting at Cara and Emory's home.

Emory Whittaker was a very successful real estate broker and developer and a savvy investor who seemed to have remained unaffected by the decline in the real estate market in the early nineties. And now, with unemployment at around five percent and the economy doing well things were more than comfortable.

He and his wife, Cara, were close friends of Gabrielle, Jonathan and Jesse. Emory had, in fact, sold Jonathan the house he and Jesse and Gabrielle lived in now and another property where Jonathan's office was located. Emory also introduced Gabrielle to them about a year and a half earlier.

Jesse and Jonathan went to Emory and Cara's new home on a dreadfully hot day, in July of 1994, to help move a valuable sculpture Emory hadn't allowed the movers to touch. He injured his back during the move, so Jesse and Jonathan were moving it for him and Jonathan was going to give Emory an osteopathic treatment for his back pain when they were finished. Emory needed to decide where the piece should go, so they put the sculpture down in the hallway and entered the library.

Straight ahead of them, as they entered, were a massive stone fireplace with an intricately-carved cherry mantelpiece and two very tall windows with window seats, whose carved fronts matched the mantel. Along both the right and left walls, to the ceiling height of sixteen feet, were cherry bookshelves, which went all the way to the end of the thirty-foot room on the left side. On the right, the shelves ended about fourteen feet from the far wall, leaving an alcove which housed a French Empire style, mahogany and leather writing desk across the corner, facing into the room. There was a large Italian, marble-topped library table just at the entrance and beyond that, closer to the fireplace, a sitting area containing six mammoth leather chairs and ottomans with pillows and inviting throws over each one.

Everything Emory did and loved was larger than life and, yet, there was a strange modesty about him. He had great wealth and definitely used it for his own pleasure but enjoyed the pleasure others found in it even more.

Only Cara recognized and understood his obsession with accumulating a fortune. It came from an unwillingness to acknowledge or touch Cara's massive trust. She came from an affluent family which had disapproved of Emory, who was abandoned and raised in orphanage care with no known lineage. Once they were married, without the blessing of her parents, he refused to let her use her money for any expenses related to running their household and caring for their sons. He insisted she use it for the things she desired and charitable contributions. In spite of having settled into a congenial relationship with her family and easing any apprehensions they had during the courtship, Emory would not compromise on this issue. Cara was exceedingly proud of his accomplishments but sometimes wished he could just accept their lifestyle in a more serene and relaxed spirit and not feel so privately apologetic and worried. She adored his wonderful capacity for loving and giving, a generous philanthropist who preferred to remain anonymous whenever possible.

Emory acquired this extensive library of books as part of an estate with the purchase of the house. Though he showed limited interest in reading earlier in life, he found a new passion and began to explore the world of literature like a child in a great wood, overcome by depth and possibilities.

Most interesting to Jesse and Jonathan was that, instead of traditional rolling library ladders for access to the higher shelves, there were what looked like cut down elevators, about three-and-a-half feet high, each with a gate, with carved acanthus leaves in cherry, on both sides of the room. Emory was proud to demonstrate his own design. A volume seeker would simply enter the "car" which measured about two-and-a-half-feet deep and four feet wide, and close the carved gate which provided safety from falling out. There was an On/Off switch and a sort of gear shift, also beautifully carved, which, when moved as labeled "Up, Down, Right, Left," navigated the hopeful reader along the wall of books to exactly where they wished to be. A fold-down shelf on one side could be lifted to become a table to place selections on for the return to ground level.

During the long renovation, Emory made his first trip up one of the pre-existing library ladders to look over the books and was so engrossed he lost his footing and almost plummeted to the floor. The certainty that their three sons would climb up the ladders as if they were jungle gyms and might have the same sort of mishap with far worse consequences precipitated the replacement of the old ladders with the cars.

Emory was making an effort to interest his sons in reading as well by enticing them with a ride on the library cars, first to choose one and then, upon completion of a book, to replace it and find another. Cara thought his idea was inspired but had a feeling the enthusiasm would be short-lived given the reading it required.

On the mantel, here and there on the bookshelves and in two huge antique curios on either side of the door they entered through, was Emory's collection of horse sculptures and bronzes, which included pieces by Frederic Remington, Patricia Crane, Jan Van Ek and a Degas. It was a room everyone longed to spend an entire rainy day in or, better still, an endless winter. Neither Jesse nor Jonathan knew who the sculptor of the new piece was, as they finally carried it in and placed it to the left of the fireplace, and Emory didn't say.

With so much to take in, neither Jonathan nor Jessie noticed an elaborate scaffold with rope pulleys to lower it until Emory looked up and called out "Gabrielle Benedict, this is Jonathan Blake and Jesse Terhune."

They both looked up as the artist, who was lying on the scaffolding painting something on the ceiling, turned her head and Jonathan was unable to take in a breath or take his eyes off her. She caught Jonathan's stare and immediately turned back to her work with a wave of her brush. Jonathan stood watching for a time, hoping she would turn her head once more. He had never seen eyes that color, not an empty and staring blue but the ocean off the Bahamas, vivid blue then blue-green all at once, with crystalline reflections of light, compelling even from the height of the ceiling.

Later, after a tour of the rest of the house, stables and gardens, Cara called to everyone to come have some lunch, insisting Gabrielle should climb down to join them as well.

As she came out to the patio, Jonathan was again unable to breathe but this time the symptom was accompanied by an intense tightness deep in his left chest. She was barefoot, carrying her sandals and wearing loose, gauzy white pants and shirt, with random smudges of paint on them. Her shirt was open and she wore a halter top, white with a design that looked like smudged paint so it was hard to distinguish the real paint from the fashion—an amusing and creative solution for occasions when her painting was interrupted by the request to join Cara and Emory and their frequent guests for lunch or dinner with no opportunity to change.

She was smiling at Cara and they were discussing the work being done on a screened gazebo adjacent to the patio and closer to the water view. This gave Jonathan a moment to see she was about five-feet-six-or-seven inches tall and had gleaming, straight, caramel hair pulled back in a loose French braid which fell almost to her waist. He was struck again by her eyes which were wide and vibrant, with long dark lashes.

Cara and Gabrielle approached the table and, when Gabrielle turned and met Jonathan's gaze, an age passed in a moment and Jonathan felt a beings most sorrowful depth and the strange certainty he knew her somehow. She started, then averted her eyes quickly and circled the table to her seat, a woman fully aware all eyes are on her, a girl desiring nothing more than to disappear. She didn't look at Jonathan again.

During lunch, Cara delighted in telling the story of how she and Emory had met Gabrielle, while on a trip to Europe. "Gabrielle spent a year wandering and painting her way around France. She painted at Cezanne's Aix-en-Provence, where Van Gogh painted the sunflower fields in Arles, and Monet's gardens in Giverny. She was working as a street painter during Festival d'Avignon, trying to earn enough money for her flight home, and painting her vision of Monet. It was from a combination of pictures she'd seen of him, with a slight paunch and a full white beard, and as described by an art critic, in 1904, dressed in '…a suit of beige-checked homespun, a blue silk pleated shirt, a tawny velvet hat and reddish leather boots.'"

Cara and Emory were strolling along the street watching the artists when they came upon Gabrielle. They assumed, from her name, she was French and began their conversation with her in what they thought was her native language. It took only a few sentences to realize they were all American. "Among her paintings, a breathtaking garden with what appeared to be a delicate sprite or spirit barely visible and easily missed, was our mutual favorite so we purchased it after an amusing reverse bargaining, with us offering then insisting on paying far more than she asked," Emory laughed as Cara said it.

"We became instant friends." Cara explained, "And, when I learned why Gabrielle was there selling her paintings for far too little, Emory and I insisted she accompany us on our return flight, easily arranged since we were flying with a group of friends on a chartered plane. Gabrielle came to stay with us while she painted two murals on the ceiling of the family room and the foyer in a previous home." Gabrielle said nothing during the telling and just sat listening, looking from one to the other with a smile."

"From then until this lunch, she has painted ceiling murals three other times, each time we've found another house we decided to live in." Emory laughed and then continued, "Before each move, I have painters come in to the house we're leaving and use paint remover and then sand and paint over the mural Gabrielle had painted, so no one else can have it. Then we commission her to paint another one in the new home."

"What?" Jesse and Jonathan both roared at the same moment, shocked at the idea of destroying a work of art so callously and selfishly and said so to Emory.

He laughed again saying, "Gabrielle understands and I always take pictures of them," but Jonathan glanced at her as he said it and thought, *perhaps not.*

Emory continued, seeming to ignore the implication of Jesse and Jonathan's reaction, "Gabrielle keeps suggesting that she paint them on something portable but I always feel I want a new painting to celebrate the change."

Being a broker, Emory had access to properties before they entered the market and bought houses like some people buy shoes. Cara would just sigh and say, "You know the things I won't compromise on," meaning it had to be on the water or with a water view and enough land for their horses and to assure complete privacy. If a property wasn't large enough to accommodate being allowed to have the horses, Emory had been known to buy out a neighbor or two, offering whatever price was too attractive to refuse to fulfill the requirement. "Beyond that, it's your decision," Cara would acquiesce and, with that, she and Emory, their three sons, two dogs, a cat, four horses and their housekeeper and her gardener/caretaker husband would move into a new house, as casually as if they were merely taking an afternoon stroll. They had lived on the Maine, New Hampshire and, now, Cape Cod coast.

In a quiet moment, Cara confessed to Gabrielle that this house, truly and for the first time, felt like home and she hoped, secretly, that Emory would come to feel the same about it. Gabrielle asked her why she didn't just tell Emory how she felt, her desire for permanency, but Cara just looked perplexed and didn't answer.

Now, Gabrielle was staying with them in their new home, creating a mural for the library ceiling and looking for a studio/apartment to rent, since she was becoming very fond of Cape Cod and wished to spend some time getting to know the landscapes and seascapes and painting them. Each trip, over the Sagamore or Bourne Bridge onto the Cape, felt like an excursion into a new, unique land to her and, yet, also a coming home.

Suddenly, Emory's face lit up as he turned to Jonathan, "Did you ever do anything with the studio addition on your house? If you're not using it for anything, I think it would be a perfect place for Gabrielle to rent."

Cara gasped, "Emory!" at his audacity and the embarrassing situation he might be placing their guests, strangers to each other, in but, after a brief and slightly awkward silence, they had all laughed. Cara knew Emory's intention was simply to find a safe and light-filled place for Gabrielle since she repeatedly refused their offers to create a space on their property.

Jonathan's home was a restored Tudor, on an acre of desirable waterfront property in Chatham. He answered Emory by admitting that, for all his intentions to fix it up and do something with it, it remained untouched. "I hadn't really considered renting it but it certainly is an interesting idea. Gabrielle, you're welcome to come, whenever you like, to see it and I will look into whether the addition might become a workable apartment/studio."

She appeared uncomfortable at first and he went on to say, "We can discuss particulars if we decide the space is right for you and renting will work for me. We might have to call it a guest house or studio or something."

She thanked him quietly, then, keeping eye contact to a minimum, said, "I may call you when my work on Emory and Cara's ceiling mural is nearing completion if I haven't already found a place."

Still rather stunned by Emory's proposal and distracted at hearing her speak finally, Jonathan answered Gabrielle, making an effort not to appear reluctant, "Good. Meanwhile, I'll talk to my builder friend about what it would take to make it accommodate a living space."

When everyone seemed finished, Gabrielle rose, "Cara and Emory, thank you so much for lunch but, if you'll excuse me, I need to go into town to purchase more paints. I'll be back later and will continue working on the ceiling in the morning if that's okay." The three of them exchanged hugs and her goodbye to Jesse and Jonathan was a brief acknowledgement of having enjoyed meeting them.

That was in July of 1994 and, a month later, Gabrielle went to see Jonathan's studio addition, a thirty-by-twenty-four-foot room, with a vaulted ceiling, loft, perfect light and an unobstructed view of the ocean. She was surprised and pleased with the space, much more workable than anything she had been shown so far. Jonathan was charmed by her smile as she looked all around the room and he slipped out for a time, to let Gabrielle have a private moment there to help to decide if it felt like a possible home for her. Already comfortable offering it to her, he waited discretely as she stood with her eyes closed enjoying the warmth of the sun through the skylights and numerous windows.

After a time, she expressed her desire to rent the space, pleased it included a small bathroom with a shower in it at one end. It was decided she would use it as a studio with a loft bedroom and share the kitchen in the main house with Jonathan and Jesse. Before she moved in, though, Jonathan had the builder install a counter with a sink, and provided a small refrigerator, toaster oven, two stove burners, and a coffee maker, eliminating the necessity of coming into the main part of the house every time she wanted a drink or light meal.

They easily reached an agreement on the rent, Jonathan using the excuse that it wasn't a legal two-family zone to ask for a small amount, since he sensed she couldn't afford very much.

More than a year had passed since Gabrielle moved into the studio. Now she was gone, leaving Jonathan with her disquieting words echoing in the empty places she no longer occupied.

Chapter 3

Emily and Jacob

Jacob's arms were so full of shopping bags he could barely get through the door and he appeared flushed and excited.

At the sound of his approach, Emily jumped, shivered and began racing desperately and aimlessly about her bedroom, as if she didn't quite know where she ought to be.

"Hello, Sweetheart!" he called cheerfully as he stacked the bags in one corner. He picked her up and placed her on the bed, kissing her forehead, "Stay right here, while Daddy brings in some very big packages."

Emily did as she was told, watching silently as Jacob made several trips outside and back into her room. He began opening boxes and sorting through the bags then left the room again to get his tool box and a hand truck he would need to carry in several pieces of furniture, singlehandedly. For the next two hours, he worked non-stop. Not a motion was wasted and he appeared to have planned every detail, each task accomplished in pre-determined order, hanging pictures, assembling four bookcases, putting up a ballet bar and mirror and placing a heavy, old children's tea table with three chairs in the center of the room.

A Bombe chest and a writing desk with a matching chair were wheeled in and the desk was positioned in front of a frameless watercolor painting Jacob hung of the seashore, with two children playing together at the edge of the water in the glow of a luminous sunset, a group of small islands, a breaker wall and sailboats in the distance.

On the opposite wall he placed another painting, a meadow bordered by a stone wall on one side and a brook and wild wood on the other. Two horses galloped through the meadow, a mare and a gelding, one the color of sugar crystals, the other a gleaming, golden brown, their silky manes and tails flying in the wind. Where the brook met the meadow, there were wildflowers, tiny white, pink and yellow blossoms on long willowy stems. And, in the forest, lush with ferns, maples and white birches, were white-tailed deer, rabbits, squirrels, a woodchuck, chickadees, a pair of cardinals, a titmouse and a downy woodpecker, all waiting to be discovered hiding, just inside.

Around both pictures, Jacob mounted pre-cut and finished casings and windowsills and hung filmy curtains, making the paintings appear to be window views.

In one corner, he placed a corner shelf and two of the six-foot assembled bookcases on either side of it. Box after box marked "Books" easily filled all the shelves with children's books, references, reading, mathematics and foreign language primers and old volumes of the classics. A light hung from the ceiling about two feet out from the corner and below it, piles of cushions and stuffed animals formed an inviting reading corner. On the corner shelf, he put a vase of silk pastel roses and baby's breath and a live potted pothos, chosen for its heart-shaped leaves and ability to withstand an environment with very little light. A sweetly smiling Madame Alexander doll, a collection of horses and a tiny, pewter sculpture of a gymnast on a balance beam sat atop the bookcases.

He opened the rest of the bags and sat two life-sized dolls, dressed in Victorian gowns and hats, on two of the chairs at the tea table and placed a delicate white, China tea set, with tiny pink rosebuds, in the center. Over the back of the empty chair, a lovely lace dress, with crinolines and a large hat with flowers and silk ribbon band and bow, much like the costumes the dolls were wearing, waited to be discovered.

At the end of the built-in bed was a footlocker and he put a bench cushion on it and filled it with games, puzzles and toys. On hooks by the ballet bar, toe shoes hung, along with several leotards and tutus.

The bags appeared bottomless and he continued to produce surprises from each of them, coloring books, several pads of plain paper in various sizes, a huge crayon box, colored pencils, pastels, paints and an easel. The last projects were to hang a huge chalkboard, with several erasers and boxes of white chalk on one wall, a bulletin board, equally as large, next to it and, on the back of the door, a calendar with squares for each day of the week large enough to make notes in.

Through all of this, Emily never moved from her bed or made a sound, a wide-eyed sculpture. Now, Jacob went over to her and lifted her down, "Go and look around, Emily, while I make your bed."

About a week before, he had painted the concrete walls a pale yellow and a new white comforter and pillow sham, with yellow and white daisies and bright green stems and leaves, turned her bed into a cheerful alcove. Throw pillows in green, white, yellow and a big daisy one turned it into a lovely garden as well. He hung mobiles with fairies and crystals over her bed and placed a new ginger jar lamp, with a fringed and beaded shade, on the bedside table, along with a daisy-face alarm clock.

Suddenly, Jacob felt so exhausted he couldn't move and sat down at the desk to rest and survey his handiwork, glancing from one corner to another and along each wall with a critical eye, deciding there was nothing he wanted to change or add. The room was miraculously transformed, from dark and dismal to enchanting, and he was extremely pleased with himself for this accomplishment.

Where was Emily? He looked around for her and realized she was standing, hands behind her back with only her eyes moving around the room, just as she thought she had been told to do, and not touching anything. He smiled at how innocent and literal children are and said, "Sweetheart, all of these new things are for you, your Happy Birthday surprise. Go ahead and play with whatever you like and I'll get our dinner." Because it was her birthday, he served her favorites, macaroni and cheese, corn and applesauce with just a little touch of cinnamon and sugar stirred in, and absolutely nothing green.

When they finished their dinner, Jacob gathered the dishes and said, "And now we must have cake." He carried the small cake, with lighted candles, into the room singing "Happy Birthday to You" in a voice only slightly more melodic than groaning water pipes.

Emily was sitting at the tea table feeding her new dollies when he entered and, with each forkful, saying to them repeatedly and in a firm voice, "And now we must have cake...and now we must have cake," as she touched each mouth with the fork, very much like a communion ceremony.

"No, Emily, not pretend cake, real birthday cake," Jacob said, rather annoyed and more sternly than intended, and, with that, placed her cake, carefully, on the desk and told her to make a really important wish. The cake was edged in pastel flowers with yellow candles and "Happy 4th Birthday, Emily" across it in green leafy letters. She stood for a long time, staring at it, with one finger on her chin, until Jacob, becoming impatient, pointed out that the candles were melting and she needed to be quicker with her wish. She kept the wish to herself, finally blowing the candles out one at a time, glancing deliberately but carefully at Jacob after each one, then chose a piece from one corner of the cake with flowers on it.

He smiled now and said, "Ah, lots of frosting – good choice, birthday girl."

With a polite "Thank you," she carried her plate to the table with her dolls but finished every morsel without pretending to share it with her tea party guests and then rose cautiously and began to explore the room again. Jacob was relieved to see her appearing happier with each discovery and he began guiding her about the room so she wouldn't miss anything. Then, realizing it probably was wiser to leave a few unfound things for days when boredom became a problem, he sat down again and watched her.

She was getting so big now but he still loved to pick her up or hold her little hand. It remained a wonder to him that she came into the world so tiny and beautiful and he'd been entrusted with such a gift. Watching her play brought memories of how mesmerized he had been when she was an infant, by her helplessness and fragility, and, later, as a toddler, by her resilience and curiosity.

Already, there was an obvious wish for independence and each day she seemed more grown up and willful - less needy. For Jacob this was a sad thing for he knew what would follow, the pulling away he dreaded and could never allow.

He allowed her to play until much past her usual bedtime then sent her to brush her teeth and wash her face while he pulled back the covers and laid out a new nightgown and slippers for her. A careful look around the room revealed things she had played with and left lying about as she moved to something new. When she returned from the bathroom, he took her hand and walked her around the room, instructing her to put every toy and pencil back in its "original and proper place," explaining she must do this herself from now on whenever she played with things, and asked if she understood. She answered with a quick nod of her head and an almost imperceptible "yes" without meeting his eyes.

Emily changed into the new nightgown and slippers and jumped from the bed, heading for the ballet mirror to look at her reflection. Jacob followed her, gently removing the elastics from her two pony tails, and began to brush her hair. Glancing at him in the mirror, Emily turned to take the brush from his hand and finished brushing her hair herself, with long dramatic strokes. *See!* he thought.

There was one last surprise for her, a "Drowsy" doll, with blond hair and pink flannel body with white polka dots. At first, her face lit up but then she realized it wasn't her old Drowsy, since it didn't have the stains, from when she left her cradled and hidden in the lilac bush for three days and it had rained. And her hair was much too smooth and neat--not the wild straight hair from making her jump up and down after pulling the string to make her talk, things like "I go sleep now, night, night" or let out her crazy infectious laugh. When Jacob left to get her a water glass, she threw the doll aside and pulled out a tiny square piece of her old baby blanket, from its hiding place behind a small tear in the boxed spring, below the mattress, and slipped it under her pillow.

When he returned, she was standing on her bed and he was about to scold her when she put her arms around his neck and kissed his cheek lightly saying, "Thank you for my birthday cake and beautiful new room, goodnight, Daddy" surprising him and bringing tears to his eyes.

And, only after Jacob kissed her goodnight, tucked her in and turned out the light, did she pick Drowsy up and snuggle her, sucking her thumb and holding her secret blanket piece with one hand and rubbing the flannel of the doll's body with the back of her hand and fingers of the other. In the dim glow of a tiny night light in the bathroom, it was easier to pretend she was her comfortable old Drowsy.

Jacob washed the dishes, cleaned up the kitchen, which was a mess from his hurried dinner and cake preparations, carried out the trash and boxes from all of his purchases and put away the cake. Although it was still early, he was wearied from the anticipation, preparation and work of creating a more cheerful environment for Emily, something to compensate for their present living situation, and decided to go to bed too.

As he always did, he went to check on Emily, before getting ready himself, and found her sound asleep and holding tightly onto Drowsy. He was happy to see that, so very happy to think that perhaps he had made her fourth birthday one she would always remember.

As soon as the door was closed again, Emily opened her eyes and glanced around at the strange, unfamiliar shapes and shadows in the darkened newly-decorated room. Deep sighs escaped from her tiny chest as she pulled out her blanket piece from under the covers, where she'd hidden it when she heard him coming. Hugging the doll closer while trying to ignore the uncomfortable feeling always hanging about in her stomach, Emily finally drifted off to sleep with a single tear resting on her flushed right cheek.

While he brushed his teeth and got undressed, Jacob thought, again, about how Emily was growing up too fast and tried to envision what he would need to do to keep her safe and protect her from all that was wrong in the world. That was all he cared about now.

Instead of getting into bed, he began pacing about, rubbing his hands together and feeling distraught. He finally managed to sit down on the edge of the mattress and whispered through gritted teeth, "Do not do this again, Jacob. Get a hold of yourself!" After a time, he heaved his shoulders, took a deep breath, pulling his thoughts back to this perfect day, which had gone exactly as he had wished it to, except for the disappointment that, still, nothing made Emily laugh out loud, a delightful sound he missed dreadfully. He forced himself to get under the covers and feel the coolness of the sheets and pillowcase and, very quickly, fell into a deep, exhausted sleep.

Chapter 4

GABRIELLE AND GIDEON

Gideon heard a knock at the door. He quickly put out the joint he'd been smoking and batted the air around with a throw pillow, as if moving it would make the distinct odor less obvious. In an effort to appear casual and pre-occupied, he picked up his guitar and began strumming random chords. The effect was lost, however, because she didn't use her key as he had expected after a call to say she was coming, but knocked again, instead.

Gabrielle stepped in slowly, empty-handed, no groceries, backpack, paint case, canvas or sketch pad, he noted. The realization she would not be staying changed his demeanor instantly, from contrived indifference to sardonic contempt and he snickered as she walked past him into the living room.

It had taken more than a month of starting to dial and then hanging up again for Gabrielle to, finally, pick up the phone and contact Gideon and, now, she tried to summon the energy and resolve she knew would be needed for this conversation. "Hello, Gideon."

"Well, Gabby!" His words were deliberately slow and whining, "How very nice of you to drop by!"

She hated that nickname and he knew it, of course, but she supposed it made him feel better to attempt to antagonize her right off.

"I'm sorry. I should have..."

"Not the appropriate response! 'Piss off Gideon' or, 'I wanted to' or even silence is preferable to 'should have' like some regrettable obligation."

"Gideon, I..."

"How long was it this time?" he continued to interrupt her, a sparring partner trying to get the bout going, "three months I was on tour and three months I wasn't...let's see, that's...six months is it? No calls and, by the way, you might have let me know you changed your post office box to some address where your mail isn't forwarded. And, I assume you're not staying, since you've brought nothing with you. So, where are you staying?"

"With David and Amber, for the moment" she answered reluctantly.

David was a studio musician who usually worked on movie musical scores but, occasionally he and Gideon had filled in on the same tours or were hired for the same recording sessions. David and his wife, Amber, were very surprised when they first met Gabrielle, because she seemed so young to be with Gideon, but they had become friends immediately. She had stayed with them a few times when Gideon was on tour and while she attended classes at the New York Studio School and they kept in touch.

"Of course, how good of my dear friends to be so loyal and hospitable to you," an interesting response, since David was never very fond of Gideon but tolerated him because Amber and Gabrielle grew close and the men were thrown together more often than he would have wished, socially and for work.

Gabrielle looked around the room, trying to remember what brought her back over the years. An old feeling in her stomach returned with the familiar smoky odor, a nearly-empty bottle of Absolut and partially-filled glass on the coffee table, alongside an overflowing ashtray with a razor blade tucked under the edge and obvious white residue lines. She called to let him know she was coming to avoid this kind of scene. Gabrielle couldn't decide if he was intentionally flaunting his lifestyle, just didn't care to hide it, or was unable to conceal his worsening addictions and clean up after himself. The latter seemed to be the most likely explanation, given the disheveled condition he and his apartment were in now compared to how fastidious he had always been. It was nearly impossible, as she stood in this environment, to recall or conjure anything resembling a desire to remain involved with this man she now felt was a stranger.

Gabrielle was so young, just seventeen, when the twenty-nine-year-old musician convinced her to run away, knowing how desperately infatuated she was with him. *Perhaps it had really been the lure of freedom and adventure,* she thought now.

In 1986, Gideon Stone came to Byrdcliffe Arts Colony, just outside Woodstock, New York, where Gabrielle was staying with her godparents, who were artists in residence there. Gideon was playing at a club nearby and had come for the day just to walk about and observe. He was a very gifted violinist but a source of great disappointment to his parents, whose plan for him was the concert stage. They were both musicians, his father a professor of music who played the French horn in a small community orchestra and his mother a somewhat-renowned concert violinist. Gideon studied at Juilliard as they wished but, while there, joined some classmates who were trying to form a different sort of rock band by combining their knowledge of classical, blues and rock music. They did quite well for a time as opening acts on some tours but never quite came together as a group and eventually disbanded, mostly due to persistent parental pressure.

Gideon became fond of the lifestyle and acquainted with many popular bands, gaining a reputation as a talented background or fill-in musician for groups who were recording or needed a performer on the road in emergency situations. Several jobs came his way playing in orchestras recording musical scores as well. He did not return to Juilliard but continued his solo career working pretty steadily because he played violin, guitar, piano, keyboard and a little percussion and was willing to take any job to be on tour and around the big players. When money and other jobs were scarce, he did an occasional solo violin performance but nothing he accomplished met his parent's expectations and they had fallen out over it a number of years before, so Gabrielle had never met them.

After spending the afternoon with Gabrielle and her godparents, Gideon invited them to one of his performances, in Woodstock. An adolescent and smitten Gabrielle could not take her eyes off his handsome face, with its sculptured features which were powerfully sensual and strong. On rare occasions when a genuine smile appeared, he was beautiful, a strange word for a most masculine being, but true. She thought him worldly and sophisticated and part of a culture she longed to see and experience.

Gideon was mesmerized by Gabrielle's striking, inquisitive eyes, her artistry and her ethereal spirit. He sensed her childlike infatuation with him and a fragility, right off, and decided he would have her. As inexperienced as she was, it took very little time to overwhelm her with his passion and to convince her to run off with him. She crept out of her godparent's house in the middle of the night, with her passport and very few of her belongings, which Gideon convinced her to do, fearing discovery. Gabrielle very quickly became fascinated with the whole lifestyle of constantly being on the road, traveling to new places and the unexpected and spontaneous nature of it. Although there was little time to see much of each city or town, Gabrielle sketched and painted and, once in a while, would convince Gideon to let her stay behind for a day or two to complete sketches for a painting, catching up with him at the next stop on the tour.

They met stars like Billy Joel, Eric Clapton, and Elton John. At one point, Gabrielle met a folk singer who heard her singing, in a beautiful, flawless voice while she was sketching, and tried to convince her to sing a duet. She was extremely shy, content with staying a discreet distance from the attention and knew nothing about performing. The song just came into her head now and then with no memory of when or where she had learned it. Her explanation and refusal disappointed him but, while he was performing, she sketched his portrait, her very first one, which delighted him and he forgave her for not joining him on stage.

After three years, the increased drinking and drug use which accompanied the lifestyle and Gideon's jealousy and controlling behavior were too much for her. One evening, as his concert began, she packed a few clothes, took her paints and canvasses and ran away, using money she secretly accumulated from paintings and sketches sold along the way.

Ever since Gabrielle had been unable to go on a class trip to France with fellow New York Studio School students, she dreamed about going to Paris to paint and study. Deciding this would be the ideal time to go, she contacted her art school classmate, Amelia, who shared the dream of an extended trip to Paris, and she quickly agreed to go with Gabrielle. Amelia possessed both the financial means and the sophistication of having traveled often with her parents to easily plan and arrange everything. She only stayed in France for a month and then went home leaving Gabrielle on her own when she decided she wanted to stay longer. After returning from Avignon with Cara and Emory, she saw Gideon now and then and wasn't sure why she had been unable to let go, completely, of their unusual and increasingly unhealthy relationship.

"Since you're just standing there staring into space, perhaps you might begin by explaining what the hell you've done to your hair and what second hand shop you rummaged through to achieve this bag lady-peasant girl fashion statement?" Gideon was very much a follower of the latest fashion trends, wore only designer labels when not on stage, and had pretty much controlled how Gabrielle dressed, wore her hair and behaved when they were together.

Gabrielle had been lost in her own thoughts and his voice startled her and brought the reality of where she was and why back into focus. "Gideon, I'm not going to play this game...I just want to talk to you..."

"So, we're going to talk. Oh, goody! Shall I make a pot of tea then or just grab a pen and paper and take copious notes?"

"Do whatever you like as long as you're listening and not constantly interrupting me."

He was shocked by her boldness and tone and decided he had to be even more forceful and not show any semblance of weakness or longing. He wondered, where this aggressive new attitude was coming from.

"Oh, I'll be listening, I assure you, Gabby. I'll be paying very close attention to every single word because I wouldn't want to miss one syllable of whatever it is you think you need to say, especially if it includes where you've been for the last six months and why I haven't heard from you. But, at least sit down first," and he gestured toward the couch.

Gabrielle chose a chair across from it instead, laid the key discreetly on the table and began, "We both know whatever we used to share hasn't existed for a long time and I felt it should be said, finally. It's not anyone's fault, Gideon, I was so young and our lives are very different now...I'm different now..."

"Really, you're different? How very interesting you should say that," he disregarded her earlier demand, continuing to interrupt and walked around her chair moving his eyes up and down her frame in disdainful scrutiny. "I have to assume you're implying different in a positive way but I'm sorry I really don't see it, Gabby. It's obvious you still need to be advised about what to wear and how to style your hair and you seem as inarticulate and shy as ever. Just exactly what is it you're referring to I'm supposed to recognize as new and presumably improved about you?"

Gabrielle took several deep breaths to steady herself before answering and then continued, "It really doesn't matter whether or not you're able see it, Gideon. It has nothing whatever to do with anyone's perception but my own. I'm learning to acknowledge my strengths and to try to put out and accept positive energy which feels supportive of my goals and expectations for myself. And I'm on a journey to try to find a real sense of purpose and peace in my life. The energy between us has become so negative and destructive for both of us and I..."

"So. I guess this Utopian 'sense of purpose and peace' means you're not running from your demons or, should I say, demon and terrors any longer? How very nice for you. How ever did you expel him from the dark corners and shadows?" Gideon could or would not let her express herself without interruption, a clever tactic to break down her resolve and disrupt her well-planned speech about leaving him.

Gabrielle breathed deeply again and continued, "You know, Gideon, on the way over here, I tried to come up with an example of what I felt was missing and wrong, apart from our extremely incompatible opinions about drugs and alcohol, and you've just given it to me – trust and kindness. You just took a most personal and painful knowledge entrusted to you and used it to belittle me and betray my vulnerability. There's really nothing more to say. I have never and will not begin now to speak to you or about you unkindly. You've played an important part in my life and I am aware of it and grateful to you for the experiences and for our time together. But we've outlived this very unusual relationship and it's time for both of us to let it go. I didn't want to say these things over the telephone and wanted to come here in person to thank you for the happier memories I'll keep in my heart." She rose from her seat, "Goodbye, Gideon."

She could see the veins at his temples were raised now and she knew his surface calm was as delicate as the tissue-thin wrapper on a package of fireworks. As she turned toward the door, he jumped up, picked up the key she had placed on the table and grabbed her arms, backing her to the wall and pressing them upward on either side of her head. He tried to make her take the key, pressing it into one palm so firmly it made an immediate imprint saying, too quietly and slowly, "I am not accepting this, Gabrielle. You can't come here, after a six-month absence, and just announce that you've decided our relationship is over." She wouldn't close her hand around the key so he dropped it and pressed his body against hers and kissed her mouth forcibly.

Her first reaction of panic made her heart beat so fast and hard she could feel it against his chest and feel his erection against her groin but she kept her mouth firm and stared unflinchingly into his eyes.

Furious at her cold response, he grabbed both arms and flung her toward the bedroom, knocking her to the floor and causing her to hit her head on the corner of a table as she fell. Her head began to bleed immediately and he started toward her, "Gabrielle, I didn't..." The forbidding look on her face stopped him mid-sentence but also rekindled his fury. As she stumbled to her feet and made her way across the living room and through the door into the corridor, he threw the key toward her and shouted, "Go ahead and run, you pathetic creature! You won't last long without me to run to...he'll find you again and you'll be back. Mark my words, he'll find you and you'll come crawling back to me!"

The elevator descent was excruciatingly slow and, with each buzz of the floor indicator, she became more frightened he might have taken the stairs and would be waiting for her when she reached the street level. She held her breath as the elevator doors opened but he wasn't there and she ran out of the building and only a little way along the busy street before she began to feel light-headed and staggered into a nearby coffee shop. The owners, Carl and Megan, were very fond of Gabrielle and Carl, horrified at the sight of blood running down her face, rushed to help her, "What happened, darling child? Do you need a doctor?"

"No, Carl, thank you. I just fell and am a little dizzy. May I have some ice for my head and a glass of water? I'm just going into the lady's room to wash my face."

"Anything for you," he said gently, supporting her arm as she walked. "Do you want me to call Megan from the back to come with you or will you be okay by yourself? You look a little pale."

Tears she didn't feel coming began streaming down her cheeks in strange patterns through the blood, "No, there's no need to call her but thank you. I'll be fine, Carl, really. I'll be right out."

Carl hurried to get water and an ice pack, made her the hot chocolate she loved with shaking hands and called Megan to come.

"She didn't fall and you know it or, if she did, that one did it to her you can be sure," Megan said, not as quietly as Carl would have wished. "She's so lovely. I don't understand why she keeps coming back to the likes of him."

Just then Gabrielle returned. Carl hushed Megan and insisted she come in the back where it was more comfortable and she would have some privacy. She was trembling so he wrapped a large towel around her shoulders and examined the wound on her head, which had a large swelling with a cut in the middle and was still bleeding. "I'm going to mind my own business and not say what I'm thinking but you know, if there's anything we can do, you only need to ask."

"Thank you, both of you. You're always so kind and, just so you know, I won't be coming back."

Carl shook his head, in relief. "Do you need me to drive you to a doctor or the emergency room? The bump on your forehead is fairly large and you could have a concussion or you might need to have some stitches to be sure this doesn't scar badly."

"No, Carl, thank you for your concern but I'm really feeling much better now and I think the cut will heal without the need for stitches. I'm certain it just looks worse than it is because of all the blood."

"Well, if you're sure then. But please drink your chocolate and rest here for as long as you like before trying to walk anywhere. Are you staying with Amber?"

Gabrielle shook her head yes and Carl continued, "That's quite a way to go if you're feeling dizzy so promise you'll stay right here until you know you're up to it." Gabrielle smiled at Carl, shook her head to acknowledge his request and sipped her hot chocolate just to make him feel better.

She did relax somewhat and tried to think of what to do next, since going "home" to Cape Cod, at this time, might threaten all she cherished, her home and studio, the people she had become so close to and how safe she felt there. When she was feeling up to it, she thanked Carl and Megan and promised she would come by again to say goodbye to them, then headed for David and Amber's house, dreading the explanation. They knew she had gone to talk with Gideon and would be furious at the obvious outcome.

They lived in a Washington Square, Greek revival row house Amber had inherited years before and it was a wonderful home and, now, a valuable asset.

On the way there, she stopped at the Washington Square Arch. From the first time she saw it, after running away with Gideon in 1986, she had felt very connected to it for some reason she never understood and had painted it and the park in every season. As she sat looking at it and enjoying the warmth of the sun on an unusually warm, winter day, Byrdcliffe came to her mind for the second time. Suddenly, she was very sure of where she wanted to go next and only hoped her godparents were still there or in the vicinity, since, shamefully, she had never contacted them after running off with Gideon. They were always so good to her and had deserved much more in return. Yes, that's where she needed to be just now.

While Gabrielle was staying with David and Amber, she was painting a portrait of their nearly-three-year-old daughter, Coco, whom she adored, and, as she walked back to their home, she began to calculate the amount of work she still needed to do to finish it.

It was hard to think about leaving this place. It had been a wonderful opportunity, both for spending time with a family she loved and to contemplate her present situation and create a design for her future in a quiet, supportive atmosphere. Amber and David never asked questions. The only reason they knew about her situation with Gideon was because of their shared acquaintance and their growing animosity toward him.

Gabrielle felt more and more certain with each step that Byrdcliffe was exactly where her journey was meant to take her next. She decided she would leave for there as soon as the portrait was completed.

Today is Sunday, she thought, as she tried to determine the work left to do and the amount of time she would need to accomplish her very precious task to her satisfaction. *I should be able to put the last touches on the portrait and leave by the end of the week.*

The sudden realization she had been gone much longer than she promised Amber and David she would be made her quicken her steps. She felt terrible, knowing they would be waiting and worrying until her return. David offered to accompany Gabrielle but she didn't want to humiliate Gideon by ending their relationship in front of anyone and refused, probably not a wise choice, given his response. She was grateful for the opportunity to escape, as Gideon hesitated at the sight of her bleeding head, and pleased with herself for finding the courage to stand up to Gideon and recapture the freedom she desired. She needed to learn to make decisions rooted in her own wellbeing in order to move ahead with her life and vowed to hold this experience as her touchstone.

Chapter 5

JONATHAN AND GABRIELLE

Frost and despair garnished the landscape and, in winter's leafless backdrop, scrub pines, like worn old men with unshaven faces and knotted knees, kept a vigil on the edge of the dunes. Jonathan sat in his study staring out of the window, past them to the frigid cerulean sea, feeling lost and affected by Gabrielle's absence more profoundly than he had anticipated. Even as he went about the necessary routines of each day, he began to feel as if he were living in an endless dream which eluded his desire to wake from it, one of those dreams about trying to get to someone or somewhere unreachable.

He assumed the length of Gabrielle's time away would be shortened by Cara's pregnancy and the promise to paint the murals for the nursery but it was mid-January and no one had heard from her since she left late in November. She'd never been gone for more than a week or two at a time prior to this strange departure.

The December clinics went very well, except there were none of the usual antics and fun during the medical exams, normally delighting the children and filling the trailer with their wonderful laughter. Jonathan's caregiving was kind and gentle, as always, but not playful so it had been a very quiet week in the medical side. The dental clinic was noisy and hilarious as usual.

Jesse was worried about Jonathan and not just because the clinics had been so different. He often noticed the way he looked at Gabrielle when she wasn't aware of it and understood how much he must be missing her now, although Jonathan kept it entirely to himself. It was a very awkward and strange time, one which he'd never experienced with Jonathan before. They were always honest and easy with each other and Jesse felt frustrated with his inability to help in some way.

He had stopped home on the morning Gabrielle left, to pick up a patient's chart, mistakenly left on his desk, and found Jonathan cleaning up smashed bottles, picture frames and various items from his bedroom and bathroom, which both looked like battlefields. Jesse offered to help but Jonathan told him, "Just leave me and everything alone." While Jesse was surprised by his response, he knew it was out of embarrassment, since it was obvious Jonathan had been crying and tore everything apart in some sort of rage. Jesse felt horrible for him whenever he thought of the scene.

One evening, in an attempt to help him talk about what he was going through, Jesse deliberately asked, "Have you heard from Gabrielle?"

Jonathan responded with a terse, "No" and immediately went to his bedroom, remaining there for the rest of the night.

By a strange coincidence, this was a very happy time for Jesse and, although he was longing to share what was happening in his life with Jonathan, he didn't feel it was appropriate just now.

Instead, Jesse spent his time trying to watch over Jonathan discreetly, since, clearly, he wasn't ready to confide his feelings for Gabrielle and the anguish her absence was causing him. Jesse cooked meals and left them and, even if he was spending the night away from the house, drove by to make sure Jonathan's car was in the driveway or stopped in briefly. He noticed Jonathan was gone the last several weekends but he was evasive when Jesse casually asked him about it, so he decided he would let it go, even when he noticed how exhausted and thin Jonathan looked when he returned home, late on Sunday.

Last weekend, Jonathan's sister, Cassy, had called, "Jesse is everything all right? No one in the family has heard from Jonathan since Christmas Eve when he called to say he wasn't feeling well and wouldn't be coming for our family gathering."

Jesse assured her Jonathan was fine, "He's just very busy with his practice and the clinics," but felt terrible about lying to her. Cassy adored her older brother and was very intuitive, Jesse thought, so it hadn't surprised him she sensed there was a problem. He left a note for Jonathan but had no idea if he'd returned her call given his present state of mind. The depth of his despair certainly became acutely evident to Jesse with that phone call from Cassy because failing to communicate with his family or celebrate the holidays with them was entirely out of character for Jonathan, especially with Cassy. He was always so protective of her and cherished their relationship.

Jonathan borrowed Cervantes's "Don Quixote" from Emory, with no explanation, and scanned it, since reading every word seemed daunting, but found nothing to help him understand why Gabrielle had gone away with such mysterious words or why she said to read it. Afterward he was angry with himself for failing to comprehend its significance since he knew she wouldn't have made this unusual request without a very good reason.

He did understand, or hoped he did, her asking him to come for her on Marginal Way and thinking of this was the one thing that kept him hopeful.

Just over five months before she left, in the last week of June, Gabrielle got a commission to paint a newly-engaged couple on the rocks of Marginal Way, where the proposal had taken place. The couple had paid for her to stay in Ogunquit, Maine, in a two-bedroom suite, in a charming old home converted to a bed and breakfast. Entering the light-filled rooms with expansive views of the ocean was like the pleasant shock of guests shouting "surprise" at an unexpected birthday party. It reminded Gabrielle of the first time she went to see Jonathan's studio addition which was now her home. And, yet, there was something so different too. Here waves challenged outcroppings as unique as each human spirit – sea and life in flux – something she knew. On the Cape there was the tranquil lure of ocean on compliant sand – something she tried to understand.

Jonathan was combining a Friday and Monday off with the weekend, for a four-day rest before beginning the exhausting three weeks of July clinics, so Gabrielle invited him to come along and he had accepted immediately.

Each morning Jonathan drank his coffee and Gabrielle a hot chocolate on the balcony, in the yellow, pink and blue felicity of sunrise over the water. After breakfast at the inn or in town, they would walk the one-and-a-quarter-mile path called Marginal Way, linking Ogunquit Village to Perkins Cove, stopping at various bends in the trail to enjoy a new view, high above the coastline, on one of the many benches along the way or from an inviting rock.

Gabrielle sketched and photographed her clients who wore the exact outfits they were wearing the day of the proposal. Meanwhile, Jonathan watched other hikers, listened to the ocean rhythms and imagined the trail's ageless trees to be old composers catching the sea breeze in their twisted limbs and conducting a seaside symphony.

He loved this rocky seacoast of Maine, so different from the Cape shore with its sandy beaches and dunes.

They shared meals of lobsters and chowder, chose bottles of obscure but pleasing wines, indulged in shared desserts and browsed in little gift shops and galleries looking for special gifts for Cara, Emory and the boys.

One afternoon, after Gabrielle finished with her clients for the day, they walked across an arched pedestrian bridge to Footbridge Beach and enjoyed a picnic supper, packed for them by the restaurant where they had eaten lunch. They stayed well past sunset, lying on a blanket reading, sometimes silent for long periods and then talking for a time. When Jonathan put Handel's *Water Music* on to play, Gabrielle became teary during *Lentamente*. Embarrassed, she admitted she had no idea why but it seemed to be connected to a recurrent dream.

Jonathan pointed out an odd coincidence, "For the last year or so, I've been having a very strange dream over and over again and *Water Music* is always playing. Tell me about your dream."

Just as she did when they first met, she looked away, avoiding further eye contact and suddenly seemed to withdraw into herself. After a time, she suggested, "Let's each write down our dream and share it at some time in the future."

It was a strange conversation, Jonathan thought, but he had agreed and then they remained quiet and contemplative until moon glow danced across the water in a shimmering path and they returned to the inn in its light.

Early one morning, they decided to wander into inland Maine, becoming lost for several hours, and came upon a horse farm where they stopped intending to ask for directions. A beginner equestrian group was just starting to assemble for a trail ride and one of the owners, friendly and warm, invited Jonathan and Gabrielle to join them. Neither Jonathan nor Gabrielle were experienced riders so a beginner trail ride was a perfect match to their abilities. After fitting them with riding helmets and having them sign a release, which gave them momentary pause, the co-owner, an incredibly fit and energetic woman, led the ride with great enthusiasm. They felt very comfortable with the pace, even when the group broke into a trot and, later, a canter for a very short distance along the trail, which wound through narrow wooded paths and across meadows. There were distant views of Mount Washington and other beautiful scenery.

A sudden wind came up, like when a storm is approaching, and the horse's mane and Gabrielle's hair flew as they cantered across a meadow and she was delighted by the feeling.

At the halfway point, the beginner trail ride brought them to an ice cream shop, strangely placed in the middle of nowhere. Their cones were included in the fee for the ride. The best part was tying up their horses to the old-fashioned hitching post there, as if they were cowboys who had just ridden a dusty trail into a nineteenth century town. They enjoyed their ice cream and laughed at their shared lack of horsemanship.

Before leaving the farm, they walked around and looked at the other horses and ponies and, at the sight of a large poster of a carousel, joked with the woman who had led the ride that perhaps a ride on a carousel steed might be more appropriate to the level of their abilities. She laughed and invited them to return any time for another ride.

The trip back to the inn in Ogunquit was fun and leisurely, as they talked about their adventure. Gabrielle and Jonathan had enjoyed the entire experience and decided they would take Emory and Cara up on their repeated invitations to learn to ride as soon as they returned to the Cape. Although she never portrayed animals in her work, Gabrielle thought she might attempt to draw or paint their horses too.

They stopped a few times along the way back to allow Gabrielle to sketch and take some photographs of the scenery and Jonathan used the time to catch up on reading some medical journals and reports so it was a long but pleasing day.

Jonathan slept late the next morning and, when he finally arose, found Gabrielle had left a note, "On Marginal Way for last meeting. Will return shortly for a late breakfast and last walk on the sand."

At the water's edge, Gabrielle frolicked, like a child, dancing joyfully in some ritual celebration of nature's brilliance and generosity, her hair wild and aglow in the wind. She sat down, at one point, and began drizzling handfuls of wet sand into mountain and forest sculptures and two children had joined her in creating a magical landscape. Jonathan was charmed by her and the privileged feeling that he was witnessing a newly discovered and sacred part of her being.

By the end of the four days spent with Gabrielle, Jonathan was completely in love with her but, until her surprising kiss and revelation on the porch as she was leaving, he had no idea she felt the same. He did notice conversation was more comfortable and sensed an awareness, though not necessarily an understanding, of moods during the months between Ogunquit and her departure in November. They both were very preoccupied with work since then, Jonathan with building his practice and Gabrielle with a number of commissions. Yet, many times, more than he cared to admit, Jonathan struggled with how he might be able to encourage something more but there was an unspoken barrier he could neither define nor intrude upon.

Chapter 6

Cara and Emory

Gabrielle's last words had been to find her on Marginal Way so, for the last few weekends, Jonathan left for Ogunquit as soon as he finished with his last patient each Friday. On those Saturdays and Sundays, he walked and sat along the Marginal Way trail all day in the bitter cold. At each turn in the path, his heart would race with anticipation thinking Gabrielle might be waiting on one of the benches or settled on a group of rocks caressing the sea with her observant gaze. Hour by hour his hopes were dashed as soundly as the crashing sea on an unyielding shoreline and his mood ebbed and flowed with the tides.

As he drove home, on Sunday night of yet another weekend spent this way, exhausted and discouraged, he decided he needed to talk with Cara and Emory. They had known Gabrielle for four or five years and she and Cara seemed close. Surely, they knew something about where she went when she disappeared. He would tell them only part of what she had said, "...if ever I don't return..." He would honor her request not to tell anyone about finding her on Marginal Way.

He didn't call first, just appeared at the door at about eight o'clock. They hadn't seen him for some time and Cara was relieved but shocked at how haggard and thin he seemed. When she offered him some left-over dinner, he realized he hadn't remembered to eat since breakfast and was famished. She piled a plate with roast turkey, stuffing, mashed potatoes and gravy, asparagus and cranberry sauce and poured him a glass of wine.

Turkey was always available in the Whittaker household, from late November until well after the New Year because, once Emory had Thanksgiving dinner, he had to have "day after" sandwiches with turkey, stuffing, cranberry sauce, mayonnaise and romaine lettuce and it took that long for his appetite for them to finally be satisfied.

The first year Gabrielle moved into Jonathan's home, they were all gathered for lunch and a leisurely afternoon at Cara and Emory's and Emory had offered them turkey sandwiches, yet again. Jonathan, Jesse, Gabrielle and Cara decided that Emory was selectively obsessive and turkey came third on the list of his passions, after houses and horses, although there had been some disagreement about what position books should occupy on the list. During this visit, they all delighted in ganging up and discussing this insight into Emory's turkey craving and other obsessions as if he weren't present and able to hear every word. Jesse added to their fun by referring to Emory as "Pilgrim," in a John Wayne sort of voice, every time turkey was mentioned. The others enjoyed this enormously because it was usually Emory who would find a sensitive subject or some other reason for unrelenting but always amusing and good-natured torment of one of them.

Cara asked no questions, just touched Jonathan's shoulder briefly as he began eating and excused herself for a moment to say "goodnight" to the children. As she passed the library, she looked in, "Emory, Jonathan is in the kitchen and I'm terribly worried about him. Would you please go talk to him while I tuck the boys in?"

Emory put his book aside and immediately headed to the kitchen because it wasn't like Cara to be an alarmist and he, too, was surprised by Jonathan's state as he entered the kitchen. Unlike Cara, though, he didn't hesitate to express his concern. "Jonathan, what the hell is happening to you? We've been very worried about you but now I'm downright shocked! You look like death. Oh, God! I shouldn't have said that. Is something wrong? Are you sick?"

Jonathan answered, "In a way," just as Cara returned to the kitchen and cringed at the last part of what Emory had said.

In all the time they had known him, they never saw Jonathan in anything but a happy and positive state of mind and Cara and Emory looked at each other, unsure of how to respond to his sad answer. Cara finally sat down next to him and rubbed his hand gently, "What is it, Jonathan? Is there something we can do?"

He quietly explained what had happened on the day Gabrielle left, omitting the Marginal Way part, and, for the first time, shared he was in love with her. He finished by asking, "What do you know about Brie, her life, or who she might be spending time with? Do you have any idea where she might have gone?"

There was a longer silence than he would have anticipated and Cara looked from Jonathan to Emory with a very strange expression. Jonathan assumed she was struggling with whether she should share a confidence or something she knew and, so, was astonished and his heart started pounding when she laid her head on her arms and began to weep uncontrollably. Emory went to her immediately, taking her hands in his, and she lifted her head and cried out, "How hideous and self-centered are we? For all these years, Gabrielle has been our beloved friend, spending time in our home, loving the boys, helping with fund-raising events I ask her to, painting your ceilings and letting you destroy her work and listening to our troubles and I, we know nothing more personal about her than the fact that she is sometimes frightened by something we can't see. How did she manage to withhold the most important parts of herself so completely, while giving so much of her time and effort to us?" Cara wondered sadly. "And, worst of all, why didn't we notice and care?" Now she was wailing and sobbing.

Jonathan felt terrible for upsetting Cara but couldn't seem to stop himself from continuing. "Can you remember a time, when the two of you were talking, when she mentioned the places she visited or think of some little thing she said that could be helpful?" Jonathan asked, persisting in spite of her obvious anguish and Emory's look of concerned warning.

Cara wiped her eyes, blew her nose and tried to think. "Greenwich Village," she said suddenly from behind a mass of tissues and diminished sobs. "Gabrielle mentioned once that she took some art classes at the New York Studio School, before she went to France, and, several times, she's mentioned places and events happening in Greenwich Village as though she had been there more recently. That's really all I can think of at the moment, I'm so sorry, Jonathan."

"No, I'm sorry for upsetting you with this and it's a great help, Cara. Thank you. At least it's something, a place to start."

Then he told them about reading "Don Quixote" cover to cover and asked if either of them had ever discussed it with Gabrielle.

Emory answered immediately, "No. But something about it must have been terribly important to her, since she placed him in the middle of her ceiling mural. That's it! Maybe it's something in the mural," and they all jumped up and headed for the library.

On the way, he brought Jonathan to the living room to show him two paintings Gabrielle had done. "We finally got around to finishing the living room renovations and hanging them, after almost two years of chaos and disasters." One was the painting they had bought from her in France. The garden was as exquisite as Emory had declared it to be.

Jonathan was captivated by how perfectly her canvas expressed the ephemeral seduction of a gardener's creation. "But I don't see the spirit Cara mentioned during our lunch on that summer day when we were introduced to Gabrielle."

Surprised Jonathan recalled that long-ago conversation, Emory laughed very strangely, "Ah. There is a mystery we cannot explain and you'll think I am completely mad when I tell you about it. Sometimes we walk in and see her as clearly and surely as we did in France and then we look again and cannot find her no matter how long we stare and try. It drives Cara crazy and she'll stand in front of the painting speaking to her and imploring her to come back. It's made a great cocktail party conversation starter. We've spent evenings with friends, in the living room of another home where the picture was hung, and some could see it right off and describe exactly what we have seen and others who, like you, saw nothing. One person suggested it was a little auto stereogram but another who said he was good at seeing the hidden images in them disagreed. I guarantee, if you come into this room a few more times, you will see her at some point and, then, you'll feel compelled to return and doubt your own sanity when no angle of observation or length of time spent staring at the painting produces even a glimpse of her. The strange part is Gabrielle will never acknowledge her existence at all."

Jonathan shuddered slightly and, to change the subject, moved to the other painting, which was of Cara on the beach at another home, her hair and sarong blowing in the wind. Emory, trying to disguise his own feelings about this painting, asked what he thought. "The portrait captures everything that is Cara, her kindness and sweetness and her playfulness are all there in the position of her head and an attitude expressed in her eyes and smile. I love that she was apparently expecting one of the boys and one hand appears to caress her pregnant stomach as she's dancing and twirling in rhythm with the wind and you can almost hear her laughter, a lovely seaside Madonna. It's extraordinary," Jonathan said quietly.

"Gabrielle's portrait work is always extraordinary." Jonathan was shocked to see tears welling up in Emory's eyes, in response to his observations, since he very rarely showed that kind of vulnerability. "She'll spend anywhere from a day to a week with a subject and their family or friends, snapping photos, sketching and just observing. Then at some point she leaves, almost disappears really, without ever consulting with anyone or asking for an opinion and returns to wherever she needs to be at that particular time to complete her work. We've referred several friends and clients to her during the last few years and each one has been extremely pleased with the finished painting, not only by the physical likeness but by the accuracy of expression and personality. She seems to have an uncanny talent for capturing essence."

Jonathan could only utter a barely audible and prolonged, "Yes…"

"The portrait of Cara is my unrivaled favorite, of course, but come now and let's study her library ceiling. I know we've all seen it many times but maybe there is something of a hint about her" Emory urged as Jonathan went back to the garden painting wishing the elusive spirit would appear.

When they entered the library, Emory, Cara and Jonathan sat in the leather chairs and looked up. On the ceiling above them, was a round painting perhaps fifteen or sixteen feet in diameter or more. In the center was a smaller circle, and, from its edges, eight lines extended out to the larger one, as if it were cut into a pie whose pieces didn't come to a point. There was another circle halfway between the outside and inside ones, creating sixteen individual sections plus the center round one, and in many of the sections there were paintings completed with some left blank inviting inspiration.

Around the perimeter of the outer circle, were grass and some leaves and, in between each section, roots and stems. As they stared at it, the painting appeared to be drawing them into a hole in the ground, down to the center, each segment a peek out of or into a tunnel or window. Jonathan began to notice the individual paintings in more detail, as Emory explained, "I love coming in and discovering a new one and have no desire for a formal design or Sistine-Chapel-type of ceiling."

This time she had done something entirely different. In the outside eight sections, there were characters from literature in strange or humorous situations--the Tortoise and the Hare, each dressed in a business suit, carrying a briefcase in one 'hand' and a latte in the other, and racing for the same taxicab. In another David Copperfield, Oliver Twist, The Artful Dodger,

Tiny Tim and a roundtable of the homeless from the streets of New York, sat dining on a great feast, in the Rainbow Room, enjoying a starlit view of New York City, and being served by Uriah Heep dressed as a waiter, while Scrooge played the harp for their entertainment. And his favorite, so far, was a tour bus, with the logo "Pilgrim Bus Lines" and a destination of Tabard Inn, Canterbury, the passengers, Chaucer's travelers, waving in the windows. Chanticleer is driving and being chased by the Fox, who is on a skateboard, holding onto the back of the bus and shouting obviously disingenuous compliments to the rooster, hoping to trick him again with flattery. Emory had just discovered Chaucer and so this one was especially meaningful to him.

The ones in the inner eight became more serious--Edgar Allen Poe's "Raven" holding the "Telltale Heart" in his talons, with "Nevermore" dripping in a beautiful elongated font in blood red; Cyrano de Bergerac, in his finest plumed hat and cape, with sword drawn toward his own heart, sitting at a writing desk, with "Dearest Roxanne" the only words visible on the letterhead, and so forth.

It took a while to solve the puzzle of what some of them were, although each was painted in great detail because of the size, and the entire mural was magnificent and completely absorbing.

Emory pointed to the ceiling to bring Jonathan's attention to what he felt was important. In the center circle, there were four windmills facing North, South, East and West but sharing one wind shaft and four common sails. In each of the four spaces between the windmills, there was a rendering of Don Quixote mounted on Rocinante and followed by Sancho Panza on a donkey. From every viewing direction, Don Quixote is leaning forward on his horse with his jousting lance tipping at a windmill and sword drawn and pointing straight ahead, creating the appearance of leading a charge toward a giant adversary. Jonathan could not recall seeing this rendition of the Man of La Mancha before. He was usually depicted either very straight and erect or slumped over and looking defeated.

Emory had "owned" several of her ceiling works of art but said this was his favorite and he couldn't wait to see the completed work. Jonathan was speechless and, with great effort, made his way through the vines and roots back to the top. Emory had provided opera glasses to appreciate the details but he wished he could climb up on the scaffolding and lay there viewing the work for much longer in quiet solitude and worried what would happen to this work should Emory find another house.

They sat in the chairs and stared at the center and then the rest of the paintings for a message or clue of some sort but discovered nothing of help.

"It's something else, I know it is," Cara said shaking her head in frustration at not being able to sort it out. "Jonathan, have you looked in her studio since she left?"

"I've never been in her studio...never invited in and I certainly don't feel comfortable invading her privacy just because she isn't here."

"But what if the answer is in there? Maybe you should look," Cara insisted.

"Ever since Brie rented the studio and moved in, I've treated that space as hers, completely, and I just don't feel right about entering it without her consent."

"And how are you feeling at this very moment because you don't look like you're 'feeling right' to me anyway," Emory put in. "Go in and have a look and you can confess what you did when she returns."

"Yes, Jonathan. She said she loved you right after alarming you with what she said about not returning. Certainly, she'll understand your concern," Cara added.

"Okay, okay, I'll consider going in and having a look around if she doesn't return soon but, if I do and she's angry about the intrusion, I promise you I will sing like a canary about whose idea it was," and he actually managed a smile, feeling reassured, after speaking with Cara and Emory, that he would be able to find Brie.

Emory had one last idea, "Tomorrow, I'm going to call Dan Saunders, a police detective and very good friend, and ask for his help to find her."

Jonathan turned abruptly toward Emory, stunned, "No, Emory, don't! I mean…it's so generous of you but there's something she's hiding deliberately and we have no idea what it is. She was very adamant about secrecy and we could be getting her into some sort of trouble if we brought the police into it."

"You're right. I'm sorry, I just wasn't thinking clearly but please keep in mind I do want to help in some way. If you want company on your search or think of something needed to aid in finding Gabrielle, whatever the cost, please just come to me, Jonathan, and it's done. She's been like a daughter to us…well to me. Cara isn't old enough to have a daughter her age but you understand what I mean. She asks for nothing but there is this compelling urge to take care of her nonetheless."

"I do know what you mean and I won't hesitate to ask if there's something that would help. Thank you, Emory." Then Jonathan turned to Cara, concerned for her health and pregnancy, "I felt very conflicted about coming here tonight and possibly causing you any stress over this and am so sorry I upset you but I didn't know what else to do. I'll find her and bring her home, so don't worry and just take care of this little treasure we're all waiting for. Thank you so much for dinner and listening and for coming up with the Greenwich Village idea."

Cara seemed calmer but tears still glistened along her lower lids, "Gabrielle couldn't have a better champion," and she hugged him for a long time, trying to reassure Jonathan and herself. "I'll call you if I think of anything else."

"And I'll call you the moment I know anything."

Jonathan went home in a better frame of mind and decided he would leave for the city on Friday, after his last patient, instead of wandering on Marginal Way for another weekend. His strong sense of responsibility regarding his patients was the only thing that kept him from heading straight to New York, in spite of the hour and his exhaustion. He had no idea how he would get through the week but hoped a very full schedule would help the days go somewhat faster. Then there were just the evenings and unending nights to deal with.

He also decided to put off going into Brie's studio for a bit longer, since he had all week and, perhaps, she'd return in the next few days before it was necessary.

What did Cara mean about Gabrielle being afraid of something we can't see? Jonathan sat up from a rare stretch of sound sleep, awakened by the thought. He knew she sometimes startled easily at unexpected noises and his first impression of her was of both a profound sadness and a subtle caution. He tried to picture it and realized she did always seem to be watching for something. And, as he thought of the days spent on Marginal Way, realized, just like Cara, nothing personal was learned and he hadn't caught it. Cara was so right about how cleverly secretive Brie had been about herself. Still, Jonathan questioned why, being so in love with her, the time ended with him completely unaware of it?

Although he was getting very little sleep, Jonathan did manage to make it through the week. A concerted effort to stay focused while he was in the office and treating patients was carrying him through the day but he frequently slipped into pondering about what Gabrielle was thinking and doing outside of the office. The great disappointment he'd felt at not being able to bring her to his family celebration at Christmas weighed heavily on him. He had been searching for just the right words to extend the invitation to her before he saw her painting in the dead garden and then she was gone. His procrastination cost him the opportunity and that, along with his hesitation when she revealed her feelings as she left, incited an anger with himself which kept returning intrusively like an unsettled weather pattern.

By lunchtime on Thursday, Jonathan had made the decision to go into Gabrielle's studio when he got home to search for anything of help. He didn't feel especially good about what he viewed as an invasion of her treasured privacy but, since there still was no communication from her, his options seemed limited to this and going to the Village for the weekend to search for her.

Mind made up, he wasted very little time and went to find the key as soon as he arrived home. He inserted it in the lock and, as it released and he touched the doorknob, a chill and foreboding almost caused him to lock it again without entering.

He shook off the feeling, speaking out loud, "This is for you, Brie. I love you, too." A feeling crept into his chest, like when he first saw her, as he found the light switch and took a few steps into the room. First, he opened the French doors to the patio to let in a little air then turned to glance around the room.

The old pine-board walls remained the same and she hadn't covered the wide plank floors in the main room, except for a few small cotton rugs, yet it had become something he could not have anticipated. On one entire wall there were staggered wood and antique brass racks, about eight feet high, holding canvases of various sizes, nearly fifty he guessed. All around the rest of the studio, leaning against furniture or on table easels, were paintings in various stages of drying. Jonathan had no idea Gabrielle was so prolific; although, while watching the process, from sketches and photos to finished portrait of the engaged couple, he came to appreciate her talent. Once, he suggested finding an agent to arrange a gallery showing. She seemed indifferent to the idea but now he realized she was probably frightened by it for some reason.

He found a small step ladder near the racks and climbed up to look through the paintings. There were landscapes, scenes from all over the country, sketches and portraits of several singers and musical groups and a portrait of an angry but uncommonly handsome man playing the violin. On the highest racks and all the way in the back, were the dead garden paintings, as if she wanted them out of her sight. There were impressionist, and post-impressionist paintings in the styles of Monet and Van Gogh, which he assumed she must have painted while in France. Then he came upon what appeared to be the painting of Monet Emory had mentioned because Jonathan recognized the description of the "...blue pleated silk shirt, tawny velvet hat..." He also found four paintings of the Washington Square Arch in Greenwich Village, in all four seasons, which confirmed

Cara's remembrance of Gabrielle conveying the impression she visited there many times. All this strengthened his resolve to go the Village to search for her.

Next, he went to a huge farm-style dining table, antiqued white and placed in front of the windows facing the water. Apparently, she used this as a desk and work table, since it was piled with papers and sketch pads. He opened the pad that appeared to be the one she was working on last and was struck by what he saw. Gabrielle had completed very detailed sketches for Cara and Emory's nursery murals before she left. She must have begun drawing them as soon as she knew about the baby and before she told him and Jesse. While there was some added pastel color, most were in black and white, dainty and enchanting, perfect for such a special baby girl. Jonathan touched the last one for a moment then, carefully, closed the pad and placed it exactly where he'd found it.

He turned back from the table and looked up toward the loft. Under it were a loveseat and two wood and upholstered chairs with an ottoman coffee table. All of the upholstery, decorative pieces, throw pillows and the bedcovers in the loft, were in shades of sand, white and soft blues and pale aqua. There were yards of billowing white curtains and everything came together to create the feeling of being enfolded in cool seascapes and breezes.

Jonathan walked around the gallery of pictures on the floor, stopping at each. The ones she started painting on Marginal Way and in Perkins Cove were finished now and Jonathan was impressed with how perfectly they represented the highlights of the days and evenings they'd shared there. Gabrielle gave him two of them for his birthday but seeing the rest touched him deeply and he closed his eyes, recalling what a sweet and exciting experience it had been. When he opened his eyes again and continued to view the paintings, he was surprised to see some very different works among the ones on the floor - geometric abstracts in vibrant, yet soft shades which reminded him of Kandinsky. It appeared she was able to paint anything she chose to try.

The idea of going through her personal papers was out of the question to Jonathan and, in fact, he was feeling more and more uncomfortable about this trespass.

Just as he decided to go, he realized all of her plants looked dead and felt this was a clear sign she hadn't anticipated being gone this long or she would have asked either he or Jesse to care for them, a terribly disturbing thought. Although he loved working on the landscaping of his yard, he wasn't at all knowledgeable about house plants but he decided to water them all anyway, in some desperate attempt to revive them and nourish a thirsty optimism.

He concluded there was nothing of help in her studio so he headed toward the door. As he glanced around the room one last time, his eyes found something that sent chills up his arms again and caused him to take in a sudden breath. He ran to the bookcases, which lined one wall, and took out the book he had focused on. It was a very old copy of "Don Quixote."

"This must be it. You meant to read your copy," he said aloud to Gabrielle, tucked it under his arm and closed the French doors, feeling much better about having entered her studio. In his haste to close the doors and curtains and then lock the entry door and return to the house, he failed to notice a folded piece of paper which slipped out of the book and fell to the floor behind him.

He had changed and gone directly to the studio when he got home, without eating dinner, so he made a sandwich and poured himself a glass of wine before settling on the sofa in his study, certain he would find the answer to the mystery of Gabrielle's request in her volume of "Don Quixote."

He thumbed through the book quickly and noticed something between the pages. He pulled it out but replaced it with a bookmark, in case it was there to mark a particular page or passage. It was a black and white photograph of a beautiful woman who looked like Gabrielle, with long dark hair and huge eyes, holding a child who appeared to be about two years old. Even in black and white, the mother's and baby's eyes seemed like they must be blue. The baby was beautiful as well and he knew it must be Gabrielle. He turned the picture over and, on the back, it said simply "Summer 1971."

A thorough search through the rest of the book for any other pictures or clues revealed nothing and a reading of the pages where he found the picture was useless too. Then he carefully scanned the entire book for any markings and again came up empty-handed. What did she want him to learn from the picture? He was angry and frustrated, again, with his inability to grasp her meaning or intent.

After a very long contemplation about Brie, whether she was safe and longed to see him as much as he longed for her, and staring at the picture until his eyes refused to focus at all, Jonathan eventually dozed off, still sitting upright. He awoke with a start, calling out "Gabrielle" and surprised to discover he had slept for nearly six hours without waking once. He jumped up realizing he called her Gabrielle instead of Brie like he usually did. The nickname started during their trip to Ogunquit, though he couldn't recall exactly how it began except it had something to do with trying to get her attention on Marginal Way, Gabrielle not carrying on the wind like Brie. She turned, recognizing his voice, but not sure what name he was calling out. It pleased her when he explained and it became his nickname for her. He was the only one who called her Brie except for Jesse who did once in a while, picking it up from Jonathan's use. These wandering wakeup thoughts changed suddenly as it occurred to him it was Friday and he would be heading for New York at the end of his work day. He looked for the picture which had, apparently, dropped as he slept and found it under the couch. He smiled at it and felt content to have this piece of her, for now, and confident of finding both Brie and the answers to so many questions this weekend.

Even the routine of showering and dressing for the office seemed comforting this morning. Thoughts of Jesse popped into his head like the sound of opening a soda can and, realizing he hadn't seen him for a while, Jonathan wondered what he was up to. Being so pre-occupied, he hadn't spent any time with his very good friend and, truthfully, sometimes deliberately ignored his comings and goings. He decided to make a point of calling Jesse before leaving for Greenwich Village.

The drive to the hospital was extremely slow, with traffic unusually congested, and though it seemed strange that his normally easy ten or fifteen-minute ride was taking so much longer, he wasn't bothered by it or worried about arriving late at the hospital or the office. He was, in fact, happier than he had been in a while, partly because of getting some sleep, and hoped there would be fewer emergencies today so he would be able to leave at a reasonably early hour for New York. It was a surprisingly warm and sunny morning for late January, probably why so many people were out and about this early which he decided was a good omen. His good luck charm, the photograph of Gabrielle was in his breast pocket. Jonathan laughed to himself feeling grateful no one knew what he was thinking, for his colleagues would certainly be questioning his ability to practice medicine, if they knew he was so desperate he was relying on omens and charms to get him through the day.

There were already several patients in the waiting room when he arrived at his office, after his hospital rounds. He was grateful because it would be one of those busy days with no time to think about how slowly the hands of the clock were moving.

Chapter 7

MORGAN AND JESSE

Morgan Jeffries could barely contain an uncontrollable urge to giggle as she spotted the adorable man who had been watching her for more than a month. In truth, she had been watching him too. If ever there were a day when she might compromise her unwavering belief that the man should make the first move, or at least appear to, today was it.

A few times they made eye contact but she only attempted this when he wasn't doing something awkward or embarrassing. She didn't want to cause any humiliation by making it obvious she noticed him then. Recently, she thought he was heading toward her to try and say something but was interrupted by meeting someone he knew, a very attractive woman and a little boy and girl who flew at him with hugs and smiles. The woman was very obviously flirting and Morgan had assumed, with a great deal of disappointment, it was his wife and children. At the end of the conversation, though, she heard the woman say, "Come on you two. We have to go meet Daddy. Say 'good-bye' to Dr. Jesse." Morgan was thrilled it wasn't what she thought and she learned a few things about him too. This funny man was a physician or dentist or PhD, children adored him and he really liked them too. Unfortunately, after the conversation, he lost his nerve, she guessed, because he left the park without trying to speak to her. Now he had a name, Jessie or Jesse. She wouldn't call him by it, though, or tell anyone she knew it because it came out of order. He should be the one to tell her and so she only repeated it, quietly to herself, in the dark hours when she laid in bed trying to imagine what would happen next. Thoughts of scanning phone book yellow pages searching for doctors or dentists with his name came and then were forgotten with sleep.

Her Aunt Sarah was concerned when Morgan first told her about him. Morgan walked Sarah's dog occasionally and, now, at the same time every Thursday evening and Saturday morning, since that's when the man who was watching her seemed to be at the park. But Morgan replied she was very sure he was harmless. In fact, she had felt, from the first time he fell over a trash can and then, embarrassed, hid behind a tree as if his very muscular build could actually be concealed by it, that, if he ever came out of hiding and spoke to her, she would marry him.

For the last two weeks, he seemed more determined but just couldn't find a way to speak to her and Morgan went from feeling sorry for him to being furious with him. It was strangely like being stood up repeatedly on a blind date or a difficult journey when unforeseeable events feel like a conspiracy of interference. While there was a growing level of frustration, Morgan had to admit there was a very titillating aspect to it as well, though she did sometimes think she was going a little insane. *Was it really possible to be so in love with someone you've never spoken a word to?*

Today, he'd definitely taken a giant and delightfully entertaining step toward showing himself and creating an opportunity for conversation. She saw him, in the distance, coming in her direction with a cute little dog. This was new and it was very apparent they both were struggling to find some common ground, though not so common they would continue to trip over each other. The dog was obviously very well trained and was doing its best to heel but the man seemed to think it should be running freely and kept letting out more leash line, which only resulted in both of them becoming more entangled in it, each time the dog tried to reposition itself properly at his side.

While the man was distracted with trying to straighten things out, Morgan and Duffy - short for his registered name, Master MacDuffy, her aunt's West Highland White Terrier, took a little detour onto the grass and sat on a bench so she could enjoy the scene. She was flattered he went to the trouble of borrowing someone's pet in order to appear to be a dog owner and, she assumed, use this manufactured commonality to, finally, speak to her.

He hadn't seen where she went and walked right by and now "his dog" decided it needed to relieve itself. He tried everything to dissuade it but was unsuccessful. He began to pick up the mess he had failed to prevent, placing his hand in a plastic bag and bending toward it with a shudder and grimace. Just as he stood up and was trying to reverse the bag, he noticed her and dropped it onto the back of the impeccably groomed dog, which shook itself, resulting in the bag and mess clinging to his sneakers and jeans.

Maybe today isn't the day, she laughed to herself when he quickly disappeared, looking completely humiliated as she pretended not to have noticed him at all.

When she returned to her aunt's house, and related the story of their latest encounter, Sarah did enjoy it but cautioned her again to be careful. Morgan just laughed and replied that, if he was someone with bad intentions, he certainly wasn't a very talented criminal. Her aunt agreed and then surprised her by suggesting perhaps Morgan should speak to him and put him out of his misery. But she still refused to make the first move since she was enjoying it all far too much to give up just yet.

"I think, on Saturday, I won't walk Duffy, I'll roller blade instead, just to throw him off and see what he comes up with next," she answered.

"Nasty girl," her aunt replied, now, with an encouraging grin.

"That's me. See you Saturday!"

"Maybe I'll have a stroll on Saturday too, apart from you, of course, just to catch a glimpse of him, poor thing, he has no idea what he's in for," Aunt Sarah said giving Morgan a quick wink and hug goodbye. *What I really want is to reassure myself he's as harmless as she thinks,* Sara thought.

Jesse couldn't have embarrassed himself more if he planned to and his only hope was that she never noticed him. He felt very clever when he decided to borrow one of Cara and Emory's dogs, Nala, a Shih Poo mix rescued from a shelter to walk in the park. They got her just as "Lion King" came out and the boys had insisted on the name Nala. While not her favorite choice, Cara gave them their way, grateful they actually agreed on something right off without fists flying. Jesse was especially fond of Nala, who was playful and very affectionate, and thought it would be the perfect opening to begin a conversation with the girl with the white dog, and, then, ask her to dinner as Gabrielle suggested.

Some time ago, he realized she walked her dog in the park, every Thursday evening around five thirty and on Saturday mornings at around eleven. It was December so it was dark on Thursdays and it wasn't always easy to find her but there she was right in front of him on the path ahead.

When he went to borrow Nala, Cara handed him some plastic bags demonstrating how to put his hand in to pick up any mess and then reverse the bag and seal it.

He'd never had a dog, which was ironic since his family was, somehow, distantly related to Albert Payson Terhune. His father adored his books when he was a boy, hence his naming his son Jesse Payson Terhune. There were no pets in the Terhune household but, ironically, his dad encouraged Jesse to read Terhune's books. Jesse, in rare rebellion, after reading *Lad: A Dog* took the position it was ridiculous to be forced to read about owning and loving a dog while being denied the experience and he refused any further Terhune books. He preferred mysteries like *The Hardy Boys* and later, *Sherlock Holmes* and Agatha Christie's *Hercule Poirot*. Sometimes, Jesse reasoned it probably was just as well, given the six-month cycle and confusion of his childhood and home, but, at other times, thought it might be nice to have something or someone who always stayed.

Anyway, following his messy dog-owner act, he ran, almost dragging Nala, out of the park and into the comfort of darkness without looking at the girl with the white dog again because he really didn't want to know if she had seen him.

He closed Nala in the bathroom, changed his clothes and threw them in the washer and then returned. He tried to use paper towels to clean her off but it only made it worse so he decided the only solution was to put her in the shower. After far too much shampoo and quite a struggle, he finally rinsed away the suds and toweled her off. He placed her on the tile floor in the foyer and went to change for a second time because, now, he was dripping wet.

When he returned, he was horrified to find Nala shaking uncontrollably. The heat was kept very low during the day when no one was at home and Jesse hadn't thought to raise it when he came in. A heating pad and the blow dryer began to warm her while he was thinking just what he needed as the ending to this awful episode was to be responsible for Cara's dog catching pneumonia. Nala seemed to enjoy sitting on the warm pad while having her coat dried with the blow dryer and fluffed with some towels. Somewhere in the middle of all this she stopped shaking, jumped up and licked his face and shook herself until she slipped on some damp tiles onto her chin. Jesse couldn't help laughing out loud because her hair was standing straight out as if she were struck by lightning or chewed on an electrical cord. He tried to smooth her down a little but she kept running away and making it clear she'd had enough handling so he just put her in the car to take her home.

When he and Nala came through the door, Cara collapsed to the floor, laughing hysterically at the sight of her favorite of all their dogs. As Nala jumped all over her, Cara took her in her arms saying, "What have you done to my poor Nala? She looks like a cheerleading pompom." Between laughing so hard and her pregnancy, she couldn't get back up. Jesse and Emory, joined by the boys, tried, very clumsily, to help her and soon they were all on the floor, laughing and enjoying the silliness. It was just what Jesse needed to lighten his mood again.

Joining them for dinner, Jesse told Cara and Emory about his dog-walking disaster in which Emory, especially, found great delight. Then Jesse declared, "I've made up my mind I am just going to walk right up to her the next time we're both in the park and begin a conversation with her".

Neither Cara nor Emory believed he would do it though, knowing how impossible it always was for Jesse, despite his determined intention, to confront his biggest fear and make the move toward fulfilling his honest and very strong desire to have a serious and lasting relationship. The nearly paralyzing result of each effort Jesse made to initiate a conversation with a woman had to be witnessed to understand the genuineness and depth of what they believed could now be considered a phobia.

On Saturday morning, Jesse was watching a striking red cardinal in a cedar tree, wishing he'd brought his camera with him to photograph this Christmas card scene and feeling very resolute about speaking to the girl with the white dog. Suddenly he spotted her moving toward and then past him very swiftly, rollerblading! He was on foot, making conversation impossible. and he decided to run home and get his blades, even though rollerblading in December seemed very strange. He was determined this was going to be the day he asked her if she would have dinner with him.

It was an especially cold and raw day, with the threat of snowflakes loitering in menacing gray clouds and chill winds and, during the short drive home, Jesse kept thinking how crazy this all was. He had watched her for some time, interacting with people in the park with her compelling smile and friendly ease and, as improbable as it seemed, he knew he was in love. He wanted so badly to find some way to speak to her.

It was impossible for him to casually walk up to a female he didn't know and begin a conversation, well, not one that was remotely coherent. Approaching a woman he was attracted to, turned words into babble, and anything within arms-reach into scattered chaos and shattered ego.

By the time he found his blades, parked his car again and put them on, she was rollerblading out of the park. Jesse decided he would follow her this time and try to catch up with her. He tried to stay at a safe distance, at first, not wanting to frighten her, but didn't take his eyes off her. Intent on his goal, he didn't realize he was blading from the sidewalk into the street until he came off the curb and collided with a bicyclist. Jesse grabbed onto the bike as they hit and his legs went between the two wheels as he slid into a sitting position under it. Neither of them was hurt because Jesse was able, with one powerful hand on the rider's shoulder and one on the bike, to hold it up and keep it from falling over. He glanced up from this strange accident just in time to see her disappear, and wondered as he apologized for his carelessness, if the person bicycling at this bitter time of year was trying to catch up with the woman he loved as well.

Morgan stayed nearby, hidden in a store window, so he wouldn't know she'd seen the collision, just to be sure he wasn't hurt. When she returned to her aunt's house and began to relate what happened, Sarah interrupted her saying she had taken a walk and witnessed the entire incident, his running to get his blades and returning as she, meanly, headed out of the park when she saw him. She was no longer leery of him and Morgan was surprised to hear her say, "Morgan, Dear, I'm going to risk the chance that you might be angry with me for saying it but I think you're being a bit cruel".

Morgan beamed and replied, "I'm not angry but I disagree with you, Aunt Sarah. I'm very sure my next plan will result in our meeting each other, finally. Besides, one day when we get married and have children, we'll have a great 'how we met' story to tell them."

Her aunt shook her head and laughed now, "I can't wait to meet this young man, who appears to be the incredibly handsome and pathetically determined fool who will be my nephew one day."

"I won't be here on Thursday but I have something very special planned for next Saturday," Morgan said.

"How do you know he'll be there? With any luck, he hit his head in the bicycle collision and it brought him to his senses or produced a serious amnesia, at least I hope so, for his sake."

Morgan adored her aunt and truly enjoyed that she had become fond and defensive of him without even meeting him. "Aunt Sarah, I'm just trying to create some pleasure and enjoyment from the torture of waiting so long for him to find the courage to speak to me. A part of me is in no hurry to start the dreaded relationship game and, in the end, it's really for him. It's very obvious he wants to do this and I'm just allowing him time to accomplish it and to have the satisfaction of having initiated our romance."

"Oh, is that it, really? Or is there some small measure of enjoying the attention and his suffering, payback to those who didn't try long and hard enough to win you?"

"Do I really seem that cynical and mercenary? I hope not but, even if there is a bit of what you say in it, I intend to do everything I can to be worthy of his effort and interest when the time comes."

"There's no question you're deserving of a wonderful man to love you and I certainly didn't mean to imply otherwise, Dear. I hope I didn't hurt your feelings but I am very aware, these days, of how precious each moment, spent well or wasted, can become when it involves the person you love."

"You didn't hurt my feelings at all. I always treasure your insights and concern. I've felt, right along, that even these frustrating and comical episodes are precious moments and shared time, which, I hope, will be an inseparable part of whatever we become together and our memory of how and when we began to love each other." She still did not share with her aunt that she knew his name.

"Oh, Morgan, I do hope so."

"And to be sure they are I've recorded the details of each of our *quasi-rendezvous* encounters in my journal so the lovely excitement and significance of these moments will be remembered long after familiarity and routine have found their way into our lives."

"That's such a wonderful thing to have done. There are so many times when I'm trying to remember something about your Uncle Casey and me I wish I'd kept a diary or journal as they are referred to these days. Now, since I've had the privilege of watching the step-by-step evolution of this romance and shared both your worst and best moments so far, I want a promise from you that a few years from now we'll have a cup of tea and share your journal to compare where your relationship is then to the expectations of this moment."

"That's a lovely idea and definitely a date," Morgan laughed. "And, now, I really do have to run. I'm so sorry but there just never seems to be enough time these days. Next week is really packed with court and client appointments, so, as I said earlier, I won't see you until Saturday. If you need anything, make sure you call me or Alex and no more trying to move things about that you shouldn't, promise?"

"I promise. Take care of yourself, Dear. You work much too hard. Thank you for all your help and for lunch."

"You don't have to thank me. You've done so much for us and it's the least I can do."

Chapter 8

MORGAN AND SARAH

Morgan did work extremely hard, very committed to her clients and their needs. After passing the bar exam and because of her excellent scholastic standing and achievements, she was invited to join a prominent law firm in Boston. She was very impressed with them and herself for a time but then, because of her ability to negotiate and earn trust, began to receive mostly divorce cases. Their clients were usually high profile and wealthy and the cases could be extremely lucrative but often contentious and she disliked that particular area of law.

During some of the cases she negotiated, though, she became interested in the child custody aspect and the rights of the child when parental battles turned bitter in the struggle to "win" custody. They often lost sight of the damage being done to their children. Slowly, her interest led her to decide to leave the law firm and open her own office to become an Attorney Guardian Ad Litem, representing children and their best interests, in difficult cases of unresolved and hostile custody issues or in cases where a child's safety was in question. Through referrals from other attorneys or mediators and sometimes through social workers or the court, her practice had, sadly, grown steadily. About twenty percent of her caseload was from the social services area, as a volunteer attorney advocate, where there was need but no financial means.

Her office and home were, for the moment, in a stone carriage house in Dennis. It was on a parcel of land that had once been part of a huge estate owned by her Aunt Sarah and Uncle Casey, husband and wife for fifty-two years until his death one year earlier.

Sarah was Morgan's maternal great aunt, sister of Morgan's grandmother, Katherine. Because of some secret family estrangement, Katherine's daughter, Elizabeth, Morgan's widowed mother, hadn't seen her Aunt Sarah since she was very small. She was struggling to raise Morgan and her brother, Alex, after their father's death. Shortly after losing her husband, Elizabeth lost her mother Katherine as well. Upon learning of her sister's death and her niece Elizabeth's financial problems, Sarah and Casey set up a trust for her and they all became very close, a family.

In addition to their house in Dennis, Sarah and Casey owned the summer home, in Chatham, where they had moved, for convenience, about two years before he died and where Sarah now lived alone. Since they never had children or any other nieces or nephews, Morgan and Alex were named their heirs and Sarah and Casey, privately, decided to turn ownership of the Dennis estate over to them immediately after they settled in Chatham, instead of waiting until their deaths. They surprised Morgan and Alex with the trust papers making it officially their property at a family gathering to celebrate Uncle

Casey's eighty-ninth birthday. Less than a month later, Casey passed away, unexpectedly, after suffering a heart attack.

Morgan and Alex inherited a gracious, sixteen-room, stone and stucco home on the water and its four-acre grounds. They decided to renovate the home and create two living spaces in a duplex style arrangement with independent entertainment and bedroom areas but sharing the kitchen and staff so it wouldn't be considered an illegal two-family home. Alex was an architect and designed the plans for the renovation, with sometimes mildly-heated but always respected input from his sister.

Once, when Morgan and Alex were visiting Aunt Sarah, they tried to convince her to return to the estate instead of living alone in Chatham but, with an interesting explanation, she gratefully, but adamantly, declined. Sarah said part of the reason she and Casey were married so long and well was allowing the other the right of solitude without presumption. Now, she was content to savor feeling loneliness when it visited and not feeling alone when others came to call.

Morgan and Alex were having the guest cottage, with its incredible views of the water, renovated as well, hoping once they got Aunt Sarah to visit, she would decide to stay there if she wasn't comfortable sharing the big house with them. Neither mentioned it, quietly accepting her refusal for now. They were puzzled, though, by her strange smile and far-off gaze as they said goodbye.

What Sarah left unsaid and lost herself in, as Morgan and Alex drove off, were the intimacies of her life with Casey, years swept up now in the passage of time and set down in the unfamiliar landscape of endless absence. Sara rarely allowed herself self-indulgent sadness, though, and, more often, remembered their days together happily as she did today. While she was engrossed in clay or stone or Mozart on her piano, Casey immersed himself in his gardens or became the tortured recluse struggling with philosophical contemplations of death, ethics and the infinite.

But there was always the wanting after a silence, one seeking out the other, the days and nights running together lost in each other's passion. Then there was the traveling to exotic places or throwing lavish, wild parties, in their Dennis home, where guests lingered for days. and, then, there would be a separating again and returning to aloneness as naturally as blood flowing away from the heart.

Chatham was where they had made their final home together and where Casey chose to die. For Sarah, it was just as it always had been, for now the coming together was in the memories, so many exquisite ones. She felt him with her, sharing the blooming of a peony or rose or a goldfinch on the thistle feeder. And, often, she felt him watching her sculpt a new piece or listening to her sing or play the piano as adoringly as he so often did when he thought she wasn't aware of it, embracing her suddenly from behind, burying his face in her hair and kissing her neck. She could feel it even now and closed her eyes savoring the delicate and fleeting moment, like a summer rain on a sunny day that produces an astonishing rainbow, lovely but transient.

How could Morgan and Alex, so young and only just beginning to understand the desire to feel and be loved, comprehend this? How could they understand why she mustn't leave this final place she and her beloved Casey shared and where he had taken his last breath?

The week passed more quickly than Morgan expected, between work and trips to oversee what was happening at her home, and, on Saturday morning, she returned to Aunt Sarah's house. After helping with a few tasks and some paperwork, she headed out to the park, hoping to see the man who had been watching her, before taking her aunt to lunch. Morgan timed it perfectly, having discovered he made a point of arriving at the park just before eleven o'clock to wait for her. She arrived early, without Duffy, and carrying her guitar, with the strap in front of her shoulder and the guitar hanging on her back. She waited until he was seated on a bench and then walked past him, heading for the other end of the park near the bandstand. From her side vision, she saw him jump up and run through the park and disappear and she bent over in a fit of laughter and almost dropped her guitar. She had to hurry now, if her plan was going to work. It usually didn't take very long for him to return. She wondered if he actually owned a guitar or would borrow that too. The thought caused her to laugh out loud again, unintentionally, and she looked around to see if anyone noticed.

Jesse, relieved she was there since she hadn't appeared on Thursday, jumped in his car and sped home thinking he just found the perfect way to meet her, at last, a real common interest, the guitar. He would sit and play his guitar and perhaps even sing something and maybe she would finally notice him and hold still long enough for him to speak to her. He was sure this was the way he would finally meet her. Now he just needed to think of exactly what he would say, once he had her attention.

He returned, found a spot in the town parking lot and crossed the street to the park determined to play his guitar the moment she was near enough to hear and then ask the girl with the white dog to dinner. He walked around the park three times, carrying his guitar in the same manner she had, before he saw her sitting on the steps of the bandstand. As he came closer, he noticed she changed and was dressed in a long red suede coat with white fur at the collar, cuffs and hood. She was a perfectly beautiful Christmas card, like the cardinal in the cedar tree. Although he could see she was playing her guitar, he couldn't hear it because the wind was blowing toward her. He was almost directly in front of her before he saw she had two large cups of coffee next to her and realized she must be meeting someone. He was trying to think quickly what to do, perhaps take the left or right path around the bandstand to make it appear he was hurrying somewhere, when she suddenly looked in his direction, stopped playing and took a sip from one of the cups and smiled.

Jesse's first impulse was to turn around to see who she was smiling at but, if there was no one behind him, he would look really foolish and, if there was, he really didn't want to know.

And then he got it...the dog...suddenly appearing at the same time each Thursday and Saturday...the roller blades...even the guitar. She'd known for some time. And then he groaned, sure, now, that she had watched him make a fool of himself again and again. It was all a mean, humiliating, excruciating and incredible game.

His heart felt like it was tumbling out of his chest and dancing there for all to see, a jester bouncing in an opened "Jack-in-the-box," and his mind tried to process and search for the perfect reaction to this turn of events knowing he was not ready to start an intelligible conversation.

Suddenly, he knew what to do and grinned at her briefly, before veering to the left, around the bandstand to the back side where she couldn't see him. This was something he could handle-a game-a competition.

He looked around for someone who seemed like they'd be up for an adventure and pulled out his pen and the piece of paper he always kept clipped to his cell phone in case his answering service called him and began writing. He spotted a young couple, Shelley and Jeff, whose daughter was a patient of his. He explained quickly what was going on and asked if they'd help him with a joke. They were delighted at the prospect of being part of this dating game. They discussed the strategy and suddenly the three of them came walking around the bandstand, where she was still sitting, as if they were good friends who had arranged to meet there, chatting and laughing as they headed back toward where his car was parked. They stood and chatted for a few moments, with Shelley facing the bandstand so she could describe what the girl with the guitar was doing.

Shelley found this fun, "She's just sitting there looking a little confused but smiling and trying to watch us discreetly." Jesse liked that. To him it meant she was, indeed, playing a game and was waiting for him to make the next move.

He handed them a note to bring to her after he left. Jesse wrote his cell phone number on one of his business cards and handed it to them. They decided Shelley and Jeff would hold onto her reply, watching from somewhere out of sight, and call his cell phone when she left the park.

Knowing they were struggling with financial problems, Jesse tried to offer them a little money, discreetly, for the time they would spend, but Shelley adamantly refused and gave him a kiss saying she thought this was all so very romantic and she hoped it had the really great ending he deserved so much. Jesse left the parking lot and drove around, anxiously waiting for his phone to ring.

Just when he was certain something was going terribly wrong, his phone rang and Shelley was laughing and could barely get out "Where are you? We have her reply. Hurry! We want you to know what she said." He drove back and found them waiting for him where they parted earlier. He picked them up so he wouldn't be spotted and drove around the block.

Now Shelley was demanding, "First tell us what your note said."

Jeff laughed and shook his head toward her, "You might as well comply right off. She won't let it go until she has her way, believe me."

Jesse laughed, "I just asked her to have dinner with me but without naming a place or time or telling her my name or phone number."

"Okay, here," she laughed too as she handed him her reply. "After she read your note and as she began to write her reply, she smiled and really seemed to enjoy crafting her answer. She said to tell you '*Check*' as she finished the note and handed it to me."

He opened it and chuckled. She'd drawn a huge smiling chess piece, with enormous eyes and long lashes in a half-closed flutter, as if flirting, and a very big grin with just "yes" in a little bubble coming out of its mouth. She hadn't provided him with her name or phone number either. Jesse yelped in excitement, scaring Shelley and Jeff at first. He did it! At last, and she said "yes." Then, he said he wanted to treat them to lunch to thank them and because he was suddenly starving. They had to pick up their daughter, who had stayed overnight with Shelley's parents, but asked for a rain check for a lunch after his dinner with the girl with the white dog or if they could help with arranging it.

As soon as he returned home, Jesse phoned Cara to report that he had finally done it.

"What did you say to her?" Cara asked, so happy for him.

"Well, I didn't exactly say anything. I wrote her a note but she did answer it." And, then, he explained, wishing he could tell Jonathan and then, sadly, missing Gabrielle. Funny, both he and Jonathan had both been dealing with thoughts about women they were in love with from afar.

Cara decided to be kind and not point out the obvious. He hadn't actually spoken with her yet and, so, would still be facing his dreaded phobia about starting a conversation with a woman. Instead, they just talked about what he planned to do next.

⸻

Morgan ran into Aunt Sarah's living room and declared she was sure this man was the love she had waited for, for so long. Everything seemed surreal and, she had to admit, a little scary now, too.

Aunt Sarah was a bit shocked at the turn of events and asked, "What will you do next?"

For the first time, she wasn't sure, "I don't want to think about that just now. I just want to feel this moment when we've finally acknowledged each other."

Jesse was leaving the next day for the December clinics and wouldn't be able to go to the park for more than a week. The advantage of this interval did not escape him. She deserved to wonder, for a short while, where he was and be the one to suffer a bit.

By the time he returned, he knew exactly what he was going to do. He got home, late on Sunday night of the weekend following their last meeting, and would have to wait until Thursday to see her, which would be twelve days.

On Thursday, not wanting to leave anything to chance, he left the office early and went directly home to pick up a few things. He arrived at the park with about twenty-five minutes to spare and met Shelley and Jeff and their daughter, Taylor. Shelley insisted they wanted to help him set up everything just perfectly. They carried a small round table and two chairs up on the bandstand, on which they put a white table cloth and a bouquet of red and white roses with Christmas greens and a bow. Jesse placed two candles, two champagne glasses, champagne in a bucket of snow on the table with a small platter of fruit, cheese, bread and napkins with holly leaves and berries on them. He stood back, pleased with the outcome. Although the original plan was an entire meal there, this changed to taking her to a restaurant for dinner, after this simple champagne, cheese and fruit appetizer, because the warm day had turned too cold to stay outdoors for very long.

When everything was ready, the three disappeared and he took out his guitar and began singing "Lady."

Morgan left her Aunt Sarah's house and walked to the park, without Duffy, as she had each night since he had failed to appear on the Thursday and Saturday following their last adventure. As she left, she called out to Aunt Sarah, "I feel sure he'll be there tonight. I'll call you tomorrow."

Her aunt was more than a little concerned as she was leaving, "Morgan Dear, may I ask that you call quickly, at some point, and just say *I'm fine?* I won't be able to rest until I know you are. Do be careful."

"I'm so sorry! That was terribly thoughtless of me not to realize, after all your support through this, how difficult this evening of waiting will be for you. I promise I will call you, at least once to reassure you."

Sarah held Morgan's cheeks in her hands and kissed her forehead, "I knew it was because you are excited and a little nervous. There is nothing like the joy of this early passion and I wish you the best possible moments this evening."

Morgan hugged her aunt. Part of her was sure his absence was just a continuation of the game and getting back at her, but her heart was skipping and she could barely breathe, wanting, so badly, to find him there tonight.

She headed directly for the bandstand, where they had last seen each other. Even from a distance, she could see two lit candles and began to run, then, regained composure, slowing to a leisurely stroll, which took every bit of self-discipline and control she could discover within herself.

He was sitting, playing his guitar, at a table set with a beautiful Christmas arrangement, champagne and food. Her face, all on its own, fell into a bigger and bigger smile the closer she got and now she could hear he was singing as well. His voice was beautiful and she realized the song was "Lady" -- the Lionel Richie words so perfect. *You have gone and made me such a fool...Lady, for so many years I thought I'd never find you...* As she reached the bandstand, he continued singing but stopped playing the guitar and reached out a hand to help her up the stairs to her seat at the table. He finished...*You're my Lady* just as he held her chair and then opened the champagne and poured it without speaking a word, neither taking their eyes off the other.

She was trembling and called upon her lawyer-in-court demeanor to try and calm herself, so her hand wouldn't shake when she reached for the champagne glass he offered to her.

What he did next shocked her and made her feel faint. He suddenly dropped to one knee in front of her and said, "I believe our ancestors and spirit guides have conspired to bring us together here, in spite of my embarrassing lack of courage and grace, because you are my one love," just that. And then she was on her knees too, with her arms draped over his shoulders, and they were kissing each other carefully, each sensing the delicate significance of beginnings. The anticipation and tension of the last month was acknowledged with each touch of lips and sweet mutual response.

When they finally rose, holding hands and looking into each other's eyes, embarrassed, at first, by their shared, uncontrollable expression of intimacy, they both began to smile again and Jesse spoke first, "Hello. My name is Jesse Payson Terhune and I'd love it if you would agree to have dinner with me tonight."

Her smile was so wide now she could barely contain it enough to speak. "Hello, Jesse. My name is Morgan Lee Jeffries, but most people call me Meg, and I've been waiting to have dinner with you for a very, very long time."

They had their champagne and a bit of the fruit and cheese, wordlessly looking at each other, smiling, looking away briefly, to gain composure, and then back again. Noticing she was feeling chilled, he took her hand and led her down the stairs saying they should be going to the restaurant. She was concerned about the table and his guitar and was about to suggest they clean it up before leaving when she turned to look back and saw the young couple who had brought her his note. They were smiling at them and beginning to clear away everything and she realized how much trouble Jesse had gone to, to plan and execute every detail.

That's strange, Jesse thought as he glanced at her from time to time in the light of the lampposts along the park walk. *She's really cute, no, beautiful and her smile is amazing but she doesn't really seem to look that much like Meg Ryan and I don't care. I just want to keep looking at her forever. Gabrielle, wherever she was tonight, had been so very wise.*

He gazed up at the starlit sky breaking into a charming and almost childlike expression which made Morgan look at him questioningly.

He felt her inquisitive look and smiled at her, kissed the back of her hand, which he was holding as they walked, and decided he would always call her Morgan.

As they strolled, Morgan wondered what he was thinking and worried what would happen once they were seated for dinner, whether he would have as much trouble with conversation and knives and forks as he did with challenges on the path to meeting her. How strange, perhaps some would say absurd or dangerous, it was to have already shared very intimate kisses but not any words to speak of.

To her surprise, he was talkative and funny and, best of all, while there had been some game playing, mostly hers, during the long struggle to meet, he lacked any hint of pretense. There was a graceful clumsiness about him, hard to describe but familiar now and both amusing and touching. He was simply Jesse, a charming mix of shyness and confidence, who enjoyed life immensely.

The conversation was relaxed and genuine and each word created and increased a desire to remain together, neither able to imagine saying goodbye. Morgan surprised herself by asking if he'd like to come to her place for a while, since he mentioned a roommate. He was so grateful she asked and accepted, without any thought of trying to pretend reluctance, and completely willing to show his obvious infatuation with her. They sat and talked and held each other until well into the night.

Finally, Morgan asked him if he'd like to stay, making it clear she did not intend to have sex with him but couldn't stand the idea of ending their time together. They went to her bedroom, stripped shyly to their underwear and, climbing under the covers quickly, fell asleep with legs, arms and hearts wrapped together.

They woke early and Jesse left immediately, skipping breakfast and avoiding awkwardness, to return home for a shower and change of clothes before heading to his office. They had agreed to meet at Morgan's house and then go to dinner as soon as they were both finished with their day. After returning home in the morning and taking a shower, Jesse packed a few things which he left in his car. He didn't bring them in when he arrived at her house, to avoid any appearance of presumption. Opening the door, the second he rang the bell, she was momentarily disappointed when she saw that he had nothing with him. Well, except for a beautiful bouquet of pastel roses and baby's breath and an enormous bag of "gourmet malt balls" from a wonderful candy shop near his office, having discovered they were a common weakness and favorite.

The moment their eyes met and Jesse saw her smile they embraced and, lips touching, forgot the flowers and candy and, unlike the shy and tentative evening before, hands and mouths caressed and kissed wildly as they moved, without separating or stopping, toward the bedroom, progressively unbuttoned, un-zippered and blissfully naked by the time they fell, breathless, across the bed, aroused by weeks of anticipation.

During the entire weekend together, they talked, showered together and made love, endlessly and easily. Apart from Morgan's phone calls to her Aunt Sarah to check on her, they had absolutely no desire to speak to or be with anyone else, so they called out for deliveries of food. Taking turns throwing on some sort of cover up to answer the door, they delighted in engaging the delivery person in long, meaningless conversations while the other waited naked and amused just out of sight.

They began to discover many things they shared in common besides the guitar, singing and rollerblades, oh...and malt balls. Each had fashioned, or refashioned their career around caring for children in some way and family and close friends were important and essential in their lives.

Politically, emotionally and morally they were mostly compatible and, in the areas where they weren't, they agreed to remain politely but adamantly "disagreeable."

From their first touch on the bandstand, they moved along the path to their future, confidently and joyfully, filling the furrows of old wounds and insecurities with rich and abundant laughter and trust.

Chapter 9

Jonathan and Gabrielle

It was noon and the morning had passed very quickly without a moment to think about Gabrielle. Now, Jonathan actually had a break for lunch, which was rare, and he decided to call Jesse. He dialed his office and asked his secretary if he was free. Jesse came on the phone immediately, "Hey! What's up?" He was hoping it was good news about Gabrielle because Jonathan rarely called him during the day.

"I just wanted to touch base…I know I've been pretty preoccupied and nasty since the holidays…I've really been missing Brie, Jess…I'm…I'm in love with her," Jonathan surprised himself by blurting it all out so early in the conversation.

Jesse was relieved he was finally opening up about it and said, "I know you are and I've really wanted to help in some way but wasn't sure how I could. Do you know where she is?"

Jonathan told him briefly about what happened the day Gabrielle left, omitting the part about Marginal Way. Jesse was a little troubled by her words and understood, now, why he had been so upset. "Have you talked to Cara and Emory? They've known Brie for a long time and might be aware of where she goes."

Now, realizing there were so many things Jesse wasn't aware of, Jonathan told him about Cara crying when she realized they knew nothing. She did remember a few conversations with Brie about Greenwich Village which seemed to indicate that she visited there quite often. Jonathan felt uncomfortable admitting to Jesse he had invaded Brie's privacy by entering her studio but described the four paintings he found of the Washington Square Arch in every season. Outlining his plan to head to New York for the weekend to search for Brie, as soon as he was finished with his patients, Jonathan said he just wanted to let Jesse know what was going on and where he'd be, in case she returned home and also said he owed Jesse a huge apology for his behavior during the last few weeks.

Jesse needed to go back to his patient but assured him, "There is absolutely no need for any apology. I'm just relieved and grateful you are finally speaking about it. Are you stopping home before you leave for the Village?"

"I'm hoping to leave the office at four and am stopping home, briefly, to change and pick up some things I packed this morning."

"Oh, good. I had a cancellation and will be through early too, definitely by four, so I'll see you at home before you leave. Thank you, my friend, for this phone call."

During a break in his schedule, Jesse called Morgan and told her about their conversation. He told her about Jonathan's call and the reason for his unusual behavior and concern about Gabrielle's absence.

They had important plans for the weekend. Jesse was meeting Morgan's mother, Elizabeth, for the first time and they were spending Saturday and Sunday at her home, in Connecticut. Although he didn't say it, Jesse was feeling he should offer to go with Jonathan to help him search for Brie but knew canceling at this late date wouldn't make a very favorable first impression.

Morgan knew exactly what the momentary silence was about and resolved his dilemma for him, "Jess, if you need to go with Jonathan, it's okay. I'll go to visit with my mom anyway and explain that you and Jonathan have a friend who's missing and have discovered something that may help to find her. She'll understand."

"Thank you for knowing. Now that he's finally let me in, I really want to help him if I can."

"Of course, you do. What time was Jonathan planning to leave?"

"He hoped to be on the road before four thirty. Morgan, I am sorry to have ruined our weekend. I do feel awful about it. Please convey my regrets."

"Don't worry. She'll picture you a sainted Samaritan when I've finished," she laughed.

"I'll call you the moment I get back."

"Okay but please call if anything happens or you find her too. I'll meet you at my house if you call when you're heading home.

"Thank you, I love you."

"Jess, please be very careful. I'm worried about the weather. It's become very treacherous out there; although, come to think of it, it actually is the perfect excuse to cancel. And I am a little scared because of the 'if ever I don't return' thing too. Sounds like one of your detective novels. I love you too, Hercule," attempting to mask her disappointment with some humor and her best attempt at a laugh.

Jesse sat for a moment, after hanging up the phone, savoring her laughter, a waterfall cascading from ear to brain to heart, with a soothing resonance.

⸻

Jonathan rushed home much later than he had intended. He was taking Monday off for Martin Luther King Day and there always seemed to be something about taking a three-day weekend that caused patients to panic and insist on seeing him on Friday. The day started out so beautifully, sunny outside and seemingly calm in the office. But, as a surprise snowstorm began to descend on the town, steady large flakes covering roads very quickly, patients began to accumulate in the waiting room. This was an unusual scenario because a snowstorm normally caused a number of cancellations and resulted in being able to allow his staff to leave early and get home safely. But instead, although the snow began to fall around noontime, it was after five when he finally left for home.

While Jesse waited for Jonathan to get home, he grabbed some snacks and placed them in a cooler with soda and bottled water. Jonathan entered the kitchen and realized, as soon as he saw Jesse's gym bag packed and the snacks, he intended to go with him. He started to protest, worried about Gabrielle's request for secrecy then reminded himself this wasn't Marginal Way. Acknowledging to himself he would welcome the company and confident of Jesse's discretion, Jonathan just smiled gratefully, wordlessly running up the stairs to change and grab the bag he had already packed.

They were out the door and into the snowstorm in ten minutes, neither considering the possibility of postponing the trip because of bad weather. Jonathan needed to go and Jesse needed to go along and that was that.

Once they were on their way, Jonathan opened the conversation with a question which took Jesse by surprise, "So, tell me about your lady love. It is a lady who's put that incessant and absurd grin on your face, isn't it?" He finished with a chuckle, as he glanced quickly away from the road and caught Jesse's astonished expression.

Jesse laughed and moaned at the same time, "I thought I had done a pretty good job of being subtle and hiding it from you but I guess not. You know me too well."

"Thank you for being so considerate through this. I did notice you, several times, coming in very excited, then, seeing me and keeping silent and it was really very selfish of me not to want to know. I'm so grateful for your compassionate attempts but it was so obvious, Jess. So, tell me all about it, especially about how you finally managed to speak to her. I'm assuming, or hoping, I guess, she is the 'girl with the white dog' right?"

Jesse told him all about Morgan and the disastrous park adventures that led up to their eventual first meeting. Jonathan laughed continually through it and really enjoyed the tale. Jesse was a great story teller and spared no details, no matter how humiliating, so the difficult drive, with several periods of being at a complete stop, went very pleasantly.

"Jess, I'm so happy for you and Brie is going to be delighted and, of course, will insist on us meeting her as soon as she comes home."

Suddenly the reality of their mission hit them again and they fell silent for a time.

"I'm sorry, Jess, I didn't mean to end your news on a down note. I really think this trip will result in Brie coming home. I wish I had been as determined about proclaiming my love to her as you were about meeting your Morgan, then perhaps she wouldn't have left. I envy you Jess. For all our tormenting you over the years about your dating problems, you're the one who persisted no matter the humiliation and frustration and has your dream. I wasn't brave enough to approach it these last six months and then, when she let me know how she felt, I stood like a petrified fool as she drove off."

"It's not the same situation at all. How could you know? I saw your longing very clearly but I didn't guess either that Brie returned your feelings. She really was inscrutable. You know I love her but, as you've talked about all this and Cara not knowing anything either, I can't believe how deliberately she withheld herself and diverted our attention from her personal life. So, my friend, along with placing blame on yourself, you should be a little angry with her, too, for her failure to trust us, and especially you, with whatever was troubling her. We've all entrusted ourselves, our problems and vulnerability, to each other and have been so close, you, me, Cara and Emory. And Brie was right there sharing all that and each one of us would have done anything for her. So, lighten up on the guilt and let's focus on the best way to handle it if we do find her. Have you thought about what you'll say to her?"

"You're right, Jess. Even when we went away, we talked for hours but it was about art or people or books and we stayed very busy. The one time the conversation became the least bit personal was about the coincidence that we both had similar recurrent dreams but, when I asked her to tell me about hers, she withdrew very suddenly and we barely talked the rest of the evening, just stayed quietly on the beach until dark. I guess I've been angrier with her than I've admitted, even to myself, about waiting until she was running out the door to show me how she felt. I haven't even thought that far ahead. I guess I'll just offer my love and help and see how she responds."

"Sounds like a plan to me. Just take my advice and avoid dogs, garbage cans and rollerblades in your pursuit. Guitars and champagne, on the other hand, seem to work very nicely," and they both laughed allowing the mood to lighten again.

They rode in silence for a time but both felt a tension build as they approached Washington Square Park and, drumming his fingers, Jesse, absentmindedly, began to hum Simon and Garfunkel's "Bleecker Street."

"Jess, do you mind if I park the car so we can walk to the Arch once before we check into the hotel and eat."

"I would have been very surprised if you'd done it any other way. The snacks were enough. I can wait. Let's go for it."

They were surprised to find so many people in the streets and the park, snow shoeing, cross country skiing and just enjoying the late-night snowfall. It was ten-fifteen and it had been a slow, tense drive in the snow but the roads definitely were not as crowded as they normally would have been on a Friday night.

Jesse reflected on the irony of helping Jonathan find his love in a park as they pulled on gloves, put on their jackets and pulled up their hoods to begin the walk to the Arch.

⁌━━⇀

Gabrielle finished Coco's portrait early Friday evening and David and Amber were viewing it for the first time. They'd known Gabrielle for many years and, of course, knew she was a talented artist but they were experiencing it very differently now, from a personal and intimate perspective. It was a painting you couldn't take your eyes from--so Coco--every nuance of her expressions and charm and mischief blended with an exquisite palate. Coco was an adorable child, with huge brown eyes, peachy cheeks and an amazing amount of shiny black hair for her age and the portrait captured every bit of it. Amber was tearful and Coco came and wrapped her arms around her legs, patting her thigh and staring up at her in concern. Amber scooped her up, holding her close and said, "Look at the beautiful picture Auntie Gabrielle painted of you. Do you like it?"

Coco sucked her thumb as she considered the painting carefully, then shook her head yes, smiling around her thumb.

"Will you give Auntie Gabrielle a lovely hug and kiss to say thank you for her wonderful gift to us?" Amber asked her.

Coco struggled out of her mother's embrace, ran to Gabrielle, throwing her arms out to be picked up, and began giving her baby kisses all over her face and giggling the moment Gabrielle had her in her arms. "Thank you for my painting, I'm beautiful."

Amber winced. It wasn't quite the 'thank you' she had in mind. She and Gabrielle smiled at each other, enjoying Coco's enchanting, childlike honesty.

"You're welcome my yummy Coco!" Gabrielle gave her lots of kisses right back and tickled her until she began the wonderful laugh that made everyone who heard it join in wherever she went. She was so happy, so well loved. Gabrielle felt sad suddenly, for she was leaving first thing in the morning, for Byrdcliffe. She was enjoying her stay so much and would miss Coco's funny little voice and hugs, especially early in the morning when they were the first to rise and Gabrielle would join her in her room to play games and read to her so Amber and David could sleep a bit longer, a rare treat for them.

It was almost ten o'clock when Amber finally told Coco she needed to be in bed and, after only the smallest of protests, she kissed Gabrielle "goodnight and good-bye" and was almost asleep, in Amber's arms, by the time they reached the top of the stairs.

Gabrielle went to her room to pack the remainder of her things and, when Amber came back downstairs and knocked on her door, she told her she was going to take a walk to say goodbye to Washington Square. Amber protested that it was late and the snow was really piling up but she knew, even as she spoke, it was no good to argue or offer to accompany her. She always went alone. Amber did insist that she wear some warm boots and went to get her a pair. She brought a scarf too and wrapped it around Gabrielle's neck, using it to pull her closer and kiss her on both cheeks and on the laceration on her forehead, which was already beginning to heal. "You're not going to see him, are you?" she asked worriedly.

"No, of course not! I meant it when I said I would never see him again. Please don't worry, Amber."

"I hope I never run into him and David said he will never work on any project Gideon is connected with no matter how appealing or lucrative. We still feel we should have phoned the police and had him arrested for assault but do understand you just want it to be over finally." With that, Amber gave her another kiss on each cheek and said, "I just wanted to say this now because I know you'll be gone with the sunrise. Thank you so much for the painting. There are no words to convey to you how beautiful it is and how much we'll cherish it. In fact, David and I were talking and decided we want to commission you to paint the three of us together when you are able but we insist on paying you for it. So put us on your list when you are resuming your work. We love you so much, Gabrielle. Please stay in touch and let us know that you're okay from time to time."

Just then, David knocked lightly at the open door and said quietly, "May I join you two for a moment?" and hugged them both. "You will be in our thoughts every day," he said, continuing Amber's thoughts, "and we'll ask spirit guides to accompany you on your journey, wherever it takes you. And you know you are always welcome to return here if there's ever anything you need, especially a place to rest."

Amber let go of the scarf and tried, unsuccessfully, to let go of her concern. "Please don't be too long or I'll worry horribly. Besides, you should have a good sleep before you go on your way."

Gabrielle was so grateful for their friendship and for the many lessons she learned from them. "The portrait can't begin to repay you both for your innumerable kindnesses and for teaching me, by example, the values of loyalty, generosity and loving and caring about others." She hugged Amber tightly and touched David's arm, "I won't be long, I promise."

As she stepped out the door, she was shocked by the change in the weather. It had been so sunny and warm this morning when she went to say goodbye to Megan and Carl and bring back coffee and hot chocolate for everyone, before putting the finishing touches on the portrait. Preoccupation with the details of it consumed her attention and she never looked outside for hours. The wind was bitter now and she was surprised and delighted by the accumulation of snow, thinking how grateful she was for the boots Amber insisted she wear and the scarf she lovingly wrapped around her neck. Gabrielle lifted her face so she could feel each snowflake touching her cheeks and nose. The trees were covered and bending and everything the snow touched was aglow under streetlights. She looked up once more at the large flakes, feeling like a tiny figure in a shaken crystal snow globe scene. With the first step toward the park, a familiar chill ran, unexpectedly, through her body and she pulled Amber's scarf around her neck and quickened her pace. This would be a very brief goodbye to the Arch.

They were completing their second trip around the Arch when Jesse stopped suddenly, raising his arm and pointing, "Oh, my God it's Brie, Jonathan. She's here!"

Jonathan threw back his hood, squinting against the snow falling onto his eyelashes, and looked in the direction Jesse was indicating, sure he must be wrong. It couldn't possibly be that easy. But it was her and he started toward her and shouted but, before he could reach her, she turned with a look of utter terror, which he thought, at first, was a response to seeing him. Then, he realized she hadn't seen him at all and was looking toward a man he had seen the first time they circled the Arch. Jonathan thought perhaps he was homeless, continually pulling at a brimmed hat, rewrapping a scarf around his face and appearing to be moving constantly to fight the cold. He was tall, though not as tall as Jonathan, with silvery gray hair spilling around his neck and in his face.

Gabrielle turned and began running away and the man with the silver hair immediately started after her. Jesse yelled, "What the hell?" and he and Jonathan followed them. "I'll go after him. You catch up with Brie," Jesse continued and then yelled "Brie!" as did Jonathan.

She didn't appear to hear Jesse or Jonathan and continued to flee but the man did and turned to look back in their direction. Realizing they were after him, he turned from the course Gabrielle chose and raced across streets and around parked cars like a running back avoiding tackles. Jesse took off after him and Jonathan continued along the path he believed Brie had taken, although he had lost sight of her, distracted momentarily by the realization of this bizarre situation and trying to get a good look at her pursuer.

At one point, in the very beginning of the chase, Jesse was nearly close enough to grab at his scarf flying behind him but it was almost impossible to make up the ground between them because the man kept turning corners and crossing streets in an attempt to get away. Jesse had to slow down, as he slipped on the ice and snow and lost his footing repeatedly, with each unexpected change of direction. Shocked by his own lack of endurance, Jesse vowed he would start dieting his holiday weight gain away and exercising regularly when he got home. Since he started dating Morgan, he rarely went to the gym, which he'd always done faithfully before because his job was very sedentary. Jesse was seeing the result of not exercising now and was falling behind with each step, barely able to breathe in the cold air. He lost sight of the man around a corner but continued to search for him for about half an hour or so, trying to follow his trail and, finally, kicking snow in frustration and cursing, "Damn... shit...shit...fuck!" when he knew it was no use. Then, of course, he realized he had absolutely no idea where he was or how to get back to the park or the car.

He dialed Jonathan's cell phone, praying he, at least, had been successful in catching up with Brie. Jonathan answered his phone immediately, "Jess?"

"Yes. Did you get her?"

"No. Once I looked away at that guy chasing her, I never saw her again. Did you catch him?'

"No. I couldn't gather enough momentum to catch up because I kept slipping. He kept taking turns and I lost him."

"I can't believe I was so close to her and now she's gone again. Shit! I just realized I have no idea where I am right now."

"I just had the same realization myself. What the hell do you suppose that was all about, Jonathan?" Jesse was looking around now for some hint of where he was.

"I don't know but we've obviously discovered that she has good reason to be so secretive and watchful. Damn, I wish we could have gotten that guy! I really wanted to beat the crap out of him, without even knowing him, for the horrible look on Brie's face. She's out there so terrified and there's nothing I can do! I'm so pissed at myself and frustrated!"

Jesse heard a crashing, "Are you okay?"

"Yeah – I just kicked some garbage cans around and knocked over a sign!"

"Hey, there's a police car parked up the street – I'm going to find out how to get back to the park because I haven't seen any sign of a cab. Should I tell him what happened?"

"No. Don't, Jess, please!"

"Okay. I can just make up some story about how I wandered so far from the car. I'll call you when I reach the park. Get to a cross street by then, I'll use the map and come get you or, if you find a cab, just call me and I'll wait for you in the car. We'll find her again, Jonathan. We'll keep looking and at least you know she's all right for the moment and close by." Jesse was very grateful that, when they began living together, Jonathan suggested they carry a copy of the each other's car keys. Actually, it had been precipitated by two phone calls to Jonathan, one in the middle of the night, when Jesse had, inadvertently locked his keys in the car and needed a ride, since he didn't have another set.

"Thanks Jess."

Jesse heard more crashing sounds and said, "I'll be there as quickly as I can."

⸻

Gabrielle ran until she was sure no one was behind her before turning back toward Amber and David's house. She took a circuitous route, glancing around her in all directions, using the time to calm herself so they wouldn't guess anything was wrong because she had taken longer than expected to return. She didn't want to involve or in any way endanger them or Coco.

Recalling the chase but not at all sure how she had been able to get away, Gabrielle remembered thinking the howling wind sounded like Jonathan's voice calling her name and wondered if it meant he was thinking of her at that moment. It certainly had given her added strength to keep running and made her feel achingly lonely for him and the combination of freedom and security she was beginning to feel in Cape Cod. More recently, she was experiencing an increased desire for a less transient and more rooted life. What had just happened made it clear going home to Chatham was definitely not an appropriate choice right now and extreme caution would have to be exercised in the morning as she began her journey back to Byrdcliffe.

When she felt ready, she entered the house and used the excuse of the cold tiring her out to retire to her room before they discovered her secret. Amber was extremely good at picking up on what expressions or eyes conveyed about a person's state of mind or concerns.

Sleep would not come easily. Determined to get some rest, Gabrielle climbed into bed, readjusting covers, molding pillows, turning and stretching then curling up on one side, a kitten preparing a place to drowse.

Chapter 10

Emily and Jacob

It was so quiet Emily could hear her heart rhythm in her head, a barking dog interrupting a delicate sleep, and she took repeated deep breaths to make it slow, to calm herself, to think. She had been studying various books on philosophy and religions and considering the idea that, perhaps, she chose to experience this particular life for a reason, an atonement and sought comfort and sense from the thought. She reassured herself with this philosophical reasoning very often lately and, for a moment, wished it had come to her mind a day or two earlier, but then realized it might have kept her from discovering the secret. The acknowledgment she could do nothing with it just yet and must come up with a plan first meant gathering information and choosing the perfect time to use it. Everything must appear as it always was when Jacob returned tomorrow.

She got up and looked in the mirror talking and smiling to see if she looked normal and convincing. Of course, she didn't and her stomach sickened at the thought that he might guess things had changed drastically while he was gone. And, then, she realized how foolish this whole thought process about normalcy was given the state of her room.

It all began with a tantrum. She hated to admit it, especially to herself, but she had lost all sense of reason and control thinking about her birthday tomorrow and what she could expect. Jacob left as he always did, trying to pretend it was just like all the other times he disappeared for a few days at a time, but she knew what would happen when he returned. There would be a dramatic production of carrying in all sorts of packages and, then, a redo of her bedroom again for her fourteenth birthday because he knew she hated what he had done to it for her thirteenth "Emily becoming a teenager" birthday and because, as an adolescent, she rarely spoke to him now.

Her bedroom had remained the same since she was four and she supposed he thought he was doing something really wonderful for her. But he hadn't thought to ask what she'd like and turned it into a disco party room. She loathed every part of it and would have preferred to keep her old ballet bar and tea table rather than the hideous setting she was forced to endure for the past year.

Jacob's obvious departure excuses and the thought of the ridiculous ritual to come was what had set her off for the two days he was gone. After a mostly sleepless night, she had torn her entire room apart, irreparably, and was overwhelmed with trying to create a reasonable explanation. It would be nearly impossible to cover up her bloodied hands, arms and legs and hide her discovery and the thought of it caused an alternate screaming and sobbing again and then she fell asleep for a time.

When she woke, she felt better and, after eating a sandwich from the cooler, began to walk around the room picking up pieces of the shattered disco ball and beads from the curtains she had torn down. There would be no way to hide the paint she deliberately hurled, in a Jackson Pollock moment, all over the bars and the floor of the disco cage he had created and the wall behind it but she got out more paint and brushes and tried to turn them all into brightly colored graffiti.

Her room, her father's version of disco in glitzy overdone adornment, was dreadful. It wasn't the music. She actually did enjoy some of it and embraced all kinds of music. But she loved folk and rhythm and blues best and would have appreciated a room that reflected her own interests. Now he would return and, without asking what she might like, create some new décor she would loathe as much as she loathed him. The thought that she hated him made her feel guilty and selfish because he had always taken care of her but she resented the life he had forced on her, on them.

A few months earlier, after a sullen and silent withdrawal from any communication with him, she asked why they lived as they did, isolated and hidden. Her words were filled with bitterness which angered him and he refused to answer. When she persisted, he finally replied, "The government believes I did something wrong having to do with money and will arrest me if they find us. It's why your mother left us and, since we have no one else, if I go to prison, they will take you away to an orphanage. Sulk and be miserable as you like, I am not going to speak of it again."

Her only knowledge of orphanages was limited to "Oliver Twist" and "Annie" but the idea intrigued her and she imagined it would be better than the life she lived now. At the very least, she would have the companionship of young people her age she longed for so often now. After this conversation, she began to refuse to call him Dad and used his name, Jacob, whenever she was forced to address him. It made him furious, which petrified and gratified her at the same time, and he would lament what had happened to the little girl he loved. He would say he was just going to continue doing what he always did, love her and make sure she had everything she needed, and it made her despise him even more.

He did win temporary favor by getting her a TV to play video tapes on and bringing home "Flashdance." He was a little uncomfortable about the more grownup scenes but knew she liked the music from it, especially the scenes about aspiring to be ballet dancer, and watched it over and over. Lately, he wasn't so sure it had been such a good idea because he felt it contributed to her attitude and he had threatened to take it away.

Before the tantrum, she had danced to it for hours, trying to calm herself by expending energy but, instead, it had turned into an uncontrollable frustration and anger and, thus, began the paint incident and the torn curtains. Bedclothes torn off and strewn about the room and still feeling the rhythm coupled with an unleashed rage, she had danced and jumped up and down on the bare mattress when the wood-frame bottom suddenly collapsed under her and her leg went through it.

She pulled back the mattress and pulled up the broken board astonished to discover, under the wooden bed bottom, a trap door with narrow steps leading to a passageway made of some sort of huge pipe.

Light from a flashlight revealed a tunnel running underground. It was very dark and eerily frightening but she began to crawl into it, constantly illuminating the path ahead and scanning for anything alive or crawling, having an obsessive fear of spiders. Twice she crawled backwards all the way back to her bed, with a pounding heart and unable to take in a good breath. Curled up with her head on her trembling knees for a while, she couldn't resist going in again to learn where it led. Not very long ago, she realized her room was a bomb shelter or safe room and now she hoped this was a secret escape passage. Obviously, her father didn't know of it or he certainly would have taken care to close it off to her.

Suddenly, it occurred to her it would be useful to try and calculate the length of the tunnel and she crawled back to her room, once again, for a tape measure. Exhaustively measuring and marking her path with the number of yards, to keep count, she promised herself she wouldn't stop this time, until she reached the end, whatever the end might be. She had removed her clothes, except for her underwear, because he would notice dirt or anything strange on them when he did the laundry. Cuts and scratches, from the sides and bottom of what must have been joints in the pipes scraping her hands and knees, did not deter her, nor did the continual imaginings of the blood attracting some predator whose den she might be invading. She continued steadily with a resolve uncommon for one so young.

After crawling for what she determined to be just over three hundred yards and stopping to enter each ten yards in a notebook she brought, the pipe ahead ended...no, turned upward and there was wood with a crack and a tiny bit of light coming through. Her heart skipped and she pushed, first with her arms, which caused only a slight give, and then managed to maneuver herself in the pipe, slowly and painfully, to get her feet up, using leg strength to cause the boards to lift and move to the side. Cautiously poking her head up, she realized the boards were actually a trap door which opened into a small shed.

Ceiling-to-floor cobwebs triggered uncontrolled shivering and a memory of reading about the difference between spider and cob webs. She had made herself research the difference hoping to learn that cobwebs were some sort of dust formation and not created by spiders and to simultaneously conquer her fear of them through knowledge. The discovery that both cobwebs and spider webs were produced by spiders, however, contributed significantly to an increased fright and anxiety with the sight of even the tiniest of the creatures. She remembered reading that they were made by two different kinds of spiders, one creating intricate spider webs and the other dragging a line with them everywhere they went. It was the dust collecting on their sticky surfaces which made the lines more visible.

This procrastination didn't lessen her dread so she pushed her mind past this momentary and unpleasant interruption of her task and tried to refocus. A sudden rush of euphoria at the thought of being free, motivated her to run right through the webs and outside without a pause, gasping for fresh air and frantically brushing her hair and body with her hands to take away the awful sensation of the webs sticking to her face and along her arms. Happily, a grove of trees and overgrown brush surrounded the shed, so her impulsive rush though the door hadn't exposed her to discovery by anyone. This also allowed her to take in the view in every direction out of the woods to find the house, necessary because she was disoriented and had no idea where she was in relation to it. She was astonished at how far she actually was from it and the distance she had crawled.

It was autumn and the trees were brilliant. She stood taking in the beautiful scene, wishing she could gather some of the crimson and yellow leaves to bring inside but resisted because Jacob might discover them during one of his periodic "inspections" to see that everything was in its "original and proper place." Perhaps an idle inquiry about whether the leaves had turned yet would allow her to ask him to bring some in for her to enjoy. A shiver shook her whole body at the thought of him, an inner and outer chill seizing her suddenly.

Staying behind bushes and trees, she headed to the house. She already knew there were no neighbors for as far as one could see and that a car traveling the road to the house could be seen for several miles as it approached but she was suddenly aware that she had lost all track of time, with no idea how long it had taken her to make the slow journey along the pipe. Still, there was no truck in sight and she was almost positive he wouldn't return until her birthday tomorrow, so she continued toward the house. Surprisingly, she found the door unlocked and a moment of intense anger arose from the realization of vulnerability should someone find their way in. Stopping to brush off any dirt from her hands and feet and be sure she wasn't still bleeding anywhere, she entered the house, aware she shouldn't touch or change anything that could be detected. A glance at a wall clock determined it had taken her more than three hours to measure and negotiate the tunnel.

She hadn't been in this part of the house for several months, ever since she tried to run away during one of the infrequent times Jacob unlocked her door and allowed her to come up and go out with him into the yard, briefly, for sun and fresh air. He caught her and, from that day, never allowed her out again.

During one of the earlier outings, she discovered a bus stopped for a time at the crossroad way in the distance where the road running up to their house intersected with another wider road. It was on Fridays, at noon, just before they would go back in for lunch. She deliberately asked to go outside on several Fridays just to be sure it always came at the same time. It did and so, on a Friday morning, she tried to make her escape, imagining she would take that bus and disappear forever. What was she thinking, running away with nothing and no strategy? Now, each time she thought about it, she was appalled at her impetuous stupidity and vowed it would be different if she ever had the opportunity again.

That was when she stopped speaking to him, when he placed her back in her room and locked the door for good, declaring wildly that she was ungrateful for all he did for her and would never again be allowed to go outdoors. Today was her first step outside since then.

The house was immaculate and she saw that there was a television now and she noticed an antenna on the roof from the woods as she approached the house. She had an old television to play her Flash Dance video but it didn't get any channels. She wanted to turn it on, since she had never seen it, but didn't know how and was afraid he would be able to tell somehow so she stepped into the living room and over to his desk instead. One goal was to discover where they were and she found some mail with his name and an address...Canada! They weren't even in the United States any more, after all his tutoring on U.S. History and patriotism! Something about this made her furious and then fearful of how she would be able to leave another country, imagining herself pursued by Canadian Mounties on horseback with bloodhounds tracking her.

A weak and shaky feeling consumed her suddenly and, as she tried to talk herself into ignoring it, her stomach rumbled loudly and she realized she was starving. She wanted to get something besides the sandwiches he always left for her in a cooler- bologna or ham in bread - no lettuce or condiments because he said it would spoil. Touching anything might alert him that something had changed. As she looked in the cabinets and drawers, she discovered money in an open tea canister. She felt a sudden weakness in her knees and dizziness and had to hold onto the cabinet for a moment to steady herself. Without disturbing the position of the bills, she was able to pull enough of them aside to see that they were all twenty-dollar bills and there seemed to be at least eight or nine hundred dollars.

"Click, click! Thump!" the sudden loud noise startled her and she accidentally emitted a scream! Her first impulse was to run but, instead, she cautiously went to the window and peeked out to see if he was home. She pulled the curtain aside slightly. Click, Click! Thump! Whirr! It was the noise of the generator coming on.

Her heart beat so hard her chest hurt and she became nervous, now, that he might return early, even though he never had before. She decided she had enough information for now, a means of escaping her room, knowledge about where they were and a source of money so she could begin to plan her escape. It would be on a Friday, when he went away again, so she could take the bus. Disappearing on a Friday would guarantee her a forty-eight hour start before he discovered she was missing, if he followed his usual routine.

A new and determined Emily went out of the house, checking carefully that nothing was disturbed, and returned to the shed, looking behind her to be sure she had left no footprints or evidence of her path. A trembling chill overtook her unexpectedly, perhaps a combination of exhaustion from the journey through the tunnel, maintaining a constant state of readiness to flee and the autumn temperature. Whatever the cause, the sudden and uncontrollable shivering alerted her to just how dreadfully cold and exhausted she had become. She knew she needed to hurry back before she made herself ill from exposure. The last thing she wanted was to do anything to cause a delay in executing her escape.

Taking a last look around at the fall landscape and sky and trying to fix the scene in her memory, Emily inhaled deeply, several times, before going into the shed. She looked for any sign that it had been entered or used and decided that the thick, intricate cobwebs she was forced to brush aside when she came through and the piles of old paint cans, rags and rusted tools indicated that no one had been in there for many years. Before entering the tunnel, she piled more things on the trapdoor to help conceal it, slid it back into place from below then climbed down to begin the long journey back to a new kind of captivity.

Jacob raced through the late evening, anxiously trying to get home. He was far later than intended and knew there was no food for Emily beyond breakfast, since his plan was to arrive home early in the morning on her birthday. The delay was caused by a police raid of a crack house, where he had been taken by a connection to choose and purchase illicit opioids and tranquilizers. Before he left, he decided that Emily's behavior was becoming unmanageable and he knew it was only a matter of time before she would try to run away again. The medication would control her mood swings and help her sleep. The idea came to him a few months before, when she tried to run away and it had taken this long for him to make contact by hanging out in bars, which he detested, and gaining the trust of someone who could help him. This definitely was not a world

Jacob cared to be a part of and he was apprehensive and anxious to get the transaction over with and return home.

He had finished all the shopping for her birthday and left the task of obtaining the drugs until last. After the buy, for much more money than it should have cost he was sure, he was about to leave with his contact "Hawk" when police in full body armor broke down the door two rooms away from them. Fortunately for Jacob, Hawk knew a back way out and found a place for them to hide.

Since they couldn't get back to Hawk's car, they were forced to wait for hours, watching until the police left. As minutes passed and then hours, he thought of Emily. Was she thinking, by now, that he wasn't returning and she would be left locked in to die there alone? He felt dreadful about what she might be going through.

There was some curiosity on Emily's part about what had happened but, instead of feeling upset, she fantasized about escape and how it might be easier than she had imagined. The enormous mistake of trying to run away without being prepared would not happen again, though, and so she wouldn't take anything for granted and would be precise in every detail. She was willing to take whatever time was needed to secure her freedom.

Hunger was echoing in her stomach, which felt painfully cavernous, and she had to fight the temptation to go through the tunnel and back into the house for something to eat. It took a constant out-loud conversation and singing "Happy Birthday To Me" over and over, reminding herself that missing a couple of meals was nothing compared to the possibility of accidentally revealing her secret should he return while she was foraging for something he might not notice was gone. Curled up on her bed and dozing lightly, she heard him come in and it surprised her she was actually a little relieved, even as her empty stomach knotted at the thought of the door opening and his first view of her demolished room.

It was nearly one o'clock in the morning and he had missed her birthday completely and this caused him more distress than anything. As soon as he realized she had torn her room apart and saw the scratches on her hands and arms, he began to beg her forgiveness, assuming his lateness was the explanation for it. So relieved she hadn't incurred his wrath and that he had misunderstood her motive, she threw her arms around his neck and said, "It's okay, Daddy." He was shocked by her response and thought perhaps he had been wrong about medicating her. Maybe her disrespect and moods were simply the result of the hormonal changes she was going through and, of course, a resentment of her lack of freedom and isolation. He hoped what he had bought for her room would make her feel happier with him and give her the ability to occupy her time with things more in keeping with her interests.

Jacob hurriedly prepared some dinner and brought in a small cake for her, even though it was the middle of the night, because he knew she must be as famished as he was. He hadn't eaten either, out of guilt and anger at himself for spoiling her birthday and feeling it wasn't right to ease his own hunger while she had nothing. Emily ate quickly and gratefully, the food soothing her anxiety. Further birthday celebration and gifts for her new room would wait until morning, after they both had gotten some rest.

Another regretful apology preceded his "goodnight" and last check on her, accompanied by a promise it would never happen again, before Jacob locked her in for the night. Once the door was closed, a huge sigh let itself out of her aching chest and Emily smiled in the dark and whispered, "You're so right, Jacob. It will never happen again."

He slept fitfully for several hours then fell into a dead sleep, waking with a start at almost ten o'clock and immediately making a large breakfast to bring to Emily, as he recalled how ravenously she had eaten their belated birthday meal and cake. She usually picked at her plate unenthusiastically, until he would finally clear away the dishes and uneaten food.

Although Emily was unaware of it, Jacob made a great effort to pay attention to what she seemed to like or showed interest in during the months before her birthday. Clearly, the disco decor he created for her thirteenth had been an enormous mistake, so it was important to make appropriate and careful choices for her room this time, gentle, natural colors for new curtains and a few simple changes to the furnishings. He couldn't wait for her to see the acoustic guitar, tapes for instruction, an anthology of folk music and tapes of performers and sheet music he had chosen as her present. He suffered over whether he wanted to encourage the interest she expressed in folk and blues but finally decided it would be another source of amusement and distraction from her resentful attitude and behavior.

After breakfast, he brought her several paint choices and asked her to choose which she preferred. While he carried out the trash from the demolished disco room and carried in new things, Emily chose a color and began painting the area around her bed, first, so he wouldn't discover anything was different and then moved to the graffiti, regretfully, for she sort of liked the way it had come out. When he finished what he was doing, he got a roller and brush and they worked together on the rest of the walls without saying anything.

A new set of bed clothes was placed on the desk and Emily stopped painting immediately to make the bed, eliminating any reason for Jacob to be in that area of the room. She stripped off the old mattress cover and sheets carefully, to avoid revealing the broken board underneath the mattress, and quickly remade the bed with the new linens. Then, just to be sure he wouldn't go over to correct her making of the bed, she asked for help with painting the graffiti wall. He had shocked her saying, "I admire the artistry of this. Are you sure you want to paint over it?"

"Thank you but yes, I'm sure."

Later, after they had completed the redecorating, Jacob brought in some of the leftover birthday cake to eat while she opened her presents. She loved his choice of a used guitar and was touched by his sudden attention to her preferences but confused and tormented by the hate, unrelenting fear and love she was always feeling toward him simultaneously. For hours each day, Emily immersed herself in the enjoyment of learning new folk songs and teaching herself to play the guitar. Jacob was grateful for the distraction and contentment it seemed to have provided.

In the month that followed, while she waited for him to take another trip which included a Friday, Emily pulled out an atlas of North America, whenever she had the opportunity, and studied it intently, carefully mapping her route back to the United States. Unfortunately, she had no idea where she would go or what she would do once she got there but was optimistic that it would all fall into place once she was free to make her own decisions. She memorized the roads, since Jacob might find any notes she made, and then put the atlas back in its exact place each time, so he wouldn't have any inkling of what she was doing. Each detail of her escape was planned as precisely as she could, allowing for alternate routes, depending on where the bus took her. It was the anticipation of how complete freedom would feel that kept her from doing something foolish and impulsive.

Her mood was changed by this hope and Jacob noticed it and assumed the experience of him not returning and then the gifts he'd brought for her had altered her perspective. Whatever the cause, he was grateful for the calm and less dramatic atmosphere and decided he would probably dispose of the pills in a few weeks, if Emily's present attitude toward him and her willingness to be pleasant and cooperative continued. The idea of having 'those sorts of drugs' in the house felt especially uncomfortable after the trauma of the raid and the delay in getting home to Emily.

Chapter 11

EMILY AND GABRIELLE

Coming out of the sleeping, darkened house into the day, the sun was blinding, reflected off the snow that had accumulated, unexpectedly, on Friday and through the night into Saturday. Gabrielle slipped out quietly, careful not to wake Coco, and placed her bags in the car. Travel plans changed as she lay sleepless and shaken from the ordeal of her walk to the Arch. She would not head directly to Byrdcliffe but would travel through Connecticut, staying a night there, then head back into New York on Route 84, as soon as she was reasonably sure she wasn't being followed.

Although she felt exhausted, the snow on tree limbs and rooftops against the cloudless blue sky filled Gabrielle with a profound gratitude for this radiant new day.

There were only a few adventurous people on the roads, which were still unplowed for the most part, and she was in Danbury, riding around Candlewood Lake, much earlier than she expected. She snapped a few photos of the snow scenes on the lake and then consulted a map and decided to travel north along Route 7 to Kent Falls. Sketching the icy falls in the crisp air was challenging for her cold hands, as was finding one rock free of snow to sit on. The afternoon sun warmed her hands and face and brought much needed relaxation and, with it, welcome daydreaming. She meandered through the Litchfield Hills, photographing and sketching stone walls and irresistible barns with icicles and snow all placed as perfectly as a movie set. At one charming pond, it wouldn't have surprised her if women in old-fashioned gowns with fur muffs and men in scarves and top hats had appeared out of nowhere, gliding and dancing across the ice to "Skater's Waltz."

After reaching the Cornwall Bridge, she headed along Route 45 into New Preston, ending at an inn, on Lake Waramaug where she had a delicious supper and found available lodging for the night. Once in her room, she warmed herself at the fireplace and thought of Cara and Emory, longing to be curled up under a soft blanket in the library with them and the boys, drinking a cup of hot chocolate and listening to one of Emory's readings.

Fatigue overtook apprehension and anticipation and Gabrielle forced herself to wash up and brush her teeth at the antique pedestal sink, which had a high ornate backsplash she wanted to remember for a painting. Slipping into warm pajamas and the inviting bed, sleep came the moment she pulled the crisp clean sheets and coverlet to her chin and remained her companion until seven o'clock, very late for her.

The decision to allow herself the luxury of staying under the covers a little longer and enjoying the pleasant moment of mindlessness that comes as one begins to awaken or fall asleep was a good one. Just as she was stirring herself from the temptation to remain in bed all day and stretching, there was a light knock on the door. When she opened it, Lily, the shy, eight-year-old daughter of the innkeeper, whispered "good morning" and showed Gabrielle a lovely tray with a flower, newspaper, a pot of hot chocolate, a cheese pastry, a soft-cooked egg in a delicate egg cup, and berries and fruit in homemade whipped cream. The little girl placed the tray on a small table, went quietly to the fireplace and, adding a log, stoked a perfect fire. *How could anyone complain or bemoan their plight on such a morning?*

Gabrielle had gone into the bathroom to wash her face while Lily was tending the fire and didn't hear her slip out of the room. Back in the bedroom, she made the instant decision to be completely decadent. Instead of sitting at the little table and chair in front of the fireplace where Lily had placed the tray, she lifted it and carefully climbed back under the covers and ate her breakfast in bed, while looking at a map of New York to decide her route to Byrdcliffe.

Her meal was pleasing on every level, aromas, colors and textures awakening her senses yet causing her to close her eyes at some points and sigh with contentment. The cheese pastry was so mouth-watering, with a hint of vanilla in the sweet cheese filling and a flaky, buttery crust, so she decided she would ask if she could purchase the recipe and if there were any left to purchase and take with her.

Warm and delightfully full, she wished she could linger here for days but knew part of the feeling was simply a shameful procrastination, for she was dreading her first meeting with her godparents. She had never called or written them after running off with Gideon and had no idea what to expect when she just showed up on their doorstep. There was a small hope the element of surprise might distract them from her inexcusable absence and neglect.

There was only a remote chance of finding them at Byrdcliffe, since her stay with them had been while they were artists in residence there. She tried to recall what she had learned about it, years ago, and remembered being told it had been established by Ralph Radcliffe Whitehead, in the early 1900's, as an experimental colony for artists and craftsmen. He named it from a combination of his middle name and his wife's, Jane Byrd McCall. Being young, she had found that fact very romantic. There were numerous buildings, barns, and artist's cottages and studios on about fifteen hundred acres and a stay there allowed artists to concentrate on their work, in quiet, supportive surroundings.

Gabrielle was hoping that someone there would remember them, and possibly her, and provide some information about where they lived now. She had no idea how she would find them otherwise.

As she was carrying her suitcase and back pack toward the car, Samuel, the owner of the inn, his wife, Claire, and Lily came out to offer their help and see her off. They chatted for a few minutes and then Samuel admitted he just had to ask her about her car.

Smiling, Gabrielle explained, "A lovely family who hired me to paint a portrait of their children realized I had no car, since I arrived at their home each morning on foot to sketch and take pictures. They asked me how I managed to travel about for my work without one and I explained that my old car finally gave out a few weeks before and I was hoping to find another one sometime soon. I didn't mention the cost factor in the delay to obtain another vehicle but, clearly, they picked up on it because the next morning, a greeting card was slipped under the door of the hotel room I was staying in while doing the preliminary portrait work. On the card cover was a cartoon-like, sad little car lying on its roof and encircled by other little cars looking down at it, with tears falling from their windshield eyes. It said *'Sorry to learn of the loss of your car'* and, inside, was a set of keys attached to a note which informed me if I looked out my window, there was a creamy vehicle, not young but as dependable as sunshine. It was a gift from the family if I wished to accept it. I ran to look and was astonished to see something I had always wanted - a cream colored, vintage 1966 Volkswagen Sundial camper bus. Of course, I refused it politely, knowing it was worth a great deal of money, in completely restored condition, except that it needed to be painted. They were so upset by my refusal and persisted so I accepted it gratefully, insisting they accept the portrait in exchange. They fought a great battle but lost, finally, when I refused to accept the car otherwise."

Gabrielle stopped her story at that point and did not share that, to her client's delight, by the time she returned a few months later with the finished portrait, she had painted the bus. The doors looked like old wooden fence gates, with a peace sign handle opening into a garden with stone walks lined with simple flowers, daisies and sunflowers and some pastel wildflowers in between. Just a few so it didn't appear overwhelming. Love and peace in words and signs were also painted on it. She had wrestled with whether or not to devalue the car by doing it but decided, since it was hers, she was free to do what she liked. Although she couldn't remember where the idea had come from, she had pictured having one forever. It wasn't the first time Gabrielle had been asked about the bus and sometimes she thought how foolish such a conspicuous possession was for someone who desired to remain unnoticed but just couldn't part with it.

Having the camper meant she never had to worry about where to stay when traveling to meet with clients if they didn't offer to provide accommodations. And, when she climbed inside and closed the door, it was like being embraced in a blanket hug.

Samuel and Claire loved the story of how she acquired it and said the painting was charming.

They had watched her sitting at the end of the dock before she checked out, sketching, at first, and, then, just staring out at the lake with her arms around her knees and found her both remarkably beautiful and incredibly sad. They understood how someone could be moved to a gesture like the bus, for, in one day and a night of acquaintance, they were touched by something about her, a gentle strength and fragility all at once. Her energy and presence were hard to part from, and caused a strange, perplexing concern.

When her story was finished, she climbed behind the wheel and they wished her safe journey and invited her to return any time she liked.

As she started down the drive and glanced in the rearview mirror, she saw Claire running after her, waving madly so she stopped and waited for her. Claire caught up with Gabrielle, reached into the big front pocket of her apron and, gasping and unable to speak from the effort, simply handed her a box with four cheese Danish and a card with the recipe for them. Gabrielle was so touched and thanked her for her generosity when she refused any money for it. Samuel and Lily caught up with Claire just as the bus started off again and they watched her drive away, still waving when she turned the corner out of sight, and resumed her imperative odyssey.

There was still minimal traffic on the poorly-plowed roads as she returned to Danbury, and took Route 84 across the Hudson River and up the New York thruway to Kingston. From there it was a short trip to Woodstock. As she reached the village, she realized this was the first time she had actually driven through it because she didn't have a driver's license when she lived here. She'd forgotten how charming Woodstock was and stopped for lunch and more procrastination, walked though one of the galleries and then stopped at a gift shop to buy something to bring with her. In her haste to leave Amber and David's house on Saturday morning, she, mistakenly, left two small still life paintings she had done, to use as gifts for her godparents, in the closet, no doubt the distraction of trying to leave without waking Coco while being sure she wasn't followed. Instead, she would have these new gifts and the cheese Danish pastries to share with them.

She started out feeling confident she would be able to find Byrdcliffe easily but wandered for quite a while without locating it. She was surprised and aggravated with herself and stopped at a candy shop, made a small purchase because she would have been uncomfortable just asking directions and finally inquired where it was. The young girl behind the counter pointed in the direction Gabrielle had been headed and told her she was very close and couldn't miss the dark brown buildings. Gabrielle drove for longer than anticipated and, just as she was wondering if she would recognize it, Villetta Inn and Byrdcliffe Theater came into view and with them the memories of something that seemed so long ago and almost surreal.

More than a month had passed since Emily had discovered the secret passage. Jacob took only one short trip and was showing no sign he intended to leave for one of his longer ones any time soon. Emily was barely making it through each endless day, waiting and hoping. She was ready now. Her escape was planned to the last detail, what she would pack and what she would do if, for some reason, she wasn't allowed to board the bus. Once on, she would inquire about its destination and how she might then get a bus to Montreal. From Montreal, she planned to take a bus or train to Albany. That's where her plans left off, for she had no idea what she would do once she was back in the United States. She had no memory of where they had lived before coming here because she was only three years old. It would be important to avoid questions or any trouble that might alert police. As much as she wanted to escape from this captivity, she didn't want to involve authorities because of whatever trouble her father was in.

The last time he left, she made a quick trip to the house and located some papers with her name on them, in case she needed some sort of identification. She intended to take them when she went into the house to get the money from the tea canister just before leaving. She would also rip out the map pages from the atlas – lots of them so he wouldn't be able to tell where she was headed and then put it in its usual place on the bookshelf. She prepared and rehearsed various stories, depending on the circumstances, in case she was questioned along the way and one for when she crossed the border back into the United States.

Looking more mature was of great concern so she experimented with pulling her hair severely back from her face in a low bun and tried to find the oldest-looking outfit she owned to wear. Every day, she exercised to "Flashdance" which was her "you can do anything if you want it badly enough" inspiration and because she assumed she would have to do a great deal of walking.

Jacob never allowed her to have any makeup but, when he was leaving the last time on a one-day trip, she asked him if she could try some lipsticks, blush and mascara and he had relented and bought her some, figuring it couldn't do any harm, since no one would see it anyway and it would keep her happy for the moment. She gave him some advertisements from the few teen magazines he let her have showing what she wanted and, when he returned, practiced various looks with the makeup until she found one that made her feel she looked more mature. This did not escape Jacob's observation and, while it astonished him to see her looking so grown up and reignited his concern about how he would keep her from becoming unmanageable again, he had to admit that she seemed very happy playing around with it. He assured himself that it was just her natural desire to see herself as growing up and beautiful, which she surely was.

All she could do was wait nervously for Jacob to announce one of his trips that would include a Friday.

There were only two weeks left until Thanksgiving and Emily was getting anxious. For no particular reason, she had set a goal of being free for Thanksgiving but that was looking less likely with each day Jacob remained at home. He reported it was bitterly cold and a wind howled continuously outside, not really incentive for leaving.

Finally, though, eight days before Thanksgiving, on a Wednesday, Jacob announced he would be leaving on Thursday afternoon for a trip and would return on Sunday. He repeatedly assured her he would not let anything interfere with his return and said he didn't want her to feel upset about his departure. He also told her he would leave extra food and water, just in case he was delayed for any reason. Emily remained quiet and patient and told him she knew he wouldn't ever leave her there on purpose and would always return. Jacob sensed something he couldn't quite figure out in her words and tone but dismissed it, deciding it was her attempt not to appear nervous about being left alone again when she was, at least, concerned and, perhaps, extremely scared.

On Thursday morning he left, reluctantly, reassuring her again and again that he would be home on Sunday, by noon. She smiled at him and even hugged him, for the very last time she thought with a sigh, and told him she would be fine. And, then, to be sure he didn't suspect anything, she asked him to bring her back some chocolate, which amused him and made him feel certain any strangeness he was feeling was related to hormonal changes and moods. Her mother had always craved chocolate at certain times of the month and often became quiet and melancholy. He had, long ago, stocked Emily's bathroom with the feminine products she would need at some point and gave her a booklet to read about menstruation because he couldn't bring himself to talk with her about it. About a year ago Jacob noticed she had begun to use them so knew she was now a young woman, which both distressed and intrigued him.

He kissed her goodbye and left, finally, promising her a treat of something very chocolate and delicious.

Emily made herself wait until early evening to begin her packing and preparations, just to be sure he didn't return for something forgotten or just to check on her. She made a small pile of the clothes she would take with her, deciding not to rip out the maps, and arranged the outfit she would wear. There wasn't enough to do to pass the time and she felt restless and anxious to begin her journey. She forced herself to eat something and then, after watching "Flashdance" one last time, climbed into bed with a book and tried to sleep.

She set her alarm for six o'clock so she had plenty of time to get through the tunnel and enter the house, but was awake by five and into the house before six. She wore sweat pants and a long-sleeved tee shirt this time because she would take them with her and discard them and wanted to avoid reopening the scratches which had just healed.

Once she was through the tunnel and into the house, she unlocked her door and re-entered her bedroom. She found a small suitcase and, remembering to take the papers she had found, she placed the clothes laid out the night before, into the suitcase and jumped into a shower. Afterward, she forced herself to eat something and drink plenty of water because she had no idea where or when she would eat next. Time went far too slowly and she was dressed and had done her make-up and hair by eight-thirty. She made her bed carefully and cleaned up her bathroom and bedroom so nothing was out of place except for the things she was taking with her.

Just as she finished packing her toiletries and was placing the suitcase on the floor, the door at the top of the stairs suddenly slammed shut with such a force she fell backward and froze, not breathing and waiting to hear the lock turned. What was he going to do now?

She waited for nearly half an hour, curled up on her bed, finally getting the nerve to move, silently, through the shelter door and closer to the bottom of the stairs to listen.

Could it be possible it wasn't Jacob who slammed the door? She heard absolutely nothing during the time she waited so she climbed the stairs and turned the knob slowly to see if it was locked again. The door opened easily so she peeked through the crack, saw nothing and finally decided she would just throw it wide open because she just couldn't bear the awful anticipation any longer. The worst that could happen was that Jacob was there and would try to find out how she had managed to get the door opened and then lock her in again. She would tell him she heard someone enter the house and she had yelled for them to unlock her door. That would explain anything he found missing. She opened the door and found the house was empty but the front door was open and the wind howled outside. Relief flooded through her and she was suddenly aware she needed to finish getting things together and leave because it was a long walk to where the bus stopped in the distance.

She hurried to the kitchen cupboard and took out the tea canister. As she reached in to remove the money a strange vision flashed momentarily and a cold feeling rushed over her, passing as quickly as it had come. She counted the bills hurriedly – eight hundred and sixty-five dollars – just the amount she had planned on. Then, she had what she decided was a brilliant idea and tore the house apart, including her room she had straightened so carefully, as if there had been a robbery. She found a crowbar and damaged the door lock to her bedroom as an afterthought so Jacob would assume she was taken away.

Back in the bedroom, she placed the money in her pocketbook, looked around once more to be sure she hadn't forgotten anything and realized she could use a book to occupy her time during the bus and possible train rides. Scanning the bookcase to select something, her eyes fell immediately on one she had been meaning to read and she pulled it from the shelf. As she leafed through it to be sure it was what she wanted, she found a picture and a folded paper taped inside the front cover. The picture was of a woman who looked very much like herself holding a young child and, on the back, it said "Summer 1971." Her heart stopped for a moment when she realized it must be a picture of her mother holding her. She quickly tore the paper from the book and opened it and found a short note from someone that said simply, "We're so very worried about you and the baby, Lyliana. Please call or write to us that you're okay. And, if there is anything we can do to help you, please let us know. Love, Nathaniel." The return address was Nathaniel Kingsley, Woodstock, New York. Now her heart was beating wildly as she placed the picture and note back into the book, tucked it under her arm and grabbed her suitcase.

She left her broken bedroom door flung wide open assuring herself Jacob would believe the scene she'd staged. That way, if he found her, somehow, and locked her up again, she would still have her secret passage to use for another attempt at escape, assuming, of course he would ever leave her alone again. Then she realized she could always escape, even if he was there, as long as she timed it correctly and this comforting thought gave her some relief.

She stepped out of the house and began running down the driveway and onto the road, then slowed her steps and breathed deeply. She reached the crossroads just before 11:45 and waited nervously turning and watching in all directions for Jacob's truck. The bus arrived, ten very long minutes later than she had expected, and she climbed in and immediately became nervous when the bus driver scowled, looking her up and down, before speaking to her. Emily's heart was pounding and she was sure he had guessed she was only fourteen and probably running away from home. He finally addressed her in French and she was grateful, suddenly, for all the grueling hours Jacob had spent drilling her in French grammar and making her read French literature aloud and answered the driver easily. His attitude changed immediately and he was very pleasant and helpful, answering her questions and explaining how to get to Montreal by bus.

    Emily settled in her seat and opened "Don Quixote" and, as she stared at the picture, a momentary flash of a woman laughing came and then went just as quickly, the second time these strange flashes had happened in one day. She reread the letter several times, as the bus traveled away from this place she hated so much, and she smiled, not just in gratitude for her freedom but because, at last, she knew exactly where she was going.

⁓

Gabrielle stopped at Villetta Inn and inquired about her godparents but neither of the two people she found there knew them and one woman stared at her suspiciously, until she explained that she once stayed at Byrdcliffe with them about ten years ago. She hesitated a moment and then she gave Gabrielle the name of someone in the Woodstock Arts Guild who might have a record of where they had moved. Gabrielle expressed her gratitude and left quickly, feeling unwelcome and uncomfortable, not at all how she remembered feeling the last time she had come but decided it was her own nervousness and distrust.

Walking along the road that divided the buildings of Byrdcliffe, she stopped several times to take more pictures of the random sculptures at different locations along the property. She started to drive off when she recognized one sculpted by one of her godparents and pulled the car over again and got out to take a picture. As she replaced the lens cover and turned toward the car, she nearly ran into a man who was standing uncomfortably close. She jumped back and away then realized she knew him.

It was "Old Joe" a homeless man and amusing character who wandered about doing odd jobs and often helped maintain the grounds at Byrdcliffe while she was there. She had always found him fascinating and was truly glad to see him again. She'd never figured out why he was called "Old Joe" as opposed to just Joe because there didn't appear to be a "Young Joe" he needed to be distinguished from. She closed the gap she had created between them when she jumped away and hugged him, "Hi, Old Joe, it's so good to see you." Then, she removed the lens cover and snapped a photo of him, thinking what a great painting it would make.

He appeared to be pleased with the idea of being photographed and smiled a mostly toothless grin, then, scowled and stepped away from her, rubbing his bearded chin and shaking his head. "Where you been, girl? You finally decide to come home to see 'em 'cuz Nathaniel's so sick, huh? Folks say he got some kinda cancer but he ain't never been the same since you left and I figure he just finally goin' from a broken heart. You broke both their hearts when you up and disappeared, you know."

Tears began to pour uncontrollably down Gabrielle's cheeks and now he regretted his bluntness. "You didn't know Nathaniel was sick?"

She shook her head slowly and asked, "Do you know where they are now?"

"Sure, I do. They live in a house in Lake George, pretty place right on the water. I do some work for them now and again. Get a pencil and write this down. It ain't hard to get there but it gets a little tricky right round the lake. I'll tell you 'xactly how to find them...they gonna be so happy to see you, blue-eyed girl."

Gabrielle wrote down his directions to the town of Lake George near Assembly Point, hugged him again, slipping a little money into his pocket as she did, and thanked him for helping her find them. He let her hug him, briefly, then pushed her toward her car mumbling he was sorry he made her cry and, then, "Hurry off now child and go make 'em happiest they been in a real long time."

Any further procrastination was out of the question and she jumped into her car and sped off toward Lake George. Traveling north, she thought of Jonathan suddenly and a loneliness joined her again. She had never felt this until leaving Cape Cod and now it was here, an uninvited companion, who intruded whenever it cared to, climbing under her covers and invading her dreams.

She thought it odd that during all her years of isolation she had never been visited by this emotion. It was just normal to be and feel alone. Then she reasoned you first needed to have something or someone you longed for or didn't want to be separated from to feel it. The closest she came to it was when she thought of her mother. She had no memory of her at all, no voice or face or event, but, whenever she wondered what she was like, why she left or where she might be, she felt a deep pain and emptiness in her chest and supposed loneliness was loitering around there too.

Old Joe's directions were perfect and she emerged from her ponderings and realized she was at their driveway much sooner than she had expected. She parked her car on the road and sat for a few moments to collect her thoughts and nerve. The view of Lake George and the mountains was breathtaking, the water so blue and the snow-covered mountains and pine trees reflected in it.

She finally got out of the car and gathered the gifts she'd purchased, the pastries, her backpack and camera and walked toward the house, each step measured and painful. She felt frightened and unsure just like when, at fourteen, she arrived at Byrdcliffe and knocked on their cabin door, at Byrdcliffe. Suddenly, the memory of how they had known who she was the moment they opened the door and how lovingly they welcomed her was a great comfort and she sighed deeply and finished the walk to the door at a quicker pace.

Chapter 12

NATHANIEL AND JEREMIAH

Jeremiah heard a car and then a car door close and was walking toward the front door as the bell rang. They weren't expecting anyone. Everyone called now before coming, to see if Nathaniel was up to company, so he looked cautiously through the sidelight, gasped, almost screamed and then threw the door open all in one huge gesture. "Gabrielle...Gabrielle! Is it you, Darling? It is...it's, it's...Nathaniel! Nathaniel! Our Gabrielle...she's here...you asked, on Christmas, for the gift of word from her and she's here!" and then sobbing.

Gabrielle began to cry too but couldn't help laughing as well at his running about and yelling. He hadn't changed a bit, well, older of course, but still as uncontrollably excitable and funny. She finally caught up with him, still running about in all directions with arms flailing and stopped him with a tight hug, "Hold still, Jeremiah, so I can tell you hello!"

"Oh, dear, I'm so sorry. I just can't believe you're really here! Nathaniel has been asking for you every day. He's very sick Gabrielle...so very sick."

"I know. Old Joe told me this morning. I saw him at Byrdcliffe and he told me how to find you. I'm so sorry for what I've done. There's nothing I can say to explain or excuse how I've neglected you both."

They held each other crying and laughing alternately until a weak voice from the other room called to them.

"Jeremiah, I had a dream that you said Gabrielle was home."

Gabrielle and Jeremiah appeared instantly at the door and she was shocked by the sight of Nathaniel so frail and small in the bed. He always seemed so huge to her – a husky bear of a man whose embraces were shrouds of security and love, a place she loved to be. She ran to him and lifted his hand kissing it repeatedly, laid it against her cheek and said softly, "It wasn't a dream, Nathaniel, it's me.

Now Nathaniel sat up slightly with a new strength, pulled her to him and burst into tears too and kissed her head rocking back and forth, "You're alive...you're alive...you're alive."

His refrain caused Gabrielle to face an awful reality. They assumed something dreadful happened to her and she couldn't have loathed herself more than she did at this moment, for failing to consider what they were left to think when she never contacted them. What they suffered all these years! There would never be a way to atone for her selfishness.

It took some time before they could all calm themselves, Nathaniel repeating his refrain, Gabrielle saying how sorry she was each time and Jeremiah pacing and crying. Then they began to talk, questions and answers like relay batons passed quickly and sometimes dropped as they raced on to the next lap.

Jeremiah finally began to tell Nathaniel that he needed to rest for a while but Nathaniel was afraid, if he slept, he'd wake to find it had all been the confusion from the morphine or a dream and she would disappear again. He only took the pain medication when it became unbearable because he hated not being in control of his intellect and actions. Gabrielle and Jeremiah both tried to convince him that she would still be there after he rested and said they'd make some dinner while he slept. He still refused and asked them to help him settle in the family room near the kitchen so he wouldn't miss a moment. Jeremiah pulled a recliner closer to the kitchen and brought Nathaniel to it by wheelchair, assisting him gently onto the chair and carefully seeing to it that he was covered and comfortable before beginning preparations for dinner.

Jeremiah and Nathaniel had been a couple since the early sixties. Both were artists, Nathaniel a sculptor and architect and Jeremiah a potter and painter. They were friends of Gabrielle's mother, Lyliana, years ago and so honored when, over the adamant protests of Gabrielle's father, she asked them to be her baby's godparents.

Gabrielle located Nathaniel and Jeremiah when she ran away from her captivity in Canada and they cared for her for more than three years, until she disappeared, suddenly, leaving no hint of why or how. When Gabrielle came to live with them, they changed her name from Emily to Gabrielle and used Benedict, which was Nathaniel's middle name, for a last name. They had obtained, through completely illegal channels, a birth certificate, passport and papers making Nathaniel and Jeremiah her legal guardians. This new identity arrangement was the reason they weren't able to call on the police to help find out what had happened to her. It infuriated them that their hands were tied but feared the possible consequences for everyone if her real identity were revealed. Mostly they were afraid she would be taken away from them, if she were found, and returned to her father. They finally decided they would simply hold onto the belief that Gabrielle had made a choice to leave for some good reason and convinced each other she would return when she felt ready to. This lasted for a time but then, as weeks turned to years, they no longer spoke of her, each suffering in silence not wanting to hurt the other by bringing up her name, until the last few weeks of Nathaniel's illness. With his frequent dreams and constant desire to see her once before his illness became worse, they again mourned the absent laughter and energy and assumed the worst, convinced they might never see her again.

Jeremiah talked about her arrival years ago and how they obtained the papers so she could stay with them as Lyliana would have wanted. They enrolled her in school, merely explaining she had been home schooled previously. When she took placement tests to determine what would be the appropriate grade level for her, she tested above senior level and the counselor wasn't sure what to do with her. Nathaniel told her Gabrielle needed to be no higher than a sophomore because she needed the social experience and she agreed and placed her in the gifted sophomore class. Nathaniel and Jeremiah, reluctantly acknowledged the excellent effort her father obviously made to educate her, if not in experience, academically. Gabrielle graduated in three years, and they were deciding on safe places for her to enroll in college just before she went missing.

During school vacations, they took her on many trips across the country, to Washington D.C. and New York, to Broadway plays, fine restaurants, galleries, operas and the ballet. She approached each new experience with unquenchable curiosity and enthusiasm – her books and imaginings come to life.

For Jeremiah and Nathaniel, it was a delight, like raising a child of their own, each day new and remarkable to her. Even eating a meal together was a learning experience in manners, conversation, flavors and cuisine and she seemed to enjoy it immensely. For Gabrielle, it was the happiness of being so adored and nurtured, yet so free which illuminated her and brought her, slowly, out of her shyness.

As Jeremiah and Gabrielle prepared dinner together, they talked and, at one point, Jeremiah said, "We have so much to tell you, things we intended to share with you once you turned eighteen but then you were gone and…"

Nathaniel interrupted him with a look that stopped him mid-sentence and a surprising strength in his voice, "There's plenty of time for all that later. Let's just catch up with what Gabrielle has been doing for now. Tell us what your life has been since you left, Darling Girl."

Gabrielle told them, first, about Gideon, being the one who took her away from them and their adventures on the road. They were incredulous and never suspected Gideon was responsible for her sudden disappearance. He was off on his tour long before Gabrielle went missing and came back to get her per their plan. Then she explained her recent final split from him and Nathaniel raised himself up on the chair as she told them about their last encounter, so angry at Gideon's outrageous behavior toward her. She put down the knife she was using and went to get him settled back and relaxed again, saying she was just fine and stronger for having faced Gideon. Now, Nathaniel noticed the laceration on her forehead, which was nearly healed, and, although it infuriated him to think of Gideon laying a hand on her, he could see that she was right. She was a more confident young woman now, despite Gideon's attempts to convince her otherwise.

Next, she told them about her art, taking courses in New York, her friends Amber and David and then explained her year in France and meeting Cara and Emory. Nathaniel seemed strangely upset about France and Gabrielle asked him why.

"Jeremiah and I booked a trip to Paris for all of us as a surprise for your graduation but you disappeared before our departure date." But, as Gabrielle's expression became sad and she began another apology, he continued, "Oh, I'm sorry, Gabrielle. There was no need to bring all that up now. I just felt a twinge of jealousy at the thought of someone else getting to see you experience France and all we talked and dreamt about doing there."

Gabrielle had forgotten their long-ago dream and realized it probably played a part in why she felt so passionate about going to Paris when she ran away from Gideon.

Nathaniel continued gently, "Tell us more about Cape Cod and your friends."

Gabrielle's tone took on an added softness, as she described her home and life with Jonathan and Jesse. She expressed her admiration for their determination to bring healthcare to the underprivileged and for their caring so much about their patients and all children. And then she tried to describe how endearingly funny Jesse was.

Searching for just the right words, Gabrielle began to tell them about the days she and Jonathan spent in Ogunquit and how, once she knew she was in love with him, she struggled for months to find a way to face Gideon and make a final break. And, though tempted to leave out the details of her last morning at Jonathan's, she told them how fear caused a completely irrational and possibly incoherent departure, running back to tell Jonathan, for the first time, how she felt and then running away before giving him a chance to comprehend or respond. She was determined not to return or contact him until she had the answers needed to understand her inability to feel attachment. Even her relationships with Emory and Cara and David and Amber were based on her occasional and usually surprising appearances.

Finally, Gabrielle spoke of the reason she couldn't go home and had come to them - how afraid she was that her father would try to take her back or, worse, hurt someone she cared about. As an adult now, there was a sense of humiliation about her childish fears and an excruciating desire for just one day to pass without thinking about him or wondering when he would appear. She came to the conclusion she needed help to confront this existence of dread, founded or unfounded, in some significant way because it dominated her life and limited the depth of trust in relationships. Her long story ended with the fact that he had been stalking her, finding her several times in the last few years, as recently as Friday night before she left. She assured them she had been very diligent about taking a circuitous route and was certain no one followed her here.

At the mention of her father, and the danger she always felt she was in, Jeremiah dropped the platter he was holding and it shattered on the tile floor startling them all. "Gabrielle, your fa..."

"Jeremiah! Let Gabrielle finish telling us about herself. We can talk about her father tomorrow." Again, Nathaniel interrupted Jeremiah, this time with a very aggressive tone.

Jeremiah looked wounded and went back to preparing dinner, after cleaning up the broken dish, and did not speak again. This was the second time Nathaniel chose to stop Jeremiah from telling Gabrielle something that seemed important to him and she looked from one to the other wondering what was going on. She was very worried about how exhausted Nathaniel looked and decided not to pursue the matter just yet. She wasn't planning on going anywhere and it could wait until tomorrow or another day if it made Nathaniel uncomfortable, for some reason, to speak of it now.

"So, I'm here cowering and hiding, just like twelve years ago, because I'm trying to figure out just who I am and how to live the rest of my life and this seemed to be the place I needed to be to accomplish that. There are so many missing pieces..."

Jeremiah didn't dare say anything and glanced over at Nathaniel assuming he would respond and reassure her.

Nathaniel lay with his eyes closed, breathing slowly and, at first, Gabrielle thought he had drifted off to sleep but, then, he opened his eyes, sighed and said, softly, "You were right to come, Gabrielle. This is exactly where you should be right now. I'm getting tired now but tomorrow there will be lots of time to talk of all that. For now, tell us more about your painting and promise me you'll sketch or paint something for us – maybe the lake or a portrait of Jeremiah, before you leave us to go back to your Jonathan."

While she and Jeremiah finished making dinner she talked about her work, what she had learned, questions she wanted to ask them both and advice she hoped they would give her. A few times she thought, Nathaniel was dozing but then he would ask her a question or comment on something she said, without opening his eyes, and she knew he was listening to every word.

He always showed remarkable patience and a capacity to appear completely absorbed in one thing and, without stopping what he was doing, listen to her when she would come running in chattering about school or just anything that seemed terribly important to tell him at that instant. He never missed a word she said and always responded without the slightest indication that she might be disturbing him.

Here he was again, so ill and tired, and still listening lovingly to her and she tried to imagine what flaw in her character allowed her to shut all of this out and leave them so saddened and deserted. Tears welled up again and it took everything in her not to crawl into Nathaniel's chair with him and rock and cry her eyes out. Her heart ached as it never had before in her remembrance.

Nathaniel mustered his energy again when dinner was ready and they ate a wonderful meal, with some of the old silliness, laughter and stories and she turned the questioning toward them and asked what they had been doing. She wanted to know all about the building of the beautiful home they lived in which she knew was Nathaniel's design. The stonework exterior and the combination of modern and rustic in stone, tile and hardwood of the interior and the openness and magnificent light an inspiration to the artist in everyone. It was a very modest size but their eclectic furniture style, which included wonderful antique focal points in each room, gave it a sense of airy grandness and comfortable charm, simultaneously.

Once Gabrielle and Jeremiah settled Nathaniel back in his bed, she climbed on for a little while lying next to him with her head on his shoulder, then hugged him for a long time and finally said "goodnight" when she noticed him beginning to doze and then fighting it.

He seemed to be gasping for breath a bit, in between sentences, and she knew they had tired him too much, "Goodnight,

Love. Welcome home. Sleep well and wake me for the sunrise, just like always, so we can spend the whole day together."

"Maybe you should sleep a little later tomorrow. I think you didn't rest enough today."

"No! No. Promise me you'll wake me for our sunrise! I can't wait to share it with you and for you see the sunset over the lake later. Promise me."

"I will, Nathaniel. I'll come to wake you. I promise. I love you. Goodnight."

Her earlier thoughts about loneliness came to mind and she questioned, again, what was wrong with her emotions and thought processes. How could she fail to feel a dreadful loneliness for this love and devotion? She needed, so badly to find, answers and reasons, not excuses, there were absolutely none that could possibly exonerate her for this…she just needed… needed. This was the problem. What was it she needed? She couldn't even articulate a reasonable answer to that question.

Chapter 13

JONATHAN AND GABRIELLE

Jesse turned the map around and around and shook his head, impatient with himself. About the third time around, he finally found the cross-street Jonathan named and headed off to find him. By the time he picked him up, Jonathan was so frozen his mouth barely worked. Jesse turned the heat up as high as it would go and aimed the vents at him, apologizing several times for the delay in locating the cross street and finding him.

He tried very hard not to but just couldn't control an irrepressible urge to laugh, "Oh geez! I'm sorry for laughing, but you looked like a snowman someone built along the side of the road when I drove up." And, then, apologized again when a few more chuckles escaped as he tried to help him remove icicles hanging from his eyebrows and hair and snow piled on every horizontal surface of his body. Needless to say, Jonathan did not find it at all amusing and as they headed for the hotel, neither spoke a word, lost in thought about their failure to catch up with Brie or apprehend the man who had frightened her so badly.

For the next three days, they spent every daylight and evening moment in Washington Square and the surrounding streets; copying the map and using it to strategize and plan the routes each would take and where they would meet, usually back at the Arch in the evenings. They stayed close by until it was time to sleep, hoping to see Brie again, although, it seemed unlikely she would return there after being so frightened. They never saw her or the man again and, finally, left for Cape Cod late on Martin Luther King Day evening, so exhausted and discouraged there was no conversation during the entire trip home.

Jesse thought about calling Morgan to let her know he was on his way but didn't want to do it in front of Jonathan, salt on a gaping wound. He would wait until he was home in his room and decided he would tell her he needed to stay home for the night, hoping, no, knowing she would understand.

They hadn't eaten since lunch so, after a quick trip upstairs and a brief conversation with Morgan, Jesse began to grill hamburgers and made a salad. He knew better than to ask Jonathan whether he wanted some because he would probably say "no" but, if Jesse just made it and put it on the table, he'd eat. He had to feel as ravenous as Jesse, broken heart notwithstanding.

During their quick meal, Jesse finally spoke, "We'll go back to New York next weekend and every one until we find her, Jonathan. She's got to be there somewhere. We should bring pictures of her and maybe Morgan will come too and we'll all canvas the area...surely someone will know her. Come to think of it, do we have any pictures of her except for the one you found as a baby?"

Jesse expected an argument or refusal of help but instead Jonathan just replied with a quiet and sad, "Okay, Jess." He didn't answer the question about a picture and Jesse could see and feel, having experienced just a taste of it, how defeated Jonathan felt after all his weeks of trying to find her and now coming so close and failing. And he was fairly sure that no recent pictures of Gabrielle existed because she would have avoided being photographed, given how elusive she was about everything else.

Jonathan had early rounds at the hospital in the morning. His head ached and he could barely move so, after cleaning up the dishes, he thanked Jesse for all his help and excused himself for the night.

Jesse sat in the living room thinking of Jonathan's "thank you" and punishing himself with demeaning adjectives like inept, clumsy and useless, so sorry that he had been of absolutely no use in helping Jonathan to find Brie. He wanted to be the hero-friend who jumped in and saved the day and, instead, he'd accomplished nothing except utterly, weak-sounding assurances that they would find her another day. Great consolation to Jonathan! He sighed and shook his head. As he searched his frustrated brain for some new idea, he leafed through Brie's copy of *Don Quixote* and picked up the picture of Brie at two years old that Jonathan left on the table and stared at it.

An impulse struck him suddenly and he went to the bottom of the stairs to be sure Jonathan's light was off and he wouldn't be coming down again. When he was sure, he went and got the key to Gabrielle's studio and, quietly slipping out of the kitchen, unlocked her door and entered.

Like Jonathan, he had never been in her studio and was touched by how beautiful and pleasant the first impression was.

Just as he described during their ride to Greenwich Village, there was a feeling of comforting sea breezes and her artistry was even more remarkable than he imagined from Jonathan's descriptions. After walking around looking at the pictures scattered and leaning all over the room, he leafed through things on her table desk. He found the sketches of the nursery and, like Jonathan, found nothing useful or revealing there. He decided it was as wasted an invasion as Jonathan declared it to be and turned to leave. The plants were all dead and it saddened Jesse unexpectedly and he took a moment to allow himself the feeling of sorrow for Brie and whatever she was going through. Then he spotted the tiniest green shoot on one of the plants and decided to water everything. Somehow the act made him feel more hopeful. He went to get some water for it but noticed all the plants were moist and assumed Jonathan must have watered them.

As he walked back toward the door and turned off the light, he felt something rustle under his feet. Shining his flashlight toward the floor, he saw a folded piece of paper near the door. He picked it up and carried it back to the kitchen, opening it the moment he was inside. It was a note addressed to someone named Lyliana expressing concern over not hearing from her and was signed Nathaniel. The return address was Nathaniel Kingsley, Woodstock, New York and it was dated September of 1973. Jesse thought it very curious that the paper was just lying there, unseen by Jonathan, and then realized it probably was in the book with the picture, originally, and must have dropped to the floor, unnoticed, as he made his way out and locked the door. He was the only one who had been in the studio since Brie left so Jesse decided it must be how the paper came to be there.

He was patting himself on the back for some excellent detective work and piecing together the clues, when the realization that this might be the reason Brie had said to read *Don Quixote* made him start up the stairs to awaken Jonathan and tell him about his discovery. He stopped halfway up, though, debating whether he should wake him or just allow him to sleep undisturbed. What would it accomplish, at this late hour, to bring it up except to cause him another sleepless night? Reason won and he stepped back down the stairs, as quietly as the creaking old boards of the staircase would allow. He went into the study, dialed Information and inquired about a telephone number for Nathaniel Kingsley and was told there was no listing for the name Kingsley in Woodstock. He was disappointed but, nevertheless, felt this was an important clue which he would share with Jonathan in the morning, after they both had a good night's sleep. He was excited and a little relieved to think he might actually contribute something to their efforts to bring Brie home after all. Certain sleep wouldn't be possible with his mind racing, he fell asleep only minutes after getting into bed, as exhausted as Jonathan from their grueling, useless weekend.

Something was buzzing obnoxiously and rays of light had made their way around the window shade and Jesse's eyelids into his subconscious, simultaneously. He jumped up, turned off the alarm and ran downstairs, afraid he might have missed Jonathan. He hadn't. Jonathan was dressed in his usual office attire, a shirt and tie, ready to begin his day with his patients and sitting at the table, staring out the window toward Gabrielle's studio while drinking his coffee. Jesse told him going into Brie's studio the night before and handed him the paper, explaining he called Information and there was no listing for this Nathaniel. They both agreed this person might be relevant to learning more about Brie and agreed they would head up to Woodstock the following weekend and see if they could locate him.

Just before Jesse came downstairs, Jonathan had been thinking about taking a sort of sabbatical to spend all his time looking for Brie but dismissed the idea as quickly as it occurred to him. He had far too many patients who were very ill and depending on him. Besides, he owed numerous coverage favors to colleagues, from taking so many weekends to search for her. In fact, next weekend was his last for a while and then he owed enough return favors to keep him working for more than a month without a weekend break.

His awareness that he was sinking deeper into a sort of depression, something he'd never experienced before, made him decide that it was time for confiding in his family and using their energy, insight and love to restore his balance. He would call Cassy today and ask her to come and stay over. She left her job as a high school biology teacher and was going back to school for her doctorate, so she had some extra time in between her classes and research and he knew she would come immediately, since she repeatedly left messages expressing concern about his absence. He blamed work for his lack of time for visits and only occasional and brief conversations with family members, never mentioning the real events taking place in his life.

His love seemed foolish and imaginary when he thought of how he would introduce the topic and explain it. There weren't any of the usual stories to tell them of dating and falling in love. Even feelings stirred by the trip to Ogunquit had remained unspoken and clearly one-sided, or so Jonathan had believed for the nearly six months leading up to Brie's astonishing revelation before driving away. It all seemed so long ago now.

He thought about Jesse and Morgan and understood the coincidental similarity of being in love with someone so surely and insanely, before any words or physical acknowledgement, an intimacy of emotion he had felt from his first eye contact with Brie, at Cara and Emory's home. Jonathan just knew his love for her existed undeniably and there was nothing he could do but try to find her again and tell her.

He could almost anticipate reactions from his family; his mother telling him to just wait for her to come back to him as she surely would if it was meant to be; his father suggesting hiring private detectives, which he would not do to guard her privacy, and his brothers and sisters offering to form a search and rescue team. It cheered him to picture the scene, a chaotic harmony, so supportive and loving.

He would call Cassy later from the office, after rounds, before starting his day, since it was very early and she was likely sleeping later these days, not having to be at school by seven fifteen. He had never understood the misguided decision by boards of education all over the country that high school students, who stay up late and do not, according to many studies, begin functioning well until late morning, should begin classes at seven-fifteen in the morning, while grammar school children, who are earlier to bed and naturally much earlier to rise should attend school beginning much later. Anyway, he definitely was going to call Cassy today.

This decision made and, with the letter Jesse found providing hope of a connection to Brie's life and finding her, Jonathan made a conscious effort to feel more positive as he headed for the hospital.

Chapter 14

Gabrielle and Nathaniel

Gabrielle woke before dawn with the momentary confusion of being unsure where she was. Then, remembering, she jumped out of bed, grabbed some clothes and went into the bathroom to brush her teeth, wash up quickly and run a brush through her hair. For the second night in a row, she had slept the entire night without waking once. She grabbed a blanket because it would be cold watching the sunrise and started out the door. Having spent so little time in the house, it took a moment, in the unbroken darkness, to figure out where Nathaniel's room was, as she reached out in front with both hands to avoid unfamiliar pieces of furniture. She forgot to ask for a flashlight before going to her room and was trying to picture what it looked like in the daylight. It would have been a good thing to request because she had no idea where the light switches were and didn't want to chance waking poor Jeremiah, who was getting very little sleep these days.

Suddenly, she tripped over something and fell to her knees dropping the blanket and, as she felt around to see what had caused her fall and to gather up the blanket, a momentary flashback of crawling through the escape tunnel for the first time came and then went just as quickly. It was the ottoman of the chair Nathaniel had rested in while they made dinner and that gave her the direction to head in to reach the kitchen. She turned on the light above the exhaust fan, which was very soft, and put Nathaniel's coffee on to brew and hot water for herself in a tea kettle reminding herself to catch it before it whistled and startled Jeremiah or Nathaniel.

Gabrielle entered Nathaniel's room silently and listened for his breathing to determine if he was still asleep, deciding, if he was, to wait until the last moment to wake him. He spoke quietly to her, "I'm awake, Love. Do you think you can help me into the wheel chair so I can wash up a bit?"

"Are you sure you're up to this, Nathaniel. It's very cold out there."

"We can watch from the sun porch – it's three season – and, if you want to take pictures, you can step outside or just open one of the windows."

"Sounds perfect, here, lean on my shoulder," Gabrielle said and she noticed that, in spite of his obvious loss of weight, standing at his full height, he still had much of the musculature of her dear giant protector and she sighed softly as she assisted him into the wheelchair and pushed it toward the bathroom, "Do you need help?"

"No, Jeremiah has everything arranged so I can manage a quick wash myself – it's just showers he has to help with and he's made accommodations even for those. He's such a good man, Gabrielle, and the best partner anyone could want. I'm afraid of what will happen to him when I'm gone. I'm so glad you're in touch again...promise me you'll stay in contact with him after...well, after...you know."

She did know what he meant but couldn't bear to think about it so soon after being reunited, "Please don't say that, Nathaniel. Jeremiah said the newest chemotherapy might still work."

"No. It won't help. The cancer has spread from my pancreas, metastasized. I've decided not to do any more trials of chemo so I'll be able to eat and enjoy the days I have left. I've already tried three rounds of experimental chemo beyond the regular regimen and look at me. My weakened condition is more from the drugs than the cancer right now, although I know that will change. The doctors said, now that I've stopped the chemo, I might actually feel somewhat better for a while before the cancer worsens. Jeremiah won't accept the truth of the situation but the doctors were very clear there's nothing more to be done. I'm sorry to be so outspoken about it with you, Gabrielle, but I need someone around who can talk with me realistically. Jeremiah just can't."

Tears welled up and she hugged him, letting out a little sob she hadn't meant to but said, "I understand, Nathaniel and, if you can tolerate the honesty of tears, I can listen to whatever you need to talk about and share." Tears had flowed torrentially ever since her arrival yesterday--a monsoon season of emotions in one day and she couldn't remember ever crying so much. "You have every right to choose how each moment of every day should be spent and what you can and cannot endure."

"Thank you, Love. Actually, I really got off the subject and didn't finish asking for something I really need from you. Please promise me you'll stay in touch with Jeremiah and take care to call once in a while to be sure he's doing okay."

"Of course, I will. I promise. Not that you have any reason to believe me or have any confidence in my word."

"Stop it, Gabrielle. You've apologized enough and I've never known you to break a promise."

"Then please know I'll look after Jeremiah and try not to use up your energy worrying about him so much. Now, you're sure you feel strong enough for this?"

"I am quite sure that sitting through a sunrise with you is just what I need." He did look better than he had last night so she closed the bathroom door behind her saying, "Call me when you're ready – I'll go get our coffee and hot chocolate ready and bring them out to the porch." She ran back to the kitchen afraid she had missed the opportunity to pull the tea kettle off the burner in time.

Gabrielle poured Nathaniel's coffee and then began looking around the kitchen for the hot chocolate packets or the tin of cocoa she was absolutely positive she would find somewhere in the cabinets because she and Jeremiah always drank it and he was as much of a chocolate addict as she was. She found both just where it seemed likely they would be, emptied a packet into her cup and added a bit of whipped cream before carrying the steaming mugs out onto the porch. Gabrielle sensed it was probably time to help Nathaniel and headed back toward his room, in case he had called to her while she was on the porch, but he was already headed down the hall and entering the living room, pushing the wheelchair and his pride toward her with a smile. He really did look better, after a night's rest and washing up, and her heart leapt with the shared secret hope Jeremiah held onto.

On the porch, she pushed her chair as close to his as possible and covered them both with the blanket. When he sipped his coffee, he realized she had added the two sugars he used to put in it but said nothing about not using sugar anymore. Instead, he enjoyed the old sweetness and reminiscence of sunrises shared years ago. He prefaced the viewing by telling her he still loved the sunrise and had sat through many thinking of her but couldn't wait for her to see the sunset over the lake later, from the stone terrace on the other side of the house.

When the sun came, finally, illuminating the porch and them, Nathaniel gasped, "Oh, Gabrielle, you're stunning—so beautiful in the light and so like your mother, your eyes are your mother and grandmother's eyes. How strange to have had all this time go by and to see the changes in you so suddenly. Your mother would have been so very proud of how lovely you are and how you're living your life."

"You speak as if she's dead, Nathaniel. Do you know where she is? There are so many questions to ask, especially why she left me...us."

"I didn't mean to make it sound so final but it is a haunting mystery because, wherever she is, I do know, without a doubt, she would never have left you willingly. She adored you more than anyone and was a wonderful mother. I wish I knew where to tell you to look for her but, until the day you came to us calling yourself Emily, all alone and running from your father, we had never heard a word. You had all just disappeared. And, then, when you didn't come back or call, we thought your father had found you again or something worse had happened, not that your father finding you wouldn't have been bad enough. We had absolutely no idea that you had run off with that Gideon person until you told us about him last night. Then, after so many years of not hearing from you, we did assume and mourn the worst, just like with your mother. I'm sorry if that sounds blunt and painful."

"No, just honest, Nathaniel, and completely understandable and I know I just keep saying how sorry I am and how meaningless it must seem after all this time. I have no explanation, even for myself, why it hadn't occurred to me what you would be thinking."

"Perhaps, with time, you'll come to understand your detachment from certain realities about relationships, Love. You've spent a lot of time surviving by detachment, I think."

"See! You always ground me and give me so much insight and food for thought with just a few words. But what I would really like is for you to tell me about my mother, whatever you remember concerning her life with my father and me, please, Nathaniel."

"Yes, Gabrielle, it's a long-overdue discussion and I'm certain it's the reason you found your way back here to us."

Chapter 15

Lyliana and Brian

Approaching her teens, Lyliana Parsons began to consider her first name rather absurd. Her mother, Diana, and her father, Lyle, had decided it would be romantic to combine their names in celebration of her birth. Although she loved them, Lyliana occasionally vented adolescent frustration by expressing disdain for their choice, not understanding at that rebellious age, the honor and love conveyed in the combination. They lived in the Congo, in Africa, Diana a doctor caring for women and children in a clinic there and Lyle a British, freelance engineer. Lyliana was with them when she wasn't in school.

Nathaniel began slowly, "Lyliana, your mother, had just returned to boarding school, in England, after spending summer break in Africa, angry and reluctant to be sent away once more. She loved Africa and the African people and missed her parents terribly when she was forced to be away from them for months at a time. The entire last month of her stay with them, she had begged Diana and Lyle, your grandmother and grandfather, relentlessly, to allow her to remain with them. They talked privately when she was asleep and agonized over the right decision but, very sadly, agreed she should return to school. As it turned out, the decision was a fortuitous one because they were murdered only one week after she left, outside Leopoldville, which was renamed Kinshasa, just as the Congo was gaining independence from Belgium in an atmosphere of revolt against attempts at Westernization."

Nathaniel had been speaking with his eyes closed, remembering, but he sensed something and, when he opened them again, realized Gabrielle had turned pale and was holding up one hand with the palm facing forward as if to stop him. He hoped this wasn't a sign this story of her parents, which would be long and possibly traumatic, was starting off much worse than he had anticipated. "What is it, Gabrielle?'

She began to speak, "It's so very odd and I'm trying to remember the exact conversation I had several months ago with a friend of Jonathan's who stayed with us for a few days. His name is Addae Dubois and he was Jonathan's very best friend all though grammar school until they lost touch, when Addae's family moved away. They were unexpectedly reunited when they ended up at the same hospital for their residency programs. He's originally from Kinshasa and he and his parents emigrated here when he was around four years old but his grandparents still live and practice medicine there. He had stopped in to say goodbye to Jonathan because he was returning to Africa temporarily to help his grandparents, who were getting older and tired, accomplish a transition of the clinic so they could consider retirement. All during dinner, on the first evening he was staying, he kept staring at me and I became so uncomfortable I finally said something. He apologized and explained it was because I looked very much like a past partner of his grandparents, whose picture hung in their clinic in the Province of Kinshasa, especially my eyes. He didn't know her name but she was a doctor who had worked with them many years before and was murdered, along with her husband and some patients, more than thirty years ago. His grandparents told Addae the loss of their friend and colleague and her husband had resulted in many children and mothers being deprived of the desperately needed medical care and the valuable help they provided travelling from village to village regularly."

"Yes, your mother told me her father had become a trusted part of the group providing driving and other help when they travelled to villages too far away for patients to reach the clinic on foot. Diana cared for the women and children, being careful to convey respect for the customs of the indigenous healers and, when possible, including them as complimentary to her medical treatment. Lyle helped with planting food crops, water acquisition and getting permission from the Elders to establish small schoolrooms with books and supplies. He came to admire the people of Africa as honorable and kind, apart, of course, from some of the beliefs and treatment of women, which Addae's grandparents were endeavoring to change, slowly. During these years, both Diana and Lyle studied and came to embrace a blending of all world religions and concepts of spirituality."

"Since I had no idea of my family history at the time and would never have imagined Africa played a part in it, I just dismissed it as an interesting dinner conversation; but, as you were speaking about my mother and grandparents, I realized it wasn't mere coincidence."

"Oh, Love, that is strange and I'm not surprised he noticed the resemblance. Diana was beautiful, just like you and Lyliana, and her eyes were exactly the color of yours from the pictures I saw." Of all the things Nathaniel might have said to Gabrielle, he was concerned what made him say something which seemed rather shallow and unimportant in response. He was worried, suddenly, that the pain medications were affecting his brain more than he realized.

Gabrielle noticed his expression and thought he was getting tired, "Are you needing to rest?"

"No, I'm fine, just lost my concentration for a moment. Let's see where was I? Oh, yes. Lyliana was almost fourteen when her parents were murdered and she had an awful time adjusting to their deaths. After their funerals, when she wasn't at boarding school in England, Lyliana lived with Diana's parents, who are your great grandparents. In 1960, they had just moved to an early commune, in California. She was happiest when she was there with them and miserable each time she was taken to the airport, for the flight to England to resume her studies. They couldn't bear her sadness and the upset each time she left and, finally, two years after Diana and Lyle's deaths, they withdrew Lyliana from her English school and allowed her to remain with them.

It was while living on the commune she learned to play the guitar and sing, composed her own original songs and collected a huge repertoire of traditional folk songs. Her British father had insisted on sending her to English boarding schools, where she also became fluent in French.

These language influences, combined with learning some of the dialects of Africa, resulted in her speaking with a lovely melodic and undefinable accent which she never lost.

Lyliana graduated from high school in 1964, and was very happy living in the peace and love environment of the commune. Sometimes, when musicians gathered there to share music, it reminded her of some of the tribal celebrations she often witnessed in Africa and she understood the commonality of all human beings and the natural and deep-rooted need for, and love of, music and rhythm in every culture. Those experiences strongly influenced the tone, words and rhythms of her songs and, I think, the haunting sweetness of her voice."

Gabrielle was pleased to learn playing the guitar and a love of folk music were things she shared in common with her mother.

"Even before entering college, Lyliana became an activist, especially for civil rights, gay rights, women's liberation and, later, against the Vietnam War. She was a guitarist and folk singer and used those talents at all sorts of demonstrations, including one of the 'Homosexual Reminder Days' in Washington, DC, which were organized to call attention to rights of employment in the federal civil service."

Nathaniel paused and sighed, "That was where Jeremiah and I met her. After one year of college, she dropped out and making music and activism became her full-time job and passion."

Nathaniel paused and asked if he was talking too much and whether Gabrielle had any questions. Gabrielle shook her head "no" and indicated he should continue.

"Lyliana spent most of her time in Greenwich Village, staying with other folk artist friends at Washington Square Hotel, which was a residential hotel during the bohemian days."

At the mention of Washington Square, Gabrielle explained her mysterious attraction to it and told Nathaniel she had painted the Park and Arch many times.

Nathaniel smiled, stroked her hand gently and waited until it was clear she had nothing else to share for the moment and continued, "Lyliana met famous artists like Bob Dylan and hung out and performed at The Bitter End, one of the more famous and infamous coffee houses. Tuesdays were open-mike nights and many stars-to-be got their start there. She became pretty popular on the folk music circuit, using only her first name, Lyliana, in tribute to her parents, finally understanding the significance of her name and honoring their gift to her and their memory. She acquired a modest but devoted following and was a very busy and happy person, finally.

Then, she and your father met, late in 1967, at The Bitter End, when he came with a group of coworkers and heard her sing."

At this point, Nathaniel interrupted his biography of Lyliana to inform Gabrielle her father's real name was Brian Masters, not Jacob. He had changed it, apparently, when they disappeared. Although he expected the obvious question from Gabrielle, she did not ask so Nathaniel chose not to tell her that Brian had changed her name as well, to Emily. He was hoping her real name would be part of the memories that might come back to her on their own and resolve some of the mysteries. For now, Nathaniel just wanted to give her little pieces of information and acquaint her with her mother, feeling this goal was enough for the first day.

He continued his story slowly, trying to remember any details that might be important to Gabrielle. "Brian fell in love with Lyliana immediately and she couldn't resist his strange infatuation, although, they couldn't have been more opposite in temperament and politic. Brian was a conservative, genius mathematician, strategist and 'game theory' proponent, who became involved in investment consulting with mutual fund companies. He loved that their last names, Masters and Parsons, were syntactically similar and both ended in the letter s. He liked things orderly. Actually, that was an understatement. His very existence seemed to depend on orderliness and Jeremiah and I found him demanding and overbearing." Nathaniel apologized to Gabrielle for saying this, since he was speaking of her father, but she assured him she recognized their impression of him as quite accurate.

"Brian's chosen profession was a source of great conflict with his family because it was a new one and not very well understood. It had been expected Brian would join his father's accounting firm and eventually take it over and his decision not to had caused a mutual estrangement from his entire family. He made very good money, though, and seemed successful and, in 1968, after dating on and off for about six months, he and your mother married, in a quiet ceremony attended by friends. Jeremiah and I were there for Lyliana's sake but were shocked she had agreed to marry Brian. No one from Brian's family attended the wedding and, since Lyliana's parents had been murdered and her grandparents had passed away, she had no family at their wedding either."

Nathaniel sat for a few minutes taking some deep breaths to restore his energy and thinking how to approach the next part of his explanation of Lyliana and Brian's relationship, "When Lyliana announced, on Easter of 1969, she was pregnant, Brian had not been happy with the news. He made it clear he had never intended to have children, although he failed to share those sentiments with Lyliana before they were married. She was shocked and unsure what would happen when the child was born.

Lyliana continued her singing and political activism, attending numerous protests. Her first protest experience had been with her grandparents who took her to Freedom Summer in 1964 to help black citizens learn to go to the polls to vote and face the hostile registrars and to bring attention to the issue in Mississippi. She had been arrested several times for sit-ins, like Sproul Hall Sit-In, at UC Berkeley, in 1968 and unauthorized marches.

Between 1969 and 1971, a series of events began to cause a noticeable change in Brian's behavior. The country was changing and social unrest and protest had become the norm. He had been very upset by Lyliana's participation in the Stonewall Riots, in 1969, although she never admitted to him that she was there. She had returned home from the Village with bruises on her face and Brian felt it was too coincidental that she was visiting friends in Greenwich Village at the time the riots broke out, in protest of alleged abusive treatment of gays by police. The initial problem had inspired more protests and is believed by some to have been the beginning of gay activism and the liberation movement, something Brian was certain Lyliana very strongly supported given her close friendship with Jeremiah, me and our friends. He did not share her views.

Then, Lyliana and fellow musicians were invited to attend the Woodstock Festival, in July 1969, and Brian felt her acceptance of the invitation and intention to attend the three-day event was a callous disregard for the danger she might have been placing their unborn child in. She had gone nevertheless.

In November of 1969, with the baby, I mean you, due at any moment, she had appeared at the 'Mobilization' peace demonstration in Washington, a protest of about 250,000-500,000 people against the 'war' in Vietnam. It was a very busy and emotional time for those opposed to the war and Lyliana joined such notable protestors as Arlo Guthrie, John Denver and Coretta Scott King.

Two days before that demonstration occurred, she had taken part in the 'March Against Death' to honor the U.S. troops killed in Vietnam. For forty hours, 40,000 people, each wearing the name of a dead soldier or a village destroyed, marched, silently, down Pennsylvania Avenue, past the White House.

These events caused Brian to become completely enraged and he had carried on for days after her return about how much he disagreed with the demonstrations about Vietnam and considered it civil disobedience with no redeeming value. He'd voiced his strong objection to her going to any more demonstrations. She had made it clear she had no intention of abandoning either her musical profession or her political beliefs and participation in causes just because she was having a child. In fact, she told Brian she felt it was of even more significance and importance now so the world would be a better place for their children.

To everyone's surprise, Brian's feelings about having children changed dramatically once you were born. He adored you from the very first moment he held you and became overly concerned about every detail of 'his daughter's' care. He began to obsess over planning your future, constantly worried about how he could ensure your well-being. Gabrielle, I hope I'm telling all of this accurately for you. It was so long ago and seems rather disjointed and out of order but I think I have most of it right."

"Nathaniel, you're doing an incredible job of remembering all those events, whether they're in order or not, but I'm afraid it's too much for you and will tire you out before the day has even begun. To learn so much about my mother...well, both of them is…is…I can't find any words to express my feelings right now."

Nathaniel continued without acknowledging her concern about him as if ignoring it returned him to his old status, the strong, irrepressible one.

"In August of 1970, I think, on the fiftieth anniversary of Women's Suffrage, Lyliana had joined the Strike for Equality March, down Fifth Avenue, in New York City. A sad irony considering what was to come. Oh dear, I am skipping all over the place, I think. I'm sorry, Love.

It wasn't clear if Brian had just hidden his displeasure with Lyliana's political activism before they were married but, now, he was unrelenting in trying to convince her to stop it all and settle into being a housewife and mother.

While all this was happening, although Lyliana had absolutely no idea, Brian was involved in one of the early insider trading scandals. One by one, his coworkers faced charges of fraud and embezzlement, for creating and using fraudulent figures to boost stock values, enabling them to acquire valuable properties and companies and to manipulate stock purchases and sales. Brian had been the genius behind the figures and, with each arrest, the scandal got closer to him and his boss. Between them, they had stashed several million dollars, an enormous amount of money back then, in various banks, in and out of the country and under different identities. We only learned this after you disappeared as we were trying to determine if he had something to do with it without alerting the police.

The increased pressure from the possibility of Brian's arrest and his growing opposition to Lyliana's continued activism caused Brian to make a unilateral decision to move. Your father's main worry was that Lyliana's constant conflicts with police would call attention to him and reveal his whereabouts." Nathaniel closed his eyes and took some long breaths again.

Gabrielle was enthralled with the endless details Nathaniel shared but was concerned about his health. She had been making notes as Nathaniel talked but, now, she put down her pen and suggested again that he rest for a time.

Nathaniel insisted he was fine and really wanted to finish if Gabrielle was holding up okay. When she said she was, he said, "I should have written this down a long time ago, because it's everything I knew about Lyliana before she disappeared, and now I don't have the energy to do it. I doubt if there is anyone else who knows this much so I need to tell you before it's too late." Nathaniel didn't see Gabrielle's pained expression at the implication and, after a pause to remember where he left off, he continued, "Brian began to have repeated and lengthy conversations with Lyliana about the world and all its evils and appealed to her sense of concern for their child, I mean you. He tried to convince her to move and live a simple life, gardening and providing a natural and safe environment for their little daughter to grow up in, much like what she herself had experienced on the commune with her grandparents.

He also told her his version of the trouble he was likely to be in, assuring her it wasn't true but he would have no way to prove it. Brian's final and most compelling argument was suggesting, perhaps, they might think about having another baby. Lyliana wanted to have a second child and was finally persuaded, trusting both in his innocence and his concerns. She actually looked forward to beginning a life devoted to you and Brian and her wish for creating a real family. He said she could always resume her interests when the children were older and struck the perfect chord with her by talking about her beloved grandparents and communal living.

In early Fall of 1972, just as one of Brian's superiors and co-conspirator was arrested, they packed up everything and disappeared. It is probably at this point that the name change took place, just conjecture on my part. Jeremiah and I weren't told where they intended to go. Because Lyliana had confided some of Brian's problems and concerns and some things she had found out on her own, we were shocked by her submissiveness and her willingness to go along with Brian's scheme.

During the first months after they moved away, Lyliana had called a few times, which is how we learned some of the things I'm telling you. But even though we begged her several times, she wouldn't reveal where they were. They just seemed to withdraw from all contact with anyone after that and finally communication stopped altogether. Lyliana's last call indicated some unhappiness and fear about an escalation of Brian's strange behavior. They lived off the land for the most part and seemed poor but, periodically, Brian would disappear for a day or two and then mysteriously return with the cash needed for food, or some bill. He refused to discuss where he had gone and how he had acquired the money.

We did manage to get one note to her, expressing our concern, at a post office box she provided briefly. The letter you found in *Don Quixote*.

In November of 1973, we received a strange package, with no return address. In it was a deed to a property, which was in her grandparent's name, with Lyliana and any future children as co-owners. It was a seven-hundred acre wooded lot, in the Adirondacks, with only a summer log cabin on a tiny lake, remote and located up a winding quarter-of-a-mile dirt driveway.

Lyliana's grandparents had hoped to establish a commune there but they passed away before they could begin the work on it. It also provided easy and fast access to Canada should the need arise to get out of the country quickly. With the deed, was a paper stating that, if anything happened to her, Jeremiah and I were designated as guardians to oversee care of the property until you and the child she was expecting were of legal age and could inherit it. That's how we learned she was pregnant. The package also contained a small jewelry box.

Jeremiah and I attempted to find Lyliana, using the information in the envelope describing the property. By then, the house was empty, although, there was definite evidence you had lived there very recently, and then just vanished. We never heard another word until Gabrielle, I mean you, calling yourself Emily, arrived on our doorstep and then, like your mother, you just vanished too."

There was more to tell Gabrielle, although Nathaniel didn't let her know it, because he felt this was enough until she could begin to remember something on her own. She had never indicated she had any memory of her mother and what had happened which resulted in she and her father living in Canada without Lyliana. Nathaniel had a feeling she held some vital clue to it all in her lost memory, although, she was only three or four and he didn't know if an accurate remembrance was even possible at that young age. Lyliana had mentioned how clever she was and that she spoke in full sentences by her first birthday. Nathaniel hoped it meant she had the vocabulary to articulate any memories.

Neither Gabrielle nor Nathaniel realized Jeremiah had joined them at some point and was sitting behind them, silently listening to what Nathaniel shared with Gabrielle about her mother and father. His growing concern about Nathanial caused him to speak up suddenly, during a pause, surprising them both. The three of them talked a little more and it was decided that Jeremiah and Gabrielle would drive up and find the property, since Nathaniel was definitely not up to it. They would make the trip the following weekend because Mary, their housekeeper and the other person who cared for Nathaniel when Jeremiah had to leave for work-related business or to run errands, was away for a family emergency and would be returning then.

Gabrielle felt overwhelmed and pleased, all at once, to learn so much about her parents. Everything Nathaniel told her about her father filled in many missing pieces about their peculiar life and his personality and compulsive behavior. It still didn't answer the most important questions, however. Why had her mother left them and never come back for her and where was she now? And, where was her brother or sister?

Her eyes were closed and she was experiencing another flash of peculiar feelings when Jeremiah and Nathaniel, simultaneously, touched her shoulders and asked if she was okay.

She startled at their voices and then recovered quickly, "Nathaniel, you must be tired and very hungry because I'm starving. What time is it?"

Jeremiah responded immediately, "It's after nine o'clock and definitely time for a break."

They had talked for nearly four hours and Gabrielle felt terribly guilty, "Nathaniel, I'm so sorry. It was thoughtless of me to cause you to use so much of your energy."

"That's why I wanted to be up early. I knew I would have the strength for it then."

But she could see the pain on his face and insisted they get him back in bed for breakfast and some pain medication. He protested, at first, but Gabrielle responded with "I'll bring my breakfast in as well and have a picnic on the bed with you. We can read articles from the newspaper to each other and do the crossword puzzle after we eat, just like we used to, if you feel up to it after the long morning."

Nathaniel was delighted by her remembrance of one of their favorite Sunday morning rituals and agreed to it all, including a little pain medication, with a smile and squeeze of her hand. They decided on omelets, crispy bacon and heaps of cinnamon toast for breakfast.

Jeremiah insisted that Nathaniel rest for the time it would take for preparation and took Gabrielle's arm and lead her from the bedroom, with a deliberate flourish, saying, "Nathaniel, you've had Gabrielle all to yourself for hours and I deserve some time too."

Gabrielle hugged Jeremiah as they left the room and watched Nathaniel close his eyes, take a long breath and relax. "That was brilliant to appeal to his sense of fair play to get around his refusal to rest, Jeremiah. You know him so well. Shall we delay breakfast a bit? Although, I will definitely need something protein to snack on, if we do, because I suddenly feel a bit shaky."

"No. We don't have to delay it. It will take a little while for all the omelets, since we all want different cheeses and vegetables, and even a short nap seems to revive him a little and probably will even more with you here, Sweetie. Here's a slice of cheese. So now, how are you after all that?"

"A little dazed, I think, but so grateful to know something about my mother and father. How long were you sitting there with us? I'm sorry I didn't notice or I would have brought you into the warmth of the blanket and our conversation."

"Thank you for saying that. I was there for most of it, sitting just outside the door for a long time, because Nathaniel seemed to have a very precise concept of how he wanted to tell you about everything. After his reactions when I said a few things last night while fixing dinner, I thought I should stay out of it. If I had come in, I might have interjected something he didn't want me to say or upset you."

Gabrielle felt terrible for him, "I'm sure whatever you might have contributed would have been just fine, Jeremiah. You've never said or done anything, ever, to hurt me and are always thoughtful of my feelings. I think part of it is because it's one thing Nathaniel can have control over, since everything else in his life now seems to be controlled by the illness, the doctors and his caretakers."

Jeremiah felt better when he thought of it in that way, since nothing like Nathaniel's vehement objection to Jeremiah's contribution to the conversation had never happened between them before. "The only reason I made my presence known was because I became concerned Nathaniel hadn't had his medications or anything to eat, not that I wasn't concerned you might be hungry too," he smiled and kissed her cheek, thanking her for making him feel so much better. He also commented on how mature and wise she had become.

"Do you know what a wonderful man you are, Jeremiah, and how much Nathaniel loves you?"

"Oh, not as wonderful as you think. There are times when I think I can't make it through another day watching him in pain and facing the repeated disappointment of the cancer not going into remission, after horrible rounds of chemotherapy.

And, too often lately, I'm ashamed to say it out loud, but I feel so angry, not with him but at the whole circumstance. I simply can't accept what's happening. Isn't that foolish? I know it is but I can't. He's giving up and I don't want him to. And, then, I realize how hideously selfish it is of me to want him to linger, suffering as he does, just so I will have him with me longer."

"Jeremiah, you've really had more burden and responsibility than any one person should have and so I repeat what a wonderful man you are and do you know how much he loves you?"

"I do know. We both do. The one thing I will have no regrets about is how we both have loved each other and cared for each other, from the moment we met and I know, beyond any doubt, he would be doing exactly the same thing I am, if it were me who was sick. It's very kind of you to say it, though, nice to know others see it as we do."

It took almost an hour to prepare everything, with the occasional pauses for their conversation. At the last minute, Gabrielle remembered the pastries she brought from the inn and placed them on the tray after a quick warming.

Gabrielle climbed up on their very high bed, which she always loved because, as she told them when she first came to live there, it made her feel like a little child in a fairytale. Jeremiah handed her the tray filled with their picnic breakfast.

Nathaniel opened his eyes and smiled at both of them, "That smells heavenly and I'm absolutely famished!"

Chapter 16

Cassy and Jonathan

Jonathan dialed Cassy's number and waited for several rings before becoming concerned that he might be waking her, even though it was almost nine o'clock. He didn't have much time to talk and had just decided to hang up when she answered. Her voice sounded a little tired, "Hello, Jonathan."

"Is that the new Caller ID thing or mind reading? Hi, Munch!" He often used this family pet name for her, short for Munchkin, a reference to her petite stature.

"Nice to know you're still on the planet, Jonboy." She was the one person who never called him that, a clear message she was angry with him.

He laughed and then apologized for his lack of communication with her. "But the reason I'm calling this morning is to invite you to come and stay for a few days or longer, if you like. I could really use some bottle-of-wine or pint-of-ice-cream-with-two-spoons talk time, if you can spare a day or two."

She sounded a little hesitant, which surprised him, then said, "I could definitely use some quarts-of-ice-cream-with-two-gigantic-spoons conversation myself. I'm packing as we speak."

"Great! You still have your key, right?"

"Yes, I think so. Hold on for a moment and I'll look for it." Jonathan could hear her moving about the room, opening and closing drawers, and then walking back toward the phone, "Yes, I have it."

"Good. I'll let Jesse know to expect you so you won't surprise him in the buff again, like last time."

"That's okay. Don't tell him. I rather enjoyed it," she laughed now.

"LaLaLa. I have my fingers in my ears and am not hearing that, little sister," he laughed too.

"How is Jesse these days?"

"Really well, actually. He finally has a lady love and is not in this world any longer. On the rare occasions when he sleeps at home, I have to deflate him and tie him in his bed so he doesn't float away overnight. He's completely out in space and in love."

She didn't laugh this time and just said, "Oh, well good for Dr. Terhune." There was definitely a strange edge to her response. Did he hear disappointment and sarcasm? Had he been missing something? Good grief! Did she have feelings for his best friend all this time and he hadn't noticed? If so, she had been as inscrutable as Brie. Well, this certainly was going to be an interesting visit.

"So, when do you think you'll get to the house? Hopefully, I'll be through, here at the office, by five-thirty or six."

"If I can manage to get to Chatham earlier, can I stop by your office and see what it looks like now? I haven't been there for ages and you hadn't even finished decorating the last time we were together up there."

"Wow! Time goes by so fast. I'd forgotten it's been so long since you've been up but you're right. It was still a work in progress. I've gone down your way the last couple of times we've gotten together. I'd love you to see it and for you to meet Linda and Carolyn, if you can make it early enough. If you don't, you can just come tomorrow.

"I'm almost out the door...well, not almost but I should be able to be there by four-thirty or five. I can't wait to see my big brother in his 'the doctor will see you now' mode. And, Jonathan, thank you so much for asking me to come. You have no idea how timely and perfect your invitation is. See you later. I'll call you if there's any problem."

"Okay, Munch. Be careful. Bye."

The melodic joy, always in her voice, was absent and, hearing that, Jonathan was even happier he had called her. While he wanted to confide in her about Gabrielle before he talked to the rest of the family, it sounded like something was very wrong and she could use some time together too. He was glad to know ahead of time, so he wouldn't be as self-absorbed and inattentive to her as he had been to Jesse all these weeks.

Before returning to his patients, Jonathan dialed Jesse's office to alert him of Cassy's visit, and asked for him, completely forgetting he was taking a one-day continuing medical education course in Boston and planned to stay over because Morgan was there as well, for a case. They hadn't seen each other over the long weekend because Jesse was with Jonathan, in the Village, looking for Brie. Well, that solved the question of Jesse being around when Cassy arrived.

Jonathan's nurse, Linda, knocked on his door, as he hung up the phone, and opened it looking slightly annoyed. He didn't realize his calls took so long and she hated when he ran behind. She was a great nurse, a perfect balance of keen judgment and caring, mature with an imposing stature, very good at keeping him on task and the patients in line. He smiled a big "naughty boy" grin at her and she responded with a "Don't try to charm me, Dr. B. Just get your ass out here now!" glare. He stood up crisply, as if responding to a military command, saluted and walked like a toy soldier, with stiff legs, toward her as she held the door. She tried to maintain her stern demeanor then burst into laughter, grudgingly, as he came nearer and pointed him to the appropriate exam room.

He was suddenly aware of feeling considerably better, probably because he was being more open about Brie, and could actually enjoy the benefit of laughter again.

―――

Cassy hurried around the bedroom, grabbing clothes to pack and then changing her mind and tossing them on the bed. The rejected pile grew exponentially with each attempt at decision while her suitcase remained empty for the most part. *Why was this so hard? For that matter, why was everything so hard lately, especially choices.*

Studying her reflection in the vanity mirror after her shower, Cassy chided herself out loud, "How could you let this happen? You are such a fool! Oh, great! Now I'm talking to myself. Jonathan, help!"

The drive from her temporary home, a tiny apartment she was renting while she studied for her doctorate, in Philadelphia, went well and, even though she made several stops along the way, she arrived at Jonathan's office just after five o'clock. There were still several patients in the waiting room so she decided she should just let the receptionist know who she was and, then, sit and read until he was ready to see her.

As Cassy approached the window, the receptionist, who wore a name tag identifying her as Carolyn, scowled a little, as if to say, whoever she was, she definitely did not have an appointment. The nurse, who had just come up to the front, on the other hand, knew who she was before she even could say her name and came out to the waiting room with a big grin. She put out her hand, "Hello, I'm Linda," then almost dragged Cassy into the back, as the patients glared in annoyance because she was taken ahead of them. She looked back apologetically, as Linda, who towered over her, closed the door behind them and introduced her to Carolyn all before Cassy had gotten to utter a word.

She found her tongue and breath finally, "I'll be happy to sit in the waiting room until Jonathan is finished for the day."

Linda, being the arbiter of timeliness, agreed, "Thank you. I'll let the doctor know you've arrived."

Cassy returned to the waiting room and glaring patients and opened her book to read.

The waiting room door opened again and, this time, it was Jonathan. He ran to her with a huge smile, picked her up and hugged her all in one motion, then turned toward the patients, "This is my little sister, Cassy," as he placed her, gently, back on the floor. And then, just to her, "It's going to be a while longer."

She smiled quickly and whispered "Brought a book just in case, but I will need to use the restroom."

"I'll tell Carolyn." Then he was the professional again and invited the next patient to follow him back into the office.

The mood changed instantly and the patients still waiting were happy to meet a relative of the doctor and to convey how much they respected and liked him.

Carolyn came out to invite Cassy to use the restroom and she took the opportunity to peek into a few open doors as she went. The feel of the office was pleasant and soothing, decorated with very subtle colors and several paintings signed simply, GB. and some compelling photographs by Krug. Several plants and a soothing water fountain in the waiting room added to the calming and natural feel *and, no doubt, contributed to more easily obtainable urine samples*, she thought, amused.

It occurred to her, suddenly, that this was actually Jonathan's medical office. *He truly achieved his goal of becoming a family doctor of osteopathy and is, obviously, as caring and concerned for his patients as I knew he would be.* She felt so proud of her big brother.

From there her mind wandered to how very different Jonathan's office was from Jesse's and how well-suited their choices of design were to each of them.

The décor of Jesse's office was a perfect reflection of his humor and personality. Entering his waiting room was a bit like entering a story book. There actually were two waiting rooms adjoined by a glass wall and doors. The adult room was furnished with dramatically oversized furniture and decorative pieces designed to make an adult look and feel very small, things like two five-foot toothbrushes in different colors and a toothpaste tube of proportional size standing in one corner. Sitting in the enormous chairs, one's feet barely touched the floor and made an adult appear childlike. Large-leafed plants reached to the high, sky-lighted ceiling. Magazines and books were oversized and in large print. No one entered without being mesmerized and it caused adults to giggle like children. The unanimous favorite was the massive dental chair in one corner, with a fake drill and supplies all super-sized, even the cotton rolls and dental mirror. Parents were always bringing friends and other family members to their children's appointments so they could experience it too, and these added visitors had, inadvertently, become a source of new patients, although it had not been the intent of the design.

In the children's waiting room, everything was the opposite, sized to make a child feel just right, although, they did enjoy the other waiting room and seeing their parents magically become very small. It was such an amusing and touching statement of respect for a child's perspective.

Cassy began to read but really couldn't concentrate on her book, since she could see the patients staring at her from her peripheral vision, so she put it down and smiled, knowing it would probably restart the chatting which began after Jonathan's introduction. It actually was enjoyable and passed the time more quickly. One by one, patients were called in and replaced by the ones leaving who stopped by for a little more conversation and to tell her how great it was to meet her.

Shortly after six o'clock, Jonathan came out and brought her back, apologizing for the wait and showed her around the entire office, proudly. She complimented the décor and thoughtful layout and made him feel very special, hugging him and saying how happy she was for him.

Before coming to Jonathan's office, Cassy made a stop at a local restaurant and purchased food for dinner, bought a bottle of wine, and then, at a small grocery, chose several pints of their favorite ice cream flavors. Traffic was light and she made the trip with plenty of time to shop and leave everything at the house with her luggage. When Jonathan suggested catching a bite before going to his house, she let him know they were already prepared for dinner. He hugged her and said, "Last one home has to use a demitasse spoon for the ice cream," and they both laughed and ran out the door to their cars, as Linda and Carolyn, who were watching them, smiled at their boss's playful and loving way with his sister.

Cassy was the first in the door, just as Jonathan meant her to be, and, still laughing, she ran to fetch a demitasse spoon from the butler's pantry for him.

They opened the salads with grilled chicken slices, "I thought we should have a healthy, dinner before beginning an evening of wine and ice cream stories," Cassy explained.

They carried their dinners to the living room and Jonathan lit a fire, as Cassy made herself comfortable, sitting cross-legged on the floor next to the coffee table and near the warmth of the fireplace, noticing and complimenting the new tiles, the mantle and the beautiful hearth stones. "The house looks better each time I see it. You've done so much work. I'm so envious of your domesticity and constantly wonder if I'll ever find a home and settle in."

"Thanks. I have a friend who's a decorator and he has been an invaluable resource. And the best part is we barter physician-decorator services. I owe him immensely, though. He's far too healthy to make it a fair exchange and so is his wife.

The contractor he suggested is another story altogether," Jonathan rolled his eyes and sighed. "He's one of those charmers who promises to be here on a certain date and gives you some arbitrary estimate and then shows up days later than promised. Then, he presents a ridiculously inflated bill and asks for additional money, every few days, before the job is anywhere near completion. The paradox is that his completed work is impeccable, he's very knowledgeable and obsessive about every detail and yet he is unreliable and borders on dishonest about the cost. There is no way I could have done all the work on the house without his expertise but most of the time I want to strangle him."

Cassy laughed and then Jonathan realized he hadn't actually responded to her lament about ever owning a home and began again, "Sorry for the rant! I love my home but ownership is not as exciting or easy as it seems. It's a huge responsibility, always requiring maintenance, repairs or updating. Mortgages, paired with student loan expense can end or indefinitely postpone dreams like travelling. You were smart to travel first. To answer your question, I'm sure you'll find a home when you're ready for the commitment."

As soon as Jonathan was satisfied with the fire and was seated, he asked a question that shocked and then amused Cassy, "So what did I detect in your tone when I told you about Jesse having a girlfriend?" He'd been curious and almost perseverating on the subject at various times the entire day, since his conversation with her.

"Well, don't beat around the bush, Big Brother, or, heaven forbid, find a more subtle approach! Okay, you probably heard a hint of disappointment. Does that surprise you?"

"Yes! Are you in love with him or something – did he ever...?"

"So much for my foolish assumption that you would have a delicate and thoughtful bedside manner. You should see the look on your face right now!" Cassy pushed him playfully and messed up his hair and then continued with a smile, "I've held feelings for Jesse for a long time but only in my demented little head have we ever made love. Much to my dismay, he's been the perfect big brother's best friend. Besides, it's much more likely he would have chosen Carly than me."

Jonathan was still processing her quick-fire answer in his slow, deliberate fashion when he realized she was saying that somehow Carly was more attractive than her. "Excuse me, but the last time I looked you and Carly were still identical twins so what does that mean? And please leave out the details of your sexual fantasies about Jesse!"

"Oh, please don't pretend you don't see that Carly is one of the beautiful, tall and athletic Blakes, like you and I am the tired-eyed, asymmetric pixie who, somehow, got a disproportionate share of the gene pool when the egg split."

"I'm not sure what funhouse mirror you look in every day but, from here, you are an admittedly tiny, but exact duplicate of Carly and so beautiful. You didn't start out as healthy and do look tired sometimes but, if you're comparing yourself to Carly, then live her life for a while. She's a great nurse and works hard but she also spends lots of time at spas and taking very good care of herself. Spend a month of pampering and see if you recognize the rested you. You work, have earned two Master's degrees and are studying for a doctorate in cultural anthropology, pretty impressive if you ask me. Is having an unrequited crush on Jesse what's made you feel this way?"

"Good grief, Jonathan, a crush? Really! You are a dope sometimes! No. He is not the reason for my feeling the way I do. I just reacted out of a little disappointment, that's all. I can't wait, now, given this response, to tell you why I wanted to come and talk to you. I can see that's going to take a huge amount of ice cream. You'd better start with what you wanted to talk to me about so I can stuff myself with double chocolate while I'm listening and get up the nerve to tell my tale of woe."

Jonathan was really curious now and got up to clear the dishes and get the pint of ice cream and two spoons but, as soon as he returned with them and sat down, she jumped up and grabbed the spoon out of his hand, retrieved the demitasse spoon and handed it to him smirking, "Oh, no you don't! You lost, remember? Anyway, smaller mouthfuls will help you tell your story more easily. So, start talking, Dr. Diplomacy," and she giggled a bit and he thought a touch of the missing melody in her speech and laughter was trying to find a voice.

He spent a long time on the story of meeting Gabrielle because, although Cassy had met her briefly once, he had never spoken to anyone about her. He talked about how she came to live in his studio addition, her artistry and their life together, leaving out Marginal Way. It was very difficult to put into words having felt a profound sadness and deep sorrow in her heart and thus in his, from the moment Gabrielle turned her head and looked at him from the scaffolding at Emory's to watching her paint in the dark garden in Autumn. He confessed he was troubled by her reluctance to trust and withholding details of her life from everyone, until he and Jesse saw her terror in the park. He knew their history together was rather sparse and lacking the romantic details Cassy would expect and so might not convey why he was so in love with her. But Cassy found it very believable that they loved each other, even with the odd circumstances leading up to and after the revelation. She was immediately drawn into the mystery of where she was and the identity of the man who had frightened her so much. She felt awful for both of them, so separated and so connected all at once and, of course, offered to join in whatever further attempts he was going to make to find her and bring her home.

Jonathan's story took up the better part of an hour and the entire first pint of ice cream, in part because Cassy's usual curiosity led to a number of questions. They decided on making some popcorn for something salty and then continuing with the ice cream indulgence, rather than opening the wine. They would save it for dinner the following evening. As they were putting the finishing touches on the popcorn, lots of butter and salt, Jonathan turned to Cassy unexpectedly and hugged her tightly, "Thank you for letting me get the whole story out."

She held onto the brother she adored so much for a very long time, becoming anxious, suddenly, thinking of what she needed to talk to only him about and how to begin her story.

They settled back in the living room, this time with Cassy curled up next to Jonathan on the couch and wrapped in a blanket, feeling suddenly vulnerable and chilly. Jonathan tried to approach his next question with a bit more delicacy and sensitivity than when he asked her about Jesse. He simply asked if she felt ready to talk about what had been causing her to feel upset. After a couple of pieces of popcorn and a few good breaths Cassy began.

The fire was smoldering with only an occasional blaze as she eased into the story by talking about her decision to pursue a doctorate in cultural anthropology.

Cassy was thrilled to learn she had been accepted into the doctoral program and was supposed to have a meeting with whomever they decided would be her temporary advisor. She'd already chosen a permanent advisor but he had a waiting list. While she waited for her place, a temporary advisor would begin to discuss her first classes, research projects and dissertation plans.

At this point, Cassy became hesitant and uncomfortable and, in what Jonathan thought was a strange change of subject, asked, "Do you remember the professor I had some difficulty with as a freshman in college?"

Jonathan immediately reacted to this reminder, wondering what made her think of him in the middle of her story and, then, connected it with what she had just been saying. "Oh shit, Cassy! Sorry! Not Michael Brighton! Is that who they assigned to you? Did you know he was at that school?"

Cassy was grateful he remembered and had made the connection so easily so she didn't have to explain that part, at least. "Jonathan, I almost died when I entered the room and he was there waiting for me. He tried to say he was completely shocked when he saw my name but I'm sure they didn't hand my file to him as I entered, so, unlike me, he was very well prepared for the meeting. I didn't know what to say, at first, but, once I'd gathered my wits again, said we should go immediately and arrange for another advisor. He begged me not to, saying requesting a change to someone else would be awkward because they would ask why and he was new and wouldn't want anything to cause problems. So, stupidly, I agreed, since it was just temporary, we should just go on with the meeting and set up my program and begin discussing my ideas for a dissertation.

Naturally, the discussion did not stay on task and he kept telling me how much he missed me and regretted his decision and the way he had ended things. I kept saying it was history and suggesting we get back to the subject of my classes but could feel myself wearing down. I really tried, Jonathan, I really did try not to listen but I had been so young and terribly heartbroken by our separation and was so in love with him. He still is as handsome and appealing and I agreed to leave with him, when we were finished, to have a drink and talk. I know! Please don't judge or be angry with me at this point or I'll die of shame right here in your living room!"

"I'm not angry with you, Munch, but I'd willingly strangle him right now! I really want to hear everything and do what I can to help. Just let me take five minutes at this point to collect my thoughts and calm down. Sit right here and don't move. I'm just going to step outside for a minute and then get us some ice water." He removed himself as slowly and calmly as he could so as not to scare her off, then, went outside and punched a tree, bloodying his hand, and returned to the kitchen, rinsed it off and started for the living room then stopped to give himself a little more time.

Cassy had started college at seventeen having graduated high school in the gifted class in three years and Michael Brighton, nearly twenty years older and her English professor, had seduced her during her second semester. He was married, although Cassy hadn't known before she got involved with him, and a chronic seducer of younger women. This was Jonathan's perception and not based on any concrete evidence. But Cassy didn't see him that way. She had been devastated when he broke it off and left, probably because of some scandal with another coed, again Jonathan's unsubstantiated assumption. The professor had helped himself to her virginity and innocence and continued to romance her until he left, coldly phoning her to say goodbye.

Jonathan had kept her secret from the rest of the family, remaining her comfort and confidant through the heartache, but did have a confrontation with Michael, which resulted in a brief hospital emergency room visit for the professor, for treatment of a mild concussion and fractured nose. Jonathan knew he would likely react in exactly the same way if he were to meet up with him right now, given this new indication he was continuing to take advantage of his position to seduce young students.

And then there was Cassy's part in it. She wasn't a college freshman any longer but an educated and intelligent young woman and it was hard for Jonathan to understand how she had fallen into this again. He wanted to rage at her for even considering having a drink with Michael Brighton and not immediately asking for another advisor but knew it would push her away and she really needed him to listen. He was dreading what she would tell him next but threw some water on his face, which felt hot and red and returned to the living room, almost forgetting to bring the ice water, after much longer than the five minutes he had asked for.

Surprisingly, she was still sitting there and appeared to be frozen just where he had left her. She looked into his eyes, so sadly, and he sat down again and hugged her. "Go on, Munch. I'm sorry I took so long but you know my history with the good professor and how I feel about him so you must have expected some reaction like this."

"I did expect it but it doesn't make it any easier. I know this is a great burden to place on you again but you're the only one I can trust. I couldn't stand it if Mommy and Daddy found out. They don't even know about what happened when I was a freshman. I know you've figured it out by now but I plunged right back into having another affair with him, only, this time he's asked me to marry him saying he was already leaving his wife. That was just two days before you called me. I'd been locked in my apartment not answering my phone or going out because I don't know how to answer him or what I feel, just that it's not the same as nine years ago. He's been calling repeatedly and even came to the apartment and begged me to let him come in and talk to me. When I refused, he sat outside my apartment building for hours. Your phone call was so well timed, providing a much-needed reason to make myself leave Philadelphia for a while, to get away and gain some perspective. I accepted your invitation and sneaked out the back way in case he was there in his car waiting to see me.

I'm such a mess, Jonathan, and I know you will have the obvious answer to what I should do but he does seem different and is acting insanely determined, where before he was so non-committal and vague, saying, repeatedly, he is in love with me. But I'm petrified and incapable of saying yes or no at the moment and I'm not sure what will happen to my doctoral program either way."

Jonathan quickly tried to think of something filled with wisdom to say but could only ask what seemed the obvious question, "Cassy, doesn't the fact that you're here, instead of in his arms, and so distraught tell you there's something wrong? I know you weren't aware of it the first time but you do know the man is still married and will have to break another person's heart to have yours. No one can tell you what love should feel like but I think, if you ask yourself the right question, the answer will find its way to you. I'm not sure what else to say except I love you and will support whatever decision you make, if you're truly comfortable with it and happy. I'm glad you came and put some distance between you and the...situation. I think you need to take some time to breathe and consider all of this. Stay as long as you like. Jesse and I aren't here that much during the week, so you'll have plenty of privacy but I'm only a few minutes away at the office if you feel like talking or need something."

Cassy said nothing and just put her head on Jonathan's shoulder. He sat, gently stroking her hair and said nothing more either.

After a time, she got up, "I'm going for another pint of ice cream and then something mindless on television. Care to join me?"

Jonathan was exhausted and had early rounds at the hospital but was hesitant to leave her just yet, "I can handle a few more spoonful's given the size of my spoon and then I'm heading up to bed. Feel free to fall asleep here, if you'd rather have the white noise of the television because the one in the guest room isn't working at the moment."

"Thanks for everything, Jonathan, especially the absence of judgment and time to think. I probably will just sleep down here then."

"Actually, I think I'll skip the ice cream and just go up to bed now. I'll bring you some sheets, a blanket and a couple of pillows."

"I'll come up with you and get them. I have to get undressed anyway...think I'll forget about more ice cream too."

Once upstairs, he handed her the linens, kissed her and wished her a restful sleep.

Every program Cassy switched to on the television was too relevant and painful so she turned it off and picked Don Quixote which was sitting on a lamp table and started to read it, hoping to discover something Jonathan and Jesse had missed, and fell asleep after the first twenty pages.

The phone rang much too soon and Jonathan tried to answer it as quickly as he could, hoping it hadn't wakened Cassy. It was four-thirty and he knew it was either the hospital or his answering service, although a part of him hoped it was Gabrielle. He was called away for an emergency at the hospital and dressed quickly and as quietly as he could then slipped down the stairs, grimacing at the creak of each old step. He'd been meaning to speak with his contractor about the stairs and what could be done to quiet them.

Cassy was awake and asked what was wrong. "One of my patients has taken a very sudden turn and I have to go to the hospital. I'm sorry the phone woke you. I'll be back for breakfast and a shower before I go to the office. Try to go back to sleep."

Surprisingly, she felt as if she could and settled back on the couch again, "Okay, but call me when you're on the way back here and I'll make breakfast while you shower. I hope everything goes well."

"Thanks. See you later," he whispered now, as if she were already asleep.

Chapter 17

Cassy and Morgan

Jesse and Morgan had risen at five o'clock to drive back to the Cape for their Wednesday appointments. "Why don't we go to my house for breakfast, since your first appointment is in Chatham, and you wanted to stop at your Aunt Sarah's house to check in with her. You can shower before we eat and maybe Jonathan will be around and I'll be able to introduce you two, finally."

"That would be great, if you think he won't mind. I don't want to cause any discomfort."

"I'm sure he'll be fine. He mentioned he would like to meet you, several times during the weekend."

Morgan was very happy she would finally be meeting Jonathan and seeing their home. Although she understood and had supported Jesse's initial decision to wait until Jonathan and Gabrielle were together again to introduce Morgan to everyone, she was relieved she would no longer be the phantom girlfriend.

They arrived at the house just before six thirty and Jesse was disappointed to find Jonathan's car wasn't in the garage and assumed he was called to the hospital for an emergency with one of his patients. Then he noticed the car parked next to the garage in the driveway and thought maybe Jonathan had some sort of car trouble. As they entered the house, Jesse smelled food cooking and expected to see him at the stove but, as they came into the kitchen, Cassy jumped and screamed and Morgan did as well in reaction.

"Cassy! Hi! Sorry we scared you! I had no idea you were visiting. It seems like ages since I've seen you! Oh, sorry. Cassy, this is Morgan. Morgan, this is Jonathan's sister, Cassy." Jonathan came in the door at that moment and Jesse continued the introductions, "Morgan, this is Jonathan...Jonathan, this is Morgan," and they all laughed.

Morgan told them both how pleased she was to meet them then circled around Jesse toward Cassy saying, "I know you from somewhere."

"Yes, you look familiar to me as well," Cassy responded, curious and smiling.

"Berkeley! You went to Berkeley, right? I think you were a few classes behind me but we both played tennis?"

"Yes, that's it. You're Morgan Jeffries, the best player on the team. I was a freshman and you were a senior. I'm surprised you remember me."

"I remember because I thought you were so beautiful and petite and never dreamed you could play tennis as well as you did, especially in your first year." Jonathan was grateful that Morgan told Cassy she was beautiful and played tennis well and hoped it registered.

Morgan moved to the kitchen with Cassy and helped her with cooking breakfast as they continued to chat. Jonathan watched Morgan and thought, in spite of what Jesse had said, she did look a bit like Meg Ryan. He liked her, right off, and was pleased Jesse had finally brought her to meet him. His expression as he watched Morgan confirmed all he had said about truly being in love with her and it made Jonathan think of Brie and wish she was with them sharing this moment.

They all sat down for breakfast together and Morgan was talking to Cassy about school, "So, let's see, what memorable teachers did you have? Was Mrs. Reilly still teaching Western Civilization by the time you came? She was a great teacher but ancient, with horrible arthritis in her hands. When she would point to one of us, we couldn't tell who it was she was calling on and, inevitably, the wrong person would respond. Mrs. Reilly would get so angry and thought we were doing it on purpose and being disrespectful but we truly weren't."

"Yes! We had the same problem and tried hard not to let her hear us laughing when it happened because we all respected her knowledge and dedication. I absolutely adored her and learned so much without even being aware I was. She had the greatest stories about her travels!"

"And, let's see. Oh, yes! What about Professor Brighton, Michael, the heartbreaker of every freshman class, extremely handsome but married and a complete cad. He seduced so many young women until one of them finally reported him and he was discreetly dismissed, or so I've heard. Did you have him for English or was he already history, pardon the pun?"

Jonathan looked at Cassy, horrified for her, and wondered, briefly, if Morgan asked her deliberately because she had heard something years before. He watched as Cassy stiffened slightly and swallowed several times and, then, was impressed with the grace and composure she summoned to answer Morgan. "I did have him for second semester English class. That's all so interesting! How did you learn all those juicy details about him?"

"Well, about the dismissal, from old college friends but I learned the rest almost first hand, actually. He made several attempts and passes at me, which I quickly put an end to, but he ended up seducing my best friend. No matter what I told her she was convinced he was in love with her and wanted to marry her. She even took a small overdose of pills, more of a melodramatic statement than a real attempt at suicide, when he moved on to the next victim. I'm surprised you never heard about it all but maybe, by the time your class came in, he was being more discreet because he knew he was very close to being dismissed."

Cassy sat with a polite smile frozen on her slightly flushed face and listened intently, responding she was surprised too and then got up, on the pretext of making more toast, and stepped out of the view of everyone for a moment. Jonathan wished there was something he could do and took the opportunity to change the subject to how much he had enjoyed hearing the story of how Morgan and Jesse had met.

When Cassy returned to the table, Jonathan didn't dare to let their eyes meet because he knew she was on the verge of tears and, if they made eye contact it might be too much for her. He had no idea how she was remaining as poised as she was because he felt as if he could easily be moved to tears for the pain she was undoubtedly feeling.

Just at that moment, the doorbell rang and they all looked surprised because of the early hour. Jonathan went to answer it and was shocked to see his friend Addae standing there. He had no idea Addae had returned from Kinshasa and threw his arms around him, delighted by his unexpected visit.

After introductions all around, and a huge hug from Cassy who was shocked to see this tall, handsome man. She was about seven and he was thirteen when she last saw him and remembered him as small for his age, very thin and always hysterically funny. She tried, constantly, to follow him and Johnathan around and sometimes pushed well past Jonathan's usually high tolerance level. Addae was startled by the lovely adult Cassy had become and happy to see her too. He apologized for the hour and explained the reason for his visit, "Jonathan, do you remember when I spent the evening with you here, before I left for Africa, and was struck by your friend Gabrielle's resemblance to a picture I remembered my grandparents had?"

"I do remember it. She was uncomfortable because you kept staring at her and asked you why."

"Well, while I was there working with my grandparents in their medical clinic, I saw the picture again and was absolutely sure, this time, there was some significance to the resemblance. Is Gabrielle here?"

"No. She's not. She went away a couple of months ago and we haven't heard from her."

"Oh, I'm sorry Jonathan. I didn't know and so am not sure, now, if this is good timing or bad but I brought the picture back with me," and with that he pulled an old photograph out of his backpack and handed it to Jonathan. "I'm here spending some time with my parents and taking a break but will return to help my grandparents finish up. I knew you are an early riser and wanted to stop in to let you know I was in town again and thought I'd bring the picture to show Gabrielle to prove I wasn't being rude or lying about the reason I kept sneaking looks at her. I also was interested to see if you both thought she might be related in some way."

Jonathan stared at the picture for a long time until Cassy asked if they could see it too. Jesse, Jonathan and Cassy, from what she could remember of their brief meeting, all acknowledged the overwhelming resemblance to Gabrielle, especially the woman's eyes.

Inevitably, the subject of the search for her was brought up and Jesse mentioned that their next step was to locate a person whose name was in a letter addressed to someone named Lyliana, whom they assumed to be Gabrielle's mother, as indicated by the date. He said he had called Information in Woodstock and asked for the number of Nathaniel Kingsley but there was no listing.

At the mention of the name, Cassy came to attention and said, "The Nathaniel Kingsley?"

"Is there a 'The Nathaniel Kingsley'? You've heard of him? Who is he?"

"If it's the one I'm thinking of, I did a report on him for an art class in college. He's a sculptor and architect. Of course, it may not be the same person but it's funny that the address was Woodstock, New York, because he was an artist in residence for a time, at Byrdcliffe Arts Colony, in Woodstock. That's where we should start. Someone there may know of him."

"Wait, we?" Jonathan picked up on the collective pronoun immediately. The fact that Morgan knew Cassy and Cassy and Addae shared information related to Gabrielle unnerved Jonathan, too many strange coincidences that kept coming up around the search for her.

"Yes, we," Cassy and Morgan responded simultaneously and then smiled and high-fived each other.

"It's time we all joined together to find Gabrielle. She's been gone far too long and you need to let us help because, if you love her, that makes her family. Maybe what's needed to solve this mystery and bring Gabrielle home is a collaborative perspective and effort. So, we are offering...no, I take that back. We are insisting you let us come along and search with you," Cassy continued, alone this time, but Morgan shook her head in agreement and then they were joined by Jesse as well.

Addae was the next to express his desire to be included and felt he had been drawn into this for some reason. "The first names of the people in the photo are Diana and Lyle and the letter Jesse found was addressed to was Lyliana, not just a coincidental combination of the two names, I think. It might make them Gabrielle's grandparents. Since I didn't know there was a concern about Gabrielle's disappearance and was only trying to prove a small point, I didn't get the last name but I'll write to my grandparents to get it. They're out in the jungle villages and might not be available by telephone so it might take a while to hear from them. The only thing I know is Diana and Lyle died just after the Republic of the Congo won independence in 1960."

After a long silence, Jonathan said, "Well, I have to admit I haven't done so well on my own and you all have certainly brought some interesting information and twists into this. It makes sense too because this Kingsley person is an artist like Gabrielle. There does seem to be a connection. I guess we could all take the drive up to Woodstock, but I do have to ask for complete confidentiality about this because we have no idea why Gabrielle has disappeared."

Jesse was very pleased with Jonathan's response to their offers of help, considering his previous refusals, and they all agreed they would leave on Friday, as early as everyone could get away from their respective commitments. Since Cassy had the most time at the moment, it was agreed that she would take care of making reservations for them and map out their route. She felt very grateful to have something to think about and do to put off having to face the undeniable implication of the new information Morgan had unwittingly provided.

The weatherman had predicted a storm and it was already beginning to snow steadily. Jesse and Morgan needed to shower and get ready for work. As Cassy was directing Morgan to the guest bathroom, they were interrupted by a call from Jonathan's answering service to say that the first three patients had cancelled their appointments. He was already finished with his hospital rounds, since he had been called there for the emergency, and was thankful for the extra time the unexpected cancellations gave him. He wanted to talk to Cassy, once Jesse and Morgan left, to be sure she was going to be okay. The stories Morgan shared about Michael Brighton had to have broken her heart, yet again, and he was worried but grateful at the same time for the harsh truth of it. And he had no idea if seeing Jesse with Morgan was troubling to Cassy as well, given their conversation about her disturbing reaction to Jonathan's news about Jesse finding a new love.

When Morgan and Jesse came back downstairs, they offered to help with the dishes before leaving but Cassy told them she had nothing better to do. They left thanking her for breakfast and with everyone saying how happy they all were to have finally met. Addae left at the same time so the house was mercifully quiet, at last.

The moment they were out the door, Jonathan came into the kitchen, where Cassy had already started washing the dishes, "Cassy..."

She interrupted him immediately, "Jonathan, don't say anything right now. Please, please just get showered and go to your office. I really need to be alone and am definitely not ready or willing to have a discussion about anything at the moment."

He could see tears starting to spill down her cheeks now that Morgan and Jesse were gone, as she busied herself with cleaning and stared out of the window, deliberately not meeting his gaze. He wanted so badly to find a way to comfort her but understood her desire not to share feelings about it, having felt that way himself about Gabrielle for so long. There just were no words so the best thing he could do, at the moment, was respect her request until she needed something or wanted to talk. "Okay, but please know you can call me if you need anything, whether I'm with a patient or not. I'll tell Linda I want to be interrupted if you call."

"Thank you, Jonathan," she did not look at him as she answered and stayed as she was so he went upstairs to get ready, extremely upset and nervous about leaving her alone. He wished Morgan hadn't mentioned her roommate's suicide episode but, of course, she had no way of knowing how her words were impacting Cassy or Jonathan.

When he came back down again, she had finished the dishes and was on the phone, already making inquiries about reservations for their trip to Woodstock. He knew staying busy until he left was her way of avoiding him and so he wrote "Call me if you need anything! I love you, Munch" on a piece of paper, placed it in front of her, kissing her on the top of her head, and left.

As he backed out of the driveway, Cassy came running out and he rolled down his window. "I'm okay, Jonathan. You looked so dreadfully worried as you went out the door, I couldn't let you leave that way. I'm not going to do anything foolish and I'll be right here when you get back, okay? So, don't spend the day thinking I might do what Morgan's roommate did. Being here with you and everyone has already helped me to begin finding a more credible, albeit excruciating, viewpoint. And I'm beginning to think that there's something at work in the Universe that made you invite me just at this time and why Addae, Morgan and Jesse showed up as they did so I need to sit quietly for a little while. Maybe it's all for Gabrielle." She stood on tiptoe, kissed his cheek and managed a small smile. "So go, Super Doc, and heal the sick."

Jonathan drove off feeling relieved and tried to regain his composure and concentration for the day.

Chapter 18

Nathaniel and Jonathan

Nathaniel seemed stronger each day and, by Tuesday, wanted to go into his studio, something he hadn't done in months, encouraged by a feeling of creativity in the energy of the house again.

Gabrielle and Jeremiah had been designing, throwing and glazing some pottery pieces, while Nathaniel was resting. It was a good bonding time with Jeremiah because it had been so long since Gabrielle worked at the wheel and they got to share some very funny moments and much needed laughs. She could see it pleased Jeremiah to be the teacher.

She was also working on some sketches for a portrait of Jeremiah and Nathaniel together. Jeremiah found a few photographs from a gallery opening the year before chemotherapy began and Nathaniel asked Gabrielle to use them for his part of the portrait and try not to impose how he looked now into her work. This was the most important portrait Gabrielle had ever painted. She wanted it to be perfect and convey everything about these two men which made them so unique and special to her and those who knew them well. She worked on it whenever she had a moment and wouldn't allow either of them to see it until it was completed.

Knowing that Jeremiah and Gabrielle were working on pieces inspired Nathaniel to begin a small sculpture, something he could manage right now. He had always wanted to do one of Lyliana but never had the opportunity and now he felt it was the ideal time to capture Gabrielle, in clay, and her expression while engrossed in her own work. Nathaniel's metal sculptures were what he was best known for but both Gabrielle and Jeremiah believed his real artistry and superb talent was in his clay and stone work.

Gabrielle was pushing his chair toward the studio, talking about one of the ceiling murals she had painted for Emory and Cara, and panicked suddenly, remembering the baby and her promise to do the nursery murals. She'd been so involved in hiding out and learning about her past, she hadn't thought about how near it was getting to the birth date. She really needed to get back to the Cape but feared that anyone she was in contact with might be in danger, if her father thought she might have confided in them about her captivity. It surprised her that Brian hadn't attempted to contact Nathaniel and Jeremiah in all the years after she ran away but supposed he assumed Gabrielle would have no way of remembering or finding them.

For the rest of Tuesday and each day for several hours, Nathaniel worked on his piece, while Gabrielle continued her work on the painting of the lake and the portrait. She finished the lake first since, unlike the portrait, she worked on it in front of them. Nathaniel wanted it hung in his room as soon as it was finished, even though it would be weeks before it was dry.

She told him she couldn't wait to paint the lake in spring and summer too. He realized, watching her work, how gifted she was and knew she needed very little advice from them at this point. She was better off using her natural instincts rather than letting herself be influenced unnecessarily. He was also stunned by how swiftly she was able to work. When he wasn't occupied with his own sculpture or grew tired, Nathaniel was content to sit quietly, resting and watching Gabrielle paint.

Late on Friday afternoon, Mary returned from her family emergency and was shocked when they introduced Gabrielle. Shortly after they left Byrdcliffe and moved into this house, Mary had come to work for them and witnessed, first hand, their despair over Gabrielle's absence. She greeted her with hugs and kisses, as if she had always known her, and Gabrielle wasn't quite sure how to react. Surprised to find them in Nathaniel's studio she remarked, "Nathaniel, you seem to look a little better. I'm sure it's you, Gabrielle, who's brought the color back in his face and the light in his eyes." She smiled at each of them and left to get settled and prepare dinner.

While they ate, Gabrielle, Jeremiah and Nathaniel planned the trip to the last home Gabrielle had shared with her parents, the land Lyliana had inherited from her beloved grandparents and left in trust for Gabrielle, the one thing left from her family. Nathaniel told them as much as he could remember about finding the remote property, since Jeremiah had only gone with him once. Although he had taken care of the taxes and legal matters regarding the land, Nathaniel hadn't gone to care for it in years, seeing that it stayed pretty much the same, though overgrown somewhat, and because it pained him too much to go there as the years passed with no word of Lyliana or Gabrielle.

Jonathan and Cassy talked, on Thursday night, first pouring two large glasses of wine from the bottle she had purchased on her way there which they never opened. As they settled in the living room after dinner, Cassy, indicated she wanted to let him know what was going on, and took a sip from her glass before beginning and grimaced and coughed. "This is awful! I'm so sorry! I'm not educated in wine selection but this tastes like... like we're likely to find 'a key on a cordovan strap at the bottom of the bottle'."

Jonathan was surprised at her reference to *Don Quixote* and she laughed, "I read the whole thing this week, trying to find some deeper meaning than just being directed to the letter and photo, unsuccessfully, I'm sorry to say. Not that I read every word or understood all of it but it was a useful distraction from the anger and hurt and the occasionally appealing desire to wallow in self-pity. It also kept me from polishing off all of the remaining pints of ice cream in a single sitting and going to the store for more, which I have been known to do."

Jonathan laughed. "Where did we learn that? I do the exact same thing when the initial emotions of a situation won't leave my head, I soothe myself with ice cream. I can't even tell you how much I've eaten since Brie left."

"Don't you remember? I think it's because Mommy used to stop everything and sit us all down with a small dish of ice cream when things got wild and out of hand and there was fighting or tears. With you and four toddlers and, even later on, I can't imagine how she did it all and I think she used it to soothe us and get things quieted down without having to choose sides or punish. She used other food and treats she baked as well but ice cream is the one I remember having most. As I recall, it always worked too because we'd all be so distracted by being allowed to choose our own flavors and toppings and, then, eating it we'd forget the anger or upset and what precipitated the chaos. It's a wonder we all didn't become quite obese. Ironically, I don't think any of us ever figured out we could have faked a good fight to get some ice cream so she must have been really good at the diversion part but obviously the stress-ice cream connection imprinted somewhere."

All this talk made them hungry for some ice cream, in light of the disappointing wine, and they went to the kitchen and chose a flavor to share and returned to their places and another warm fire. This time Cassy handed Jonathan a regular spoon and smiled.

She began to talk, slowly, pausing between sentences for a spoonful of cookie dough and the accompanying moans of pleasure. "I've taken some measures to resolve the situation at school, first, contacting the Chairman of the Department, Professor Browne and telling him I wished to have another temporary advisor assigned to me. When asked why, I simply said I didn't feel Michael Brighton saw my goals and future in the same way I did and I needed someone else's perspective until my advisor of choice, Professor Peter Andrews, was available. As possible leverage, I mentioned taking a summer course with Professor Andrews and that it was he who suggested putting myself on his waiting list. I said I wondered if perhaps the professor might be asked to suggest another temporary advisor.

Professor Browne, though obviously curious, asked only one further question, "Did you, by any chance do your undergraduate work at Berkeley?"

I answered him quietly, but emphatically, 'Yes, I did' and understood the implication of his question.

He had assured me he would call me back, after making a few inquiries, and definitely arrange for another advisor, as I requested. Before ending the call, I made a point of thanking him for his assistance and kindness."

She was pleased with herself for finally doing what felt right, emotionally, morally and academically and not trying to protect Michael. Whatever fallout this might cause was most certainly deserved since his conduct with her, even at this point, was inappropriate, at best, and probably cause for dismissal again. She didn't wish to contribute directly to it, feeling that she bore fifty percent of the blame this time, but, if it raised any questions or suspicion and he was continuing to act as despicably with young women on this new campus as he had with Morgan's friend and all the others, she hoped he would realize the inevitable consequences of his reprehensible behavior.

Jonathan was relieved to learn of Cassy's decisive actions and how resolute and strong she seemed, "I will continue to do anything to support you through this but please promise me you will call immediately if Michael Brighton doesn't comply, in every way, with your wishes."

She agreed with a huge hug, "I am so grateful to Morgan, even though she has no idea what she did, for revealing the real Michael Brighton. It's embarrassing it took someone else's view to see the situation for what it truly was. Maybe, in the future when I've gotten to know her better and feel I can trust her, I'll let her know she helped. Now let's finish this ice cream and get a good night's rest for our trip to Woodstock tomorrow."

Jesse, Morgan, Cassy and Addae were waiting for Jonathan to get home on Friday when the doorbell rang. To their surprise, Emory stood on the porch with a bag, saying that he and Cara had decided that he should go along to help look for Gabrielle as well. Jonathan smiled and shook his head when he entered the house and saw them all gathered and ready to leave for Woodstock, at around six o'clock. Luckily, Jonathan and Jesse had an eight-passenger vehicle they sometimes used for the clinics and so they were all able to fit comfortably into it for the trip. Jonathan had to admit the ride actually was fun with continual talking and laughter and positive outlook on their mission. So much better than all his rides alone to find her.

The group had stopped for a late dinner, halfway to Woodstock, and didn't arrive at the hotel until almost one-thirty. Jonathan inquired about Byrdcliffe and the desk clerk gave him a map and a pamphlet and explained how to find it. They were all exhausted and agreed to meet in the lobby at seven o'clock to have a very quick breakfast and then go straight to Byrdcliffe.

Walking toward the elevator, Jesse came up to Cassy and put his arm around her shoulder, "Is everything okay, Cassy? I feel like you're mad at me or something. Have I done anything to upset you?"

Cassy was embarrassed he had to ask such a question because it meant she behaved in some way that made him uneasy. He didn't deserve it. He was really like one of her family. She explained her quietness and any lack of enthusiasm as preoccupation with trying to regain some emotional stability after ending an unhealthy relationship and apologized if she'd made either Jesse or Morgan at all uncomfortable because she thought they were an adorable and perfect couple.

Jesse hugged her saying he was relieved it wasn't him but sorry some guy, who was obviously out of his mind, had hurt her so badly. Cassy hugged him right back, then included Morgan, saying how happy she was for them and, to her surprise, realized she meant it.

Cassy had never honestly considered Jesse as a real love interest. Jonathan was right to call it a crush, left over from her teenage years she supposed. She smiled slightly remembering some of the schoolgirl fantasies she and Carly had shared about him, giggling in the dark about what it would be like to actually kiss him on the mouth or see him naked. Cassy laughed out loud at that thought and reminded herself to tell Carly about the last time she had stayed at Jonathan's home.

She had let herself in with her key and surprised Jesse, coming, naked, out of the shower and he had grabbed the dresser scarf from a chest in the hallway to cover himself, scattering the candles and other decorative pieces all over the hallway. The scarf was crocheted lace and didn't do much to create a cover and Cassy continued to her room and laughed into a pillow until she was able to regain her composure, wishing Carly was there to share the moment.

Dinner that night was very awkward and Jonathan asked if anything was wrong. Cassy lost control again, almost choking as she began to laugh and tried to explain what happened. Jesse was so embarrassed he knocked over his wine glass. She wondered, suddenly, if he had told Morgan about the incident and laughed to herself at the thought of Jesse trying to explain it.

Jonathan, ever watchful, helped her carry her luggage into her room and asked immediately, "Everything okay with you and Jess?"

"Yes, dearest big brother, just fine. I'm really doing much better tonight. Of course, the two glasses of wine with dinner didn't hurt either. I need to start writing down the names of wines we enjoy, like the one we had this evening, so the next time I want to bring a bottle of wine somewhere I won't make hideous choices like the one last night. So, how are you doing with the prospect of learning something new about Gabrielle from this Nathaniel? Take some advice and prepare yourself for the worst so anything better will seem quite okay."

"Yes, oh wise and learned sage, I'll go immediately to my room and put myself to sleep by considering all the worst things I could possibly learn. Any suggestions what I might start with?" and he laughed.

"I guess that did sound pretty idiotic but you know what I mean. As unthinkable and ridiculous as it may seem to you, I'm still shocked by what Morgan revealed about Michael and I guess I'm just reacting to it. I don't really think you'll learn anything terrible, even if someone is pursuing her, but did it occur to you and Jesse it may have been a detective or the police who were watching and following her and for some good reason? Although, I suppose it's unlikely a policeman or detective would run away when they realized they'd been discovered, huh?"

Jonathan hugged her and laughed at her *Nancy Drew* detective work and then thanked her for being so passionate and concerned with solving the mystery and helping to find Gabrielle. They said good night, finally, and Cassy decided she would meditate and think very positive thoughts for Jonathan and Gabrielle before going to sleep.

Gabrielle and Jeremiah were up early. Jeremiah was explaining and writing down directions for Mary, as if she'd never taken care of Nathaniel before. She rolled her eyes, shook her head and smiled at Gabrielle and kept reassuring him she was only gone for two weeks and still remembered how to care for him. He apologized and she hugged him, completely aware of his stress level for the last few months and understanding how nervous he became each time he had to leave Nathaniel for more than an hour, the fear he might not be there should death pay an anticipated but premature visit.

The property was in the northwest part of the Adirondacks and it would probably take most of the day and evening to get there, spend whatever time Gabrielle needed and return. Jeremiah was nervous, too, about how Gabrielle might react to being there after all this time. He and Nathaniel talked, late into the night, about all of the possible scenarios and what Jeremiah would do under various circumstances to help her through them. Unfortunately, Jeremiah's cell phone wouldn't be usable there in an emergency and that worried him too, so he appeared distressed, although, he was trying very hard to disguise it by remaining in motion and busying himself with little last-minute chores and details.

Gabrielle assumed his distraught look was because of leaving Nathaniel and offered to go to find the property herself so he could stay. Jeremiah surprised her by responding quite adamantly, "Absolutely not. I wouldn't dream of letting you go on the trip alone."

Nathaniel was awake when they went to check on him before leaving. He had a very bad night, probably from so much activity in the studio and then talking so late with Jeremiah, and looked very tired. Gabrielle suggested he rest all day and not go into his studio to work. He agreed very quickly so they both knew he must be in considerable pain.

They left and got into Jeremiah's car, after loading a basket of food and emergency supplies Mary insisted they take with them.

Gabrielle had forgotten about her car being parked on the side of the road at the end of their long driveway because none of them had gone anywhere since her return. It wasn't visible from the house and, as they approached it, she realized Jeremiah was staring at it with a shocked expression. "Are you okay?"

He recovered quickly and started to laugh peculiarly. "Yes, I'm okay but we need to move your car off the road to the driveway and bring Nathaniel to the window to see it. Gabrielle, that...that car...where did you get it?"

Stunned by his obvious upset, she explained the story of the car, in a brief version.

"So, you did the painting? It wasn't like that?"

"Yes, I did it. Why? What's the matter, Jeremiah? You're scaring me a little."

"Oh, I'm so sorry, Gabrielle, but your mother owned a Volkswagen bus with painted flowers and peace signs like this and I thought...I'm just surprised."

"Okay, but do you think we should show it to Nathaniel when he's so tired. Will it upset him as much as it did you?"

"You have to move it and it's better if he sees it while we're still around."

"I'm sorry. I never gave it a thought, so foolish of me to leave it parked there, since it's so distinctive."

She got out of Jeremiah's car and pulled it down the driveway in front of Nathaniel's side of the garage.

They went to Nathaniel's room and he was surprised to see them, thinking, at first, he had slept all day and they were back. Jeremiah told him about the car and helped him to the window so he could see it. He was surprised by it but quickly noticed and pointed out several differences.

When he learned Gabrielle had done the painting, he smiled and found it touching she was so like Lyliana, a little dolphin swimming beneath its mother by some unexplained instinct. Something about the thought pleased Gabrielle too and it made Jeremiah look at it differently and calmed him down.

Nathaniel was already apprehensive about how Jeremiah would manage if Gabrielle began to have any memories. He wasn't worried about him dealing with it intellectually, just emotionally. Now he was even more concerned and suggested perhaps they could find a way to bring him along. Gabrielle and Jeremiah insisted he remain at home and rest and assured him they would be just fine.

Jeremiah understood why Nathaniel said it and realized he needed to appear more confident and ready for the journey, to ease Nathaniel's mind, so he jumped up, smiled and exclaimed cheerfully, "Well, we're off to the wilderness! Get some rest!"

Gabrielle and Jeremiah hurried to the car before Nathaniel could insist on accompanying them and drove off quickly.

The laughter coming from their table was infectious, if a bit too loud, as Morgan and Jesse shared the story of finding each other with Cassy and Addae who hadn't heard it. Jonathan and Emory didn't mind hearing it again because Morgan's perspective was even funnier than Jesse's. They all thoroughly enjoyed their breakfast and the company, even though they didn't stick to the original schedule. By eight-thirty, they were on the road and heading for Byrdcliffe.

Approaching the first of the dark brown buildings the desk clerk had described, they saw a sign "Villetta Inn" and thought that might be a good place to start. They went to the door and rang the bell and a woman answered. Jonathan asked for Nathaniel Kingsley and she scowled immediately and without inviting them to come in said, "What is it with this Nathaniel person? I'm definitely going to have to find out who he is because you're the third person in a week to ask about him. I'll tell you exactly what I told the other two. I have no idea who or where he is but you might want to check with the Woodstock Arts Council to see if they have any information."

Jonathan looked worried and asked whether one of the other people had been a young woman with long hair and beautiful blue eyes. She looked surprised and said yes, as a matter of fact that was a perfect description of someone who had asked for this Nathaniel about a week or so before. Then he held his breath and asked if she remembered what the other person looked like and she was getting suspicious and annoyed by all his questions and wasn't going to answer. He explained that he was a physician, just to make them seem more credible, and that the young woman may be in danger and Cassy, Morgan, Emory, Addae and Jesse confirmed his statement with nods.

She thought for a moment, "Late last night an older man, fairly tall with silver-gray hair asked about him too." They all felt sick suddenly and thanked her rushing toward the car with the hope they could find this Arts Council office before Gabrielle's pursuer did.

As they reached the car, an old man approached them and asked, "You lookin' for Nathaniel and the blue-eyed girl?"

"Yes, do you know them?" Jonathan asked."

"Might...might not...why you askin'?"

Morgan stepped in suddenly, "What did you say your name was?"

"Didn't, but for you, pretty lady, it's Old Joe."

"Oh, my goodness, it's you, Old Joe! Gabrielle has told us so much about you."

"You know the blue-eyed girl?" he wasn't sure of them at all.

"Yes, we do. We were supposed to meet her here, in Woodstock, last week but weren't able to get here and now we don't know where to find her."

"Hold up! Hold up! That's way too much to hear so fast girl...slow up a bit. She was here last week, like you say. Gave her directions to Nathaniel's...he's her godfather, you know."

"Yes, Old Joe, we know. Can you tell us how to find Nathaniel's house too. We'd be so grateful."

"I can but not sure if I should. She didn't know Nathaniel's pretty sick and I made her cry...felt bad about that."

"Uh, huh. She's very fond of you and I'm sure she knows you didn't mean to hurt her and I think she'd be very happy that you helped us find her. She probably could use some friends around, if he's that sick."

"Prob'ly right about that. You sure are a pretty little thing and you seem real nice too, so I guess it's okay. Write this down."

When they were finished writing the directions, Cassy stepped forward and pressed a twenty-dollar bill into his hand thanking him for his help and asked if anyone else, besides Gabrielle and them, had asked for directions to Nathaniel's home.

"Nope."

Holding another twenty-dollar bill where he could see it, she said, "There might be someone else, a man with silvery gray hair and almost as tall as him, pointing up to Jonathan, asking how to find Nathaniel. He's someone who might hurt the blue-eyed girl and Nathaniel wouldn't want him to know where he lives. Can you remember not to tell him anything?" and she held the twenty-dollar bill out casually.

"Geez, I'm old not senile but I'll let you get away with saying that cause you're pretty too. I won't tell no one else nothing 'bout where he lives. Sure, I can do that," and he took the bill as casually as it was offered. Cassy kissed his cheek as if it sealed a deal and he grinned saying, "Sure are a lot of pretty ladies looking for Nathaniel," and walked away mumbling, "Sure is good money in givin' and not givin' directions lately."

Jonathan hugged Morgan and said, "You must be one amazing attorney. That was brilliant. Thank you so much. I would never have thought to pretend we knew who he was."

Morgan replied with a laugh, "Well, it's probably not one of my talents I'm proudest of but I have learned how to talk to people to get the information I need for cases."

Then Jonathan hugged Cassy, "And you, little sister, thank you for thinking to give him the money to find out if he'd given her pursuer directions and, cleverly, getting him to agree not to tell anyone else. I am so grateful for your presence here and know how fortunate I am to have you all in my life. Thanks for insisting on coming along because this would most likely have gone very differently without you."

They all jumped back in the car and raced to get to Nathaniel's house and, hopefully, to Gabrielle before the man with the silver hair learned how to find them. They found the house just as easily as Gabrielle had and, as they pulled down the driveway, Jonathan yelled, "There's Brie's car!"

Emory suggested Jonathan should go in alone, since Old Joe had indicated Nathaniel was very ill. He rang the bell and an adorable red-haired, green-eyed lady answered the door and Jonathan assumed she must be Gabrielle's godmother. He introduced himself as a friend of Gabrielle's and asked if she was there. She looked a little alarmed, glanced toward the van full of people and discreetly locked the storm door then said she was not and asked who he was and why he was looking for Gabrielle.

He told her his name was Jonathan then pointed to her car and asked if she was sure Gabrielle wasn't here. Since she just stood, silently, staring at him and obviously reluctant to answer any questions, he asked if Nathaniel was well enough to see him.

She said, "Stay there and wait. I'll see if he's awake and if he wishes to see you when I tell him who you are," and slammed the door and locked it.

Jonathan waited anxiously until she returned and opened the door cautioning, "Nathaniel will see you but please don't stay too long or upset him."

Jonathan promised her he wouldn't and followed her to Nathaniel's room. Nathaniel smiled and greeted him warmly, saying that he knew all about him, not wanting to waste any time and glad that he had appeared because he was really worried about Gabrielle's journey to her past. He knew Gabrielle had told Jonathan nothing and, although he would have liked to honor her privacy and silence and allow her to tell him, he needed to give him some idea of the situation. Nathaniel told him, briefly, about her captivity, her mother's disappearance and her father chasing her.

Nathaniel was surprised when Jonathan told him, "Jesse and I saw both Gabrielle and the silver-haired man in Greenwich Village a week ago. Gabrielle looked terrified and was running away from him but, when we yelled to her, she didn't hear us. Jesse and I weren't able to catch up with either of them." He also told him about finding the book and Jesse finding Nathaniel's letter to Lyliana, which had enabled Jonathan to find him. He referred to Mary as Nathaniel's wife and them both being Gabrielle's godparents and Nathaniel laughed and told him she was his housekeeper and he and his partner, Jeremiah were her godparents. Jonathan apologized for his mistake and they both laughed.

Nathaniel explained, "Jeremiah and Gabrielle have headed to the property she once lived on as a small child and I'm afraid it might be very traumatic for her emotionally should her memory of those lost years return. I think you and your friends should go directly there right now." He told Jonathan to make a copy of the map and the directions to the property, which were on his bedside table, and called to Mary to show Jonathan where the copier was. He made two copies, just in case, and returned to Nathaniel's room to place the originals on the table again.

Jonathan thanked him and asked if there was anything he could do for him before he left. Nathaniel sat up a bit and, as Jonathan offered his hand, he took it and pulled him to him, whispered something, while slipping a small box into his hand

and then with a warm hug said, "Just find her as quickly as you can and help her through this. Then take her home and love her."

"I can do that." Jonathan walked with Mary out of the room as calmly as possible then told her quietly, because he hadn't wanted to upset Nathaniel about Gabrielle's father already being in Woodstock, "Lock the door behind me and don't let anyone into the house, especially a silver-haired man asking for Gabrielle. If he does come, call the police immediately."

Mary, who had heard Nathaniel's revelation to Jonathan, looked slightly alarmed and answered, "You know, I had never heard the whole story of how or why Gabrielle came to live with Jeremiah and Nathaniel or why she left but I certainly understand their fears and grief over it now. I'll do as you say. Go with angels at your side."

Jonathan ran back and jumped into the car, explaining as much as he could while handing the maps to them to figure out a route, then drove insanely out of the driveway, throwing them all backward. They were astonished by his behavior and obvious desperation and Jesse offered to drive. Jonathan felt he had spent too long with Nathaniel, although it couldn't be helped because he needed to give Jonathan some idea of what wasn't shown on the map that he needed to know and what he might encounter once he found Jeremiah and Gabrielle.

As only a sibling can, Cassy raised her voice, "Geez, Jonathan, calm down and slow down or you'll have us in an accident or stopped by the police and we'll be delayed even more from getting to Gabrielle!"

Jonathan had to admit he was being uncharacteristically irrational and apologized to everyone. He needed to occupy himself with the driving but slowed down somewhat, explaining that Gabrielle and Jeremiah had a little over an hour head start on them and they really needed to get there as quickly as the car and police radar guns would allow.

Jeremiah and Gabrielle were a "little lost" as Jeremiah put it and he thought they might need to find a place with a telephone to call Nathaniel for clarification of his directions.

"Is there such a thing as a little lost? Isn't lost pretty much just lost?" Gabrielle tried to make a joke of it so Jeremiah wouldn't get upset and then declared it an adventure. She assured him she didn't mind if they had to turn around twenty times and pointed out, cheerfully, "Jeremiah, we can try again another time if we aren't successful in finding it today and you want to get back home. There really is no hurry since I'm not going anywhere.

Jeremiah pulled over and they studied the map, finally discovering their mistake, and decided they needed to backtrack about nine miles and start again. Gabrielle noticed Jeremiah's jaw tighten and his expression was a worried one so she reminded him that Mary was taking very good care of Nathaniel, just as she always did but added they could start for home if he was too worried.

Realizing she was absolutely right, he relaxed somewhat, smiled and made an effort to get into the spirit of the adventure from Gabrielle's perspective. Of course, she had no idea what was about to happen and patiently sympathized with Jeremiah's changes in mood as he became the face of cheerfulness and enthusiasm for her sake.

They doubled back to a point they were sure was right and started toward their destination again on the corrected route. It was Gabrielle who spotted the stone pillars Nathaniel told them to look for. There were large metal loops imbedded in them as if they had been connected by a chain or gate at one time. "Stop! Stop! There they are, Jeremiah, just as he described them. This must be it!"

Jeremiah couldn't stop in time and had to back up to turn into the dirt drive. As he drove between the pillars, Gabrielle's head hurt suddenly and she had a flash again—this time of a woman's face and she felt quite faint. She moaned strangely and Jeremiah stopped the car and turned to her. She was pale and her lips had lost all their color. "Take some water, Gabrielle. Do you want a little bite to eat too before we continue?"

Her heart was pounding and she wanted to tell him to turn back and go home but instead said, "Yes, Jeremiah. Could you back out again and pull over somewhere, just for a bit? Let's eat the lunch Mary packed and take a little time. Is that okay?"

"It's completely okay, darling. We're going to do this at your pace and, if it's too much right now, we'll just head home and do it again another day, when you feel ready just as you said earlier. I'll get the basket. Please pour some water for me too, if you feel up to it."

Jeremiah's hands were shaking as he retrieved the picnic basket from the trunk and he breathed a few times and tried to remember what he and Nathaniel had discussed about how to help Gabrielle through this experience. He smiled to reassure her and asked which kind of sandwich she wanted, chicken salad or turkey with cranberry sauce and it made her feel better because she was distracted by the thought of Emory and his turkey obsession and smiled to herself at the warm thought. There was a thoughtful silence during the car meal, neither knowing what to say and both wondering what to expect once they started down the drive again. As she ate, Gabrielle discovered she really had been hungrier than she realized, having skipped breakfast, and decided the strange feelings were simply low blood sugar.

When they finished, Gabrielle said she was ready to continue and Jeremiah pulled back into the driveway and started toward the house. Along the drive, as they came near to the tiny cabin, Gabrielle spotted metal sculptures that looked very familiar and then realized they were of Don Quixote and Sancho Panza. She jumped out of the car, before it had even stopped completely and ran to one of them. "Did...did Nathaniel sculpt these, Jeremiah?"

"Yes. Your mother always adored the book and he made them for her before she met your father. She lived on the road most of the time and, so had kept them in the barn on a friend's property, always asking him to sculpt a new piece for her, which he always did gladly. Nathaniel loved doing them for her but hadn't realized, until he came to care for the property after you were all gone, she had brought the entire collection of them here and placed them all around the property."

"The statue of Don Quixote and Sancho Panza are exactly like the ceiling painting I'm doing for Cara and Emory's library ceiling."

"Really? There's also a working windmill that he made that's located further back in her flower garden and I believe we'll find a stone fountain with flowers and birds on it you just have to see in the garden. Nathaniel sculpted it with so much love and wishes for her happiness and gave it to her and Brian for a wedding present."

Since he had said her father's name, Jeremiah thought now would be a good time to tell her something they decided he should. "Gabrielle, you know your father changed your name to Emily when he took you to Canada and then we changed it to Gabrielle when we bought counterfeit papers to establish an identity for you but your real name, the one your mother gave you when you were baptized, is Dulci, well, Dulcinea really, from *Don Quixote*."

The moment he spoke the name Dulcinea, Gabrielle fainted, falling to the ground before he could reach her.

Chapter 19

NATHANIEL AND BRIAN

Nathaniel's pain was the worst it had ever been and, after Jonathan left, he decided he needed to take something to relieve it. There were moans coming out of him he was not consciously causing and wanted to be sure it wasn't still happening when Gabrielle and Jeremiah returned. He didn't want to alarm them. He called to Mary to ask for her help because he and Jeremiah agreed the pain medication shouldn't be left at his bedside, in case he became confused. Mary took one look at him and said she thought he should take two of them, which he was allowed to do, to break the pain cycle he always let get too far and, to her surprise, he agreed. She brought the bottle of medication and a fresh container of water, pouring a glass and handing it to him before tackling the pill bottle, which she found very difficult to open. Just as the top finally came free, Nathaniel reached out to see if he could help her and knocked the bottle out of her hand and onto the floor. She gasped and bent to pick it up but it had turned upside down on top of the decorative return grate in the floor and the contents fell into the duct. Horrified that Nathaniel wouldn't have his medication, Mary lifted the bottle, discovering two of the pills resting on top of the grate. Picking them up, carefully, she brushed them lightly and handed them to Nathaniel without telling him what had happened. Mary knew his worry about what might be happening with Gabrielle was adding to his increased pain and the addition of more stress was the last thing he needed.

A call to his doctor, as soon as she left the room, to get a refill, was the best action. It was almost time for it anyway. She arranged the bed pillows, emptied his urinal and asked if he wanted anything, as she unplugged his phone making sure he didn't notice. He smiled appreciatively and said no and settled back to wait for the medication to allow him to rest. Mary's heart broke when she realized Nathaniel was moaning periodically and, then, grimacing at the sound of his own pain.

She left the room and went into the kitchen to find the doctor's number. Jeff Schneider was a very close friend of Nathaniel and Jeremiah's and returned the call immediately. He could hear how upset Mary was, as she explained what happened, and he said he would call the pharmacy immediately and okay the refill a few days early. Jeff had wanted to give Nathaniel a larger supply to have on hand but he refused them. Mary described the moaning and how much pain Nathaniel appeared to be in and the doctor decided he would drop a new prescription, for a slightly higher dose and a larger quantity, at the pharmacy, personally. He would let the pharmacist know she would be picking it up for Nathaniel and suggested she wait about a half an hour and then phone to be sure it was ready before leaving. He apologized for not being able to bring the medication over himself but explained he was just called to the hospital for an emergency and would stop at the pharmacy on the way. Mary thanked him again and again, relieved to know Nathaniel would have his medication.

Feeling guilty about leaving Nathaniel alone for the time it would take to go to the pharmacy and return, Mary knew Jeremiah would be furious when he learned what had happened but there was no other solution. She needed to pick up the prescription before the pharmacy closed or there would be no medication for the night. It was Saturday and they closed early, long before Jeremiah and Gabrielle would return. She decided she'd wait about forty-five minutes to leave just to be sure Nathaniel was resting comfortably and would sleep until she returned. She knew she should probably wake him and tell him what happened and let him know she was going but just couldn't bring herself to do it. After only thirty-five minutes, she phoned the pharmacist, to confirmed the prescription was ready for her to pick up and then went to check on Nathaniel. He was breathing comfortably and sleeping soundly so she felt better about leaving for a brief time.

She jumped in her car and hurried off, saying a prayer all the while and asking Blessed Mary to watch over him until she returned.

As Nathaniel lay dozing and finally comfortable in a drug-induced haze, he heard a question repeated to him, "Nathaniel, where did you say Gabrielle was."

He couldn't seem to open his eyes but he replied speaking in a slow, slurred voice, "Jonathan, what happened? I thought you'd left. I told Mary to help you copy the directions from my bedside table. It's all there just look for the stone pillars, hurry Jonathan!" He heard him move to the other side of the bed and he couldn't tell if he was dreaming it again or if he was really there. He called his name again, "Jonathan, are you still here."

"Yes. I'm here but I'm going right now. Thanks, Nathaniel."

Something was wrong...that wasn't Jonathan's voice. Nathaniel tried very hard to open his eyes and finally managed to just in time to glimpse the blur of a tall silver-haired man leaving his room. The horror of what might have happened took several minutes to penetrate the fog of the double medication but then an adrenalin rush hit him and with it the realization Gabrielle's father now had the directions to find her and Jeremiah. Nathaniel waited until he felt Brian had left and then began calling for Mary again and again and, when she didn't respond, was sure Brian must have done something to her to gain access into the house.

He picked up the telephone and tried to think of someone he could call for help but discovered it wasn't working for some reason and, at the same time, realized the directions were no longer on the bedside table. It hadn't been a dream so there was no choice now. He had to get himself up somehow and see what had happened to Mary and find some way to warn Gabrielle and Jeremiah Brian was on his way to the property, since cell communication was out of the question. The only hope was Jonathan and his friends had gotten enough of a start to find them before Brian did. Luckily Nathaniel was dressed and pulled himself into the wheel chair, to conserve as much energy as possible and prevent a fall from the effects of the mediation, and wheeled himself toward the kitchen shouting Mary's name again.

Since she wasn't responding to his repeated calls to her, Nathaniel was desperate, now, to find a way to warn Jeremiah and Gabrielle of what he had done and to find out what had happened to Mary. He decided he needed to get up out of the chair and look around the house and outside. He'd been feeling better and taking longer walks each day but not by himself yet, so he was surprised by his own strength and stood easily and went to the door, discovering Brian had smashed the doorknob to get in. Mary's car wasn't in the driveway and he tried to make sense of it because, obviously, Brian had found a way here and so, wouldn't have needed her car. Then again, Brian might have gotten a ride and kidnapped Mary and hijacked her car.

He remembered looking at the clock as Mary handed him the pills and, again, when he opened his eyes and saw Brian leaving his room and calculated that about fifty-five minutes had elapsed between those events and now another five or ten minutes had passed. *Why is that important?* "Think, Nathaniel, damn it!" he was shouting at himself. Then he realized he was trying to calculate when Brian had been there and how much time had passed since he left. He walked, slowly, to the other end of the house to their studios checking each room as he went and found nothing.

When he returned to the kitchen, he noticed his empty prescription bottle on the counter by the telephone and a note in Mary's handwriting with his physician's telephone number and "ready in forty-five minutes??" scribbled next to it. She must have discovered he was out of pain medication, which really surprised him because Jeremiah was so meticulous about taking care of things like his prescriptions. Now he remembered he had knocked the bottle out of her hand when he tried to offer his help to get it open. Back in the bedroom, Nathaniel saw the cap lying on the return grate in the floor and concluded the remaining pills must have spilled into it and also noticed the telephone had been unplugged. Mary had, apparently, called

Jeff, his physician and friend, for a refill and had gone to the pharmacy to pick it up. Perhaps she wasn't here when Brian came in. Before jumping into the car to leave for Gabrielle's property, he wanted to be sure that was the case and she was all right. He phoned the pharmacy and inquired whether anyone had been in to pick up a prescription for Nathaniel Kingsley and was told that Mary O'Connell had signed for it and left about ten minutes before.

Nathaniel felt free to leave now and grabbed a coat, left a brief note for Mary and went into the garage. He pushed the remote button and as the door opened saw that Gabrielle's car was parked in front of his side, blocking him from leaving. It hadn't occurred to him, when they were looking at it from his bedroom window, where it was parked but, of course, he hadn't anticipated needing to drive his car. Would it be possible to maneuver his car back and forth until it was on Jeremiah's side?

Mary returned just then, speeding down the driveway. She ran toward the house, first noticing the front door had been smashed in then saw the opened garage door and Nathaniel standing next to his car. Her face went ashen and she immediately began to apologize for her absence. He stopped her with an uncharacteristic abruptness, "Mary, dear, it's okay, I figured out what happened to you but we have a much bigger problem right now. Gabrielle and Jeremiah may be in grave danger and we need to get to them immediately."

"What do you need me to do?"

"I can't get my car out because Gabrielle's is blocking it. Can we take your car right now? I'll drive."

"We can take my car, Nathaniel, but you're not driving. I mean no offense, but I'm a much faster driver than you and, anyway, you shouldn't be operating a motor vehicle. It says so right here on your pills. Get in quick and navigate and I'll have you there in no time at all."

Nathaniel couldn't disagree because, not only was she a faster driver, but she was right about the pills too. He knew he still wasn't clear-headed and, actually, felt a little relieved as they sped away from the house and he explained what happened while she was gone. They were going without a map because Brian had taken it so he explained, from memory, the route she needed to take and what she needed to look for and she stopped for a moment to write it down when it became clear it was a rather involved route. Nathaniel said he was reasonably sure he got up right after Brian left and was still trying to figure out how much of a head-start he had. Mary said she was only away thirty to forty minutes so he couldn't have gotten very far after leaving.

She continued apologizing for leaving him alone but he assured her that he was really quite glad she wasn't there because he had no idea what Brian would have done if she tried to prevent his entry and brazen attempt to find Gabrielle. Nathaniel said he felt reasonably sure that Brian left him unharmed because he felt confident that he was dying and wouldn't remember or would think it was a dream. He hadn't opened his eyes and looked directly at him, and appeared to believe he was speaking with Jonathan. Mary shuddered as she considered what might have happened.

Nathaniel rubbed her shoulder and told her to feel free to commit any infractions of the speed limit she cared to so long as she felt safe, to make up the time since Brian's head start. His only hope was that Brian wouldn't remember exactly how to get there after so many years, assuming he never returned at any point. Luckily, the map wasn't too helpful, which is why he had gone over, in detail, how to find it with Jeremiah and Gabrielle and then Jonathan. Those reviews were enabling him to explain it to Mary easily, in spite of the medication.

He kept talking to reassure himself until Mary finally said, "Nathaniel, why don't you put your head back and take advantage of the remaining time of pain relief from the medication for a little sleep, so you'll feel able to handle whatever happens once we get there. I'll wake you when we're close or if I have any questions," and she turned on a classical music station to distract him. He was, admittedly, very tired and put his head back and closed his eyes, feeling certain he wouldn't actually be able to fall asleep.

Mary glanced at him as he rested and thought about how lucky she was to be a housekeeper for him and Jeremiah. She adored both of them for their kindness to everyone and their many artistic talents. Before Nathaniel became so ill, he had been drawing plans for a house for her which she wanted to build on a tiny piece of property she owned on the other side of the lake. He understood exactly what she wanted and created a beautiful, cozy little home, just as she pictured it. The building of it was put on hold, though, when Nathaniel was diagnosed with cancer and his treatments began.

She was very worried about Nathaniel and, like Jeremiah, was having an increasingly difficult time accepting that nothing more could be done for him and seeing him suffer. Her other major concern was what would happen to Jeremiah when Nathaniel was gone and Mary was glad Gabrielle had returned to them at such a critical time.

Nathaniel thought of something, suddenly, and raised his head again, "Mary, don't pull into the driveway if you find it and I do happen to doze. I don't know what will be happening by then and I want to be able to assess the situation before we make our presence known."

"I'll wake you before we get near the stone pillars or I'll pass them and park down the road, if I come upon them sooner than expected. Now try to relax, Nathaniel."

The low billowing clouds looked like snowy foliage resting on leafless branches and the sky was remarkably blue, Mary thought, as she drove and sang softly to the first act of "La Traviata" which she had put in when she lost radio signal. After a time, she noticed by his breathing Nathaniel had fallen asleep and she was relieved he was getting some much-needed rest. She drove as fast as the roads allowed her, determined to reach the property before Gabrielle's father.

Chapter 20

Dulcinea and Gabrielle

Jeremiah ran to Gabrielle and lifted her head gently, calling her name. She opened her eyes slowly and asked what happened. "You fainted, darling. Are you feeling okay now? Maybe we should stop right now and go home."

"No! I'm all right. I want to look around some more, please Jeremiah."

"Whatever you think is best but I'm staying right by your side this time, in case you feel faint again."

"Yes, I think that's a good idea," and she managed to get up but still felt a little shaky.

She found the windmill and stroked it looking up to the top of it and said, "I remember this, Jeremiah. It seemed much bigger then but I remember I used to play under here and listen to the wind turning the sails," and she closed her eyes and listened for the sound of them but they were in tatters after all these years and she heard nothing. As she waited, another image flashed of someone lifting her in the air, singing and laughing and Jeremiah felt her knees begin to buckle. He held her up calling her name and asking if she was feeling faint again. She shook herself from it and explained what had happened.

"That's good, Gabrielle, you're beginning to remember your mother. Are you up to continuing to walk around?"

"Yes, let's go on."

They walked toward the side of the house. It was a tiny cabin really and she was surprised that it didn't seem familiar at all. They continued toward where the fountain was and Jeremiah explained, as they reached it, that this was once Lyliana's flower garden. As Gabrielle stepped into the garden to walk toward the fountain a flood of memory overcame her and she fell to her knees and began digging in the dirt, which still had traces of snow, screaming and sobbing, alternately. Then, burying her face in her dirt-covered hands, she began rocking back and forth and screaming, "I did it...I did it...it's my fault...it's my fault...I killed Mommy...I gave him the jar...," in a childlike voice, then, vomited suddenly and began choking and sobbing, sitting back on her knees and rocking and whispering to herself in between sobs. She didn't appear to be aware of Jeremiah or anything around her now.

Jeremiah was paralyzed by her words, at first, and then horrified for her and wasn't sure whether he should speak to her or let her continue to remember.

Just as he decided to let her stay there a little longer, he heard something and turned to see five or six people running up the dirt driveway. He slipped away and ran toward the group to stop them from seeing her, putting his hands up to indicate they should come no further, but one of them continued toward him saying he was Jonathan and Nathaniel had given him directions to find them. Jeremiah, relieved and grateful he had come, put his finger to his lips for quiet, explaining in a whisper what had just happened. Jonathan followed him, silently, closer to where Gabrielle sat sobbing and rocking in the garden and the others followed, staying a bit behind when Jonathan waved his hand behind him, signaling they shouldn't come any closer just yet.

Jeremiah continued, "Gabrielle's real name is Dulci or Dulcinea and I think that's who she is right now."

Jonathan felt a chill run through him while he listened to her sobbing and learned her name. He looked around and noticed the sculptures, the Windmill, *Don Quixote* on *Rocinante* and *Sancho Panza* on *Dapple*. Breath left him and his chest ached recalling the images in the center of Brie's library ceiling painting of these identical figures.

Suddenly Gabrielle or Dulci began screaming again, "No, Daddy, stop! Stop it! When she began to cough and vomited a second time and then crawled away and began digging in the dirt again, sobbing and screaming, Jonathan decided it was time to go to her.

As he approached, he spoke quietly to her, "Dulci, it's me, Jonathan, I'm right here and I'm walking toward you, sweetheart," and, when he reached her, he knelt beside her, touching her back lightly and then stroking it gently.

She turned staring up at him blankly, as if she didn't recognize him for a time, her head twitched back and forth and she began to tremble then faintly spoke his name, "Jonathan?"

"Yes, sweetheart, it's me," and he put one hand on her face and moved the hair out of her eyes with the other and began whispering, "It's all right now...shhh...everything will be okay now...shhh...," as she drew in the spasmodic breaths and gasps that come after crying so hard.

Just when he thought she was calming a little, she began to sob, crawled away from him and cried out in the childlike voice again, "I did it...it's all my fault...Mommy hid money so we could run away but, then, she used some to buy me a birthday present and Daddy found out and wanted to know where it was...he hit her and hit her saying 'where is it' over and over...and I thought he meant my new doll "Drowsy" so I ran and got her from the lilac bush I hid her in and brought her back to Daddy but he grabbed her away from me and threw her in the woods ...and Mommy was laying on the ground in the garden all bloody and he was hitting her again and he wouldn't stop...'where is it, Lyliana, where is the money... tell me right now'...and he was hitting her and she couldn't say anything and she was looking at me and I didn't know what to do...I pulled and pulled on Daddy's arms...Stop, Daddy...and he pushed me away...and I fell down next to her head and Mommy was staring at me and then…then her arm moved and her fingers were pointing to the windmill so… I thought…I thought she wanted me to get it so I went under the windmill and dug it up...a big jar of money and it was heavy...and I brought it to Daddy so he would stop hurting her...but he took it and started screaming at her and hitting her with it over and over...and the jar broke and there was more blood all over Mommy," Gabrielle was screaming now, "...and then she didn't move anymore and Daddy started yelling 'look what you've made me do, Lyliana...look what you made me do'...and I ran to Mommy and started shaking her 'Mommy! Mommy, please wake up' then he grabbed me and dragged me into the house...and I was covered in blood and screaming I wanted to stay with Mommy but he slapped me and told me to shut up...and he stood me at the kitchen sink on a chair and put all the money, with dirt and blood all over it, into the sink and told me to stay there and wash it all and my clothes and myself until there was no more blood or dirt anywhere...and then he went back outside..."

Gabrielle's mouth was wide open, emitting sobs and moans of gaping agony until she was hoarse and no sound was left in her. She laid her head on Jonathan's chest, sobbing, quietly now and whispering, "I broke the secret...it's my fault...it's my fault."

Tears were streaming down everyone's faces as they listened to her holding onto each other in shock. No one moved or made a sound.

Jonathan had his arms around her and rocked her saying, softly but in a voice slightly more emphatic than a whisper, "No Dulci, it wasn't your fault. You were a baby and tried your best to save her...she loved you and wanted to take you away and you kept the secret all that time. But then he was killing her in the garden, even before you got the jar from under the windmill and gave it to him; and she was staring at you to tell you how much she loved you and that she knew how hard you were trying to save her but there was no way to stop him, no way at all. She was a grownup and she couldn't stop him so there was no way for a tiny little girl to do it. Brian killed Lyliana, not you, Gabrielle." He deliberately used the name Gabrielle at the end to bring her back to the present and, then, he was silent too, as she absorbed his warmth and what he had been saying to her. Gabrielle's gasps and sighs began to lessen in intensity and he could feel her body starting to relax against his.

Slowly, she became aware of her surroundings and realized Emory, Jesse, Addae and two women, one who looked familiar and the other who looked like Meg Ryan, were standing nearby with Jeremiah, who approached her with a towel and some water. She said she wanted to be out of the garden now and

Jonathan helped her to stand, supporting her because he could feel how weak she was, but she collapsed anyway and he picked her up and carried her toward the front of the house to a stone bench. There she gratefully accepted the water from Jeremiah, rinsing her mouth, drinking some and then pouring some on her hands, which were covered in dirt and using the rest to soak the towel to wash her face.

She was embarrassed to look at anyone at first, until Jesse stepped forward, took her hands and kissed them. They all gathered around her, smiling and reassuring. She looked at them now, one at a time, realizing one was Jonathan's sister Cassy, whom she had met only once when she first moved into Jonathan's house. Then she smiled at Jesse and the other woman, assuming he had finally spoken to the girl with the white dog because, even closer, she looked very much like Meg Ryan. Addae was there and she remembered she would need to tell him about her grandparents. Then she looked for Jonathan, who had gone to his car to get a jacket for her because her coat was a mess now and he thought it would make her feel better.

Jeremiah came and sat next to her taking her hand. Unsure of what he had heard, Gabrielle said to him, "My mother is dead, Jeremiah. My father killed her in the flower garden and then told me she left us," and tears came again but quietly now.

Then she began talking, quickly and hoarsely, as thoughts suddenly occurred to her. This was definitely Gabrielle speaking and she was looking at Jeremiah. "The money...the money I took from the tea canister when I ran away from my father and came to you and Nathaniel...that was the money from the garden...he made me iron it when it was dry and put it in that tea canister," and she shuddered, "it never occurred to me until now."

Jeremiah spoke gently to her, "Gabrielle, do you see what happened? Your mother helped you run away from Brian with the money she'd saved, even though it was many years later. Her energy must have been right there guiding you the whole time and that's why you picked *Don Quixote* to take with you and found the picture and Nathaniel's letter, so you'd know where to go to find us. You seem to have been sensitive to her energy your whole life."

Gabrielle was grateful to Jeremiah for the thought and felt sure he was right. It explained so many things. She felt some energy return and an awareness of everyone and everything, rushing, swirling, dizzying…beginning to fill her and she felt like she was breathing, really breathing, for the first time in her remembrance.

She was quiet and gazing far away, as Jonathan returned from the car. Everyone thought she was okay and ready to leave, but she stiffened suddenly, stood up and screamed, "No, Daddy!" and put her hands up in front of her as if she were protecting herself from a blow.

They all assumed she was having another flash-back but turned in the direction she was looking, stunned to see a silver-haired man running toward them from the woods with a gun pointed directly at Gabrielle!

Chapter 21

Brian and Gabrielle

What followed Gabrielle's scream of "Daddy, no!" sounded like a battlefield roll call...Jesse catapulting his entire body between Gabrielle and Brian, yelling "Get down, Brie," as a shot rang out. Morgan screaming "Jesse!" as he fell to the ground. Cassy screaming "Jonathan!" when she saw him reach Gabrielle and push her away as a second shot was fired in their direction. And, finally, Emory yelling "Cassy, Morgan, Addae, Jeremiah, get down!"

Brian stopped for a moment and looked around trying to locate Gabrielle again, keeping the gun moving from person to person. Suddenly, from behind Brian, came an enormous roar and cry, like an enraged wild animal and the sound of something crashing through the woods as Nathaniel came storming out of the trees and right at Brian yelling, "I'll kill you, you bloody bastard!" While Nathaniel had lost some of his bulk he still was of impressive stature and, in one motion he grabbed the arm that held the gun and wrestled with Brian to take it away.

They struggled ferociously and then fell to the ground together as a third shot rang out and Jeremiah and Gabrielle both cried out an agonizing "Nathaniel!"

Time seemed to be suspended and everything appeared to happen in slow motion as Jonathan moved toward Jesse, who lay face down and motionless on the ground. They all began to move cautiously and tried to determine whether Nathaniel or Brian had been injured by the gun going off and whether Brian still had the weapon in his hand.

The question was answered immediately when Brian jumped up, suddenly, frightening them all and still holding the gun. He was looking around wildly and began screaming incoherently, "Gabrielle...Gabrielle...it was all for you...I did it all for you and you left me...I killed your demon for you...when he found you again, I murdered him...and you didn't come back to me...I loved you and you didn't care...," and he stared for a moment.

Gabrielle stood up now and kept repeating with what little voice she still had, "Oh, God...Oh, my God...it was you all this time...these last years that I kept running because my father always managed to find me...it was you!"

Everyone was stunned and confused by the exchange and, when Brian suddenly pulled off the scarf that covered his face and threw off his hat which also removed the silver-gray hair, a handsome and much younger man screamed, "I loved you Gabrielle and you never loved me back" and, as they all gasped in shock and bewilderment, the gun was aimed directly at Gabrielle once again.

Gabrielle seemed unable to move or protect herself and, as two more shots were fired at her, it was Emory and Addae who dove toward Gabrielle, knocking her to the ground. At the same time, there was another roar as Jonathan leapt from his crouched position next to Jesse, straight at the gun, which propelled both he and the gunman backward with such force they all could hear the breath forced out of each one as they crashed against the statue of Don Quixote. There was no movement and complete silence for what seemed an endless interval. Then, Jonathan jerked backward suddenly and turned to face them with blood pouring from his torn jacket and there was a collective and horrific scream as Gideon Stone, impaled on *Don Quixote's* sword, stiffened, dropped the gun and fell forward, off the sword and onto the ground, dead.

Chapter 22

Gabrielle, Emily, Dulcinea

She was in the garden, painting, and, even from the kitchen window, Jeremiah could see her canvas held the promising colors of the bulbs he had planted, which bloomed optimistically early this year, and an incredible sunset. He made two mugs of hot chocolate with heaps of whipped cream and headed out to the terrace because he knew she must be chilled without the warmth of the sun.

She was just gathering her things and he called her name to be sure he didn't startle her as he approached. Once on the terrace, they both began to speak at the same time, then, excused themselves and asked the other to go ahead simultaneously, too, and finally just smiled at each other. Jeremiah waited for a moment and then indicated again Gabrielle should speak first.

"I'm leaving tomorrow, Jeremiah."

"Good." Gabrielle looked stricken for a moment and he continued quickly, "It's time for you to go home to Cape Cod."

"Just for a while and I'm not going to Cape Cod," now Jeremiah looked stricken and she went on, "There's somewhere I have to be and something I have to find in order to go back to a beginning."

Jeremiah waited for her to continue and then realized that was her entire explanation. "Gabrielle, what is it you're still struggling with that keeps you from returning to your home and to Jonathan, if I may ask?"

"You may always ask, Jeremiah, but whether or not I have a reasonable answer is another matter. Are you sure you want to know? It's a very long list."

"I've got nothing more important than you on my calendar for the next few decades. Tell me what's on your mind, Sweetheart."

"So many thoughts dance me around in sleepless night hours. I'm feeling much better, Jeremiah, I really am. Your friend, Dr. Schneider, has spent so much time with me and has been an enormous help in guiding me toward insight. Through his kind and patient counsel, I've found beauty in the shadows which were once menacing and turning an unfamiliar corner is losing its terror and is beginning to stimulate the pleasant anticipation of unending possibilities. And, for the first time in my life, when I draw in a breath and exhale, there is a relaxation in every part of me I have never experienced. I was always on alert before and incapable of ease, while trying to keep up the appearance of being just fine.

That being said, I continue to struggle with a number of things, like how I can integrate the mourning and sadness with the incredible loathing I feel for the man who brutally murdered my mother and happens to be my father. I do understand now why I always felt an underlying apprehension and, even when I was angry and rebelled somewhat around the age of thirteen, knew there was a clear and unspoken line never to be crossed. And then a fragment of fear overcomes me, thinking Brian isn't really gone and Gideon lied or only imagined he murdered him. Then I am ashamed of the thought and consumed by an overwhelming guilt for hoping Gideon spoke the truth. When I think of what he did to my mother, he is Brian. But, when I think about losing my whole family, I can hardly bring myself to say it, but I will suddenly feel a desire to see Jacob again and am disgusted with myself for a betrayal of my mother's memory."

She was silent for a little while but Jeremiah didn't feel it was time for a reply just yet.

"I'm also trying to understand why I had a relationship with Gideon Stone, who, like my father, was so controlling and felt compelled to murder those who disappointed them by trying to leave.

Jeremiah continued to listen and wait, because he understood how difficult this was and how much work she had done to learn to share herself with people she cared about. He watched her reach inside herself and struggle to characterize her feelings and, then, find the appropriate words to describe them. She had spent a lifetime keeping secrets and avoiding scrutiny and he admired how determined she was to accomplish this important step toward being able to trust and move on with her life.

"And, then, there's trying to accept that my hopes and dreams of finding my mother are gone. The desire to be reunited with her has had an enormous influence on what motivates my life and now I feel rather aimless and lost. I'd always hoped I would be someone she was proud of. I do think I'm beginning to find an answer to a question which has come up, repeatedly, over the last years and much more so now. I've wondered about purpose, feeling my whole reason for existing surely isn't just to paint pictures. Hearing from all the people who were touched by my mother's music and, more profoundly, by her activism and compassion, has led me to ask myself what I would want to leave as my legacy. I thought it would be caring for impoverished children in need of medical attention like the ones I met at Jesse and Jonathan's clinic but now I believe it will be about helping to protect abused and battered women and children, changing the laws which don't protect them and providing more safe places for them to go. I think it's a part of what I am supposed to do. Sorry, I seem so scattered."

"You're doing just fine, Gabrielle. Please go on."

"The biggest challenge has been learning, after all the insanity and pain and, after years of working to be just Gabrielle with no past, who Dulcinea Masters, Emily Michaels and Gabrielle Benedict, reacquainted, were, are and will be.

And then there are the choices I've made in my life and the unbearable cost to those I care so much about as a result of them. Most importantly, I can't imagine finding a way to live with what I've done to you and how, even though you say it's time, I would ever be able to leave you here all alone."

Jeremiah waited for a while and, realizing she had finished, began to speak, "I'm honored by your trust in me and your willingness to have this conversation, Gabrielle.

Let's try to put some order and coherence to some of what you've spoken of today, first, your father. He was your only human contact for nine years, as Jacob, the only memory you have of family and he did care for you and, heaven knows, gave you an incredible education. Although I feel the same loathing you do for what he did to you and our dear Lyliana, I must tell you, just as Nathaniel did, we never saw a man more turned about and love-struck with a child than he was when you were born. Of course, you feel love for him and mourn him now that you've learned of his death. It's very natural and not something for which you owe apologies or explanations. Unfortunately, the fact that you learned of his death just as you remembered what he had done to your mother makes it all hideously complex and confusing but you can't just turn love, in whatever form it has presented itself, on and off like a light switch. I would be much more worried if you were able to than the fact that you have reasonable concerns about your feelings.

And there's something I have wanted to tell you since you came up here after Nathaniel's funeral. The guitar you brought with you, the one your father gave you for your fourteenth birthday is your mother's guitar, Gabrielle. First, I was completely shocked and then moved to tears when I realized you had it in your car but didn't feel I should tell you right away. Giving you that gift must have been a very hard decision for your father to make but somewhere in him he knew it was the right thing to do because it belonged to you. And he had kept your mother's books, which she adored and it allowed you to find *Don Quixote* and us. I believe there is good to be found even in those who seem to be the worst of human beings and believe it's true for Brian.

As far as running off with Gideon Stone, he was handsome, gifted and, most importantly, domineering and controlling, which was familiar to you."

"Let me interrupt you for a moment, Jeremiah. For the three years before running away, I was with you and Nathaniel, two gentle, loving men, who were anything but controlling and gave me so much love and freedom, and yet I made the insane choice to leave."

"Gabrielle, you were just seventeen and, I realize now, quite overwhelmed with all of your freedom. None of us would want to have to reveal or explain the many, many risky and insane things we did when we were that age. And you're forgetting you did leave him, after a time, and went to France, knowing there was something wrong. Then you made a very decisive attempt to end your relationship with Gideon once you knew you were in love with Jonathan. All of your choices in relationships as an adult, your friends like Amber and David and Cara and Emory, and, certainly, your attraction to Jonathan have been with extremely loving and kind people. And, when you felt you needed help sorting out the mysteries of your past which had haunted you for so long, you knew the answers were here and returned to us. You've learned just as you should and grown into a tender and caring adult and are not accountable for the actions of those who did not."

"How can you say that? By coming here as I did, I put you and Nathaniel in danger and have taken everything from you."

"And, so, you intend to spend the rest of your life denying yourself all you deserve and staying here with me as atonement for some perceived transgression?

We all had freedom of choice, Gabrielle. Nathaniel and I knew you were in danger from someone we thought to be your father who was pursuing you. Nathaniel could have chosen to send someone else to warn us about his mistaken revelation of where you were. Instead, he chose to come himself, to storm out of the woods and stop the person he thought was Brian from murdering you. He ended his suffering, which Mary has told us was far worse than either of us knew, in such an heroic and loving way, saving the life of his precious, Darling Girl.

I know a good deal of your guilt is because I had confided in you, when you first came, that I couldn't imagine or accept the loss of Nathaniel's presence in my life. The truth is you haven't taken anything from me. No one can take away what Nathaniel and I shared for over thirty years. It's still here all around me and in my memory and heart. And I still have you, Gabrielle. You are and always have been like our own child, a blessing we never would have experienced if you hadn't chosen to come to us, and a source of great happiness and pride. Speaking of pride, you mentioned that finding your mother and making her proud has been your motivation. I can assure you, having known Lyliana for so many years, that you are exactly as she would have wished you to be, loving, talented, perceptive and empathetic.

What I need most from you now, Gabrielle, is to honor Nathaniel's love for you by living the life he saved as well and as happily as you can. That's how you can take care of me and help my heart to heal, by loving and being loved and by smiling again so I can see his love for you genuinely reflected in those beautiful eyes and in your incredible spirit.

You've been a heroine, too, at almost four years old, trying to save your mother and, at fourteen, escaping from your captivity and now you must be one again and do this thing I ask. I'm going to try, as well, to keep the memory of Lyliana and Nathaniel alive by reflecting gratitude for the privilege of having shared the precious moments we were given with them."

They were both crying now and holding each other while darkness fell over the lake and, one by one, lights appeared along the shore, as households began their evening rituals. Stars joined the breathtaking spectacle they never took for granted. "Look at the stars. Nathaniel and Lyliana are with us as surely as those stars are, 'Angel's eyes in the night sky', even when clouds make it seem like a starless night."

Gabrielle looked into Jeremiah's eyes and thought about what she had learned since returning. While Nathaniel captivated her, from the first day they found her on their doorstep, with his exuberance and unending sense of mischief, it had been Jeremiah, kind and wise, who created the family they became, quietly caring for both of them. They stood a little while longer, holding hands and watching the stars and she touched his face and kissed his cheek, no further words needed between them.

Jeremiah felt her shiver slightly, "Come inside, now, Sweetie. You're ice cold. Let's have a lovely supper and some wine while I tell you about my plans to get a home computer and learn this new internet thing. Have you used one?"

Gabrielle smiled at the thought of Jeremiah being the first among their friends to try it and confessed she hadn't, although she said Emory was looking into getting one too. She didn't know much about it yet but it made her happy to think of Jeremiah being able to occupy himself with something, knowing how absorbed he would be in no time.

⸻

Jonathan rose early to shower and dress before breakfast, in preparation for his first day back in his office. It had been nearly two months and he was glad for the resumption of routine and occupation. It was Thursday and he was returning for a short week to begin with. As he washed and the cloth went across his chest and abdomen, where the scars were healing well, he shuddered suddenly, still shaken and slightly nauseous at the memories it evoked. Then, as it always did, thankfulness for his fortunate recovery and a profound reverence for each new day came over him and he finished his shower with renewed energy.

The same sword which ended Gideon Stone's reign of terror had penetrated Jonathan's diaphragm, as he lunged at the gun and impaled them both on the sword of Nathaniel's sculpture of *Don Quixote*. Part of his two-month recovery had been coming to terms with the fact that he was responsible for the death of a man, regardless of the circumstances and accidental element of it. The taking of life was in direct conflict with what his existence and work were devoted to.

It remained such a baffling and traumatic occurrence for everyone involved. The echoes of the mournful screams and horror, from the first gunshots to the moment when Jonathan had pulled himself from the sword and Gideon fell to the ground dead, were reverberating, still, in the consciousness and dreams of each of those present that day.

After Jonathan dropped to his knees, injured and in shock, he remembered hearing Mary screaming. She ran toward them all from the driveway, yelling she had already called the police from the nearest house as Nathaniel had instructed her to do when they peered through the woods and realized 'Brian' was there and brandishing a gun. He also remembered sirens blaring in a bizarre duet with Mary's cries as she found Nathaniel and then nothing, until he awoke in the recovery room after surgery to repair a nicked artery and remove a portion of his lung damaged beyond repair.

It had been a chaotic scene, apparently, as the police arrived, guns drawn and ordering everyone still standing to get on the ground, until Jeremiah was able to explain that the shooter was disarmed and, he believed, dead. The difficult part was afterward, at the hospital, because police were very anxious to question everyone to sort out the complex explanation of what had happened.

Gabrielle remained in shock and barely able to speak, having remembered and witnessed, in an incredibly short span of time, the circumstances of her mother's murder and Nathaniel's death during his struggle with 'Brian.' Then there were Gideon's continued attempts to shoot her striking those trying to protect her, the bizarre revelation of his real identity, his confession of the murder of her father and his horrific end. And, even as the police tried to question her, she faced the possible loss of Emory, Jonathan, Addae and Jesse, who were all in operating rooms undergoing simultaneous surgeries for repair of injuries sustained during their attempts to shield Gabrielle from Gideon's rampage and frighteningly accurate aim.

It had been Jeremiah, once again, in spite of his sorrow over Nathaniel's death, who succinctly detailed what had transpired and the identities of everyone involved. His strength and goodness were inspiring to everyone during the weeks before and following Nathaniel's funeral, which had been quite a large event attended by many friends and admirers of his work. And, through all of this, he cared for Gabrielle, who remained as weakened and sad as she was when Jonathan carried her from the garden and placed her on the bench before the confusion of Gideon's attempted revenge.

Once Emory, Addae, Jesse and Jonathan were in recovery, Gabrielle had become fixated on her obligation and promise made to Nathaniel to take care of Jeremiah when he was gone. She had returned to Lake George with him to mourn the unbearable loss of Nathaniel, after reuniting with him only one week earlier.

It might have helped if Gabrielle had been with Jonathan but she chose to remain behind, with Jeremiah, while the very intensive and bewildering police inquiry was completed. The investigation quickly cleared Jonathan of any wrongdoing legally. Despite Gideon proclaiming he had murdered Gabrielle's father, no evidence was uncovered to either prove or disprove this and the question of whether Brian was dead remained unresolved, although the police had looked into it very thoroughly. It did open up an inquiry regarding Brian Master's aliases and revealed his status as a fugitive from justice for his part in the financial scandal, embezzlement and tax evasion years before.

Worst of all, Gabrielle's remembrance of how her mother died resulted in an immediate homicide investigation into the possibility of the murder of Lyliana Masters. An intensive search of the property Gabrielle had inherited, with cadaver dogs, did not result in the recovery of her mother's remains from the garden as everyone had anticipated. The most unexpected "evidence" found were shards of glass from a broken jar like the one Gabrielle described and, nearby, the buried remains of a fetus, a tiny baby boy. It was a chilling discovery because he had been "mummified" - wrapped in cheesecloth and then with two-inch black electrical tape, each wrap precisely one-half inch below the previous one. An immerging technology determined the baby's DNA matched Gabrielle's but years washed away any definitive blood from the pieces of the jar for further investigation of what happened to her mother.

Gabrielle and Jeremiah fulfilled what they thought Lyliana's wishes would be by having her brother cremated and Cara let Gabrielle know she was welcome to keep the urn or sprinkle the ashes in a beautiful and secluded Japanese garden on their property so she had a quiet place to think of Lyliana and him whenever she wished. Gabrielle chose to scatter some of the ashes there and in the garden at Johathan's, in the ocean where the garden met the shore and to the winds, reminders of her mother's love of flowers, peace and freedom.

There was a memorial for her mother and the baby, attended by more people than Gabrielle and Jeremiah had anticipated, which occurred as a result of the publicity about the shooting. There were hundreds of letters sent to Gabrielle, from people all over the country, who remembered her mother and related fond memories and tales of Lyliana as a young folk singer and activist. It was a wonderful connection to her mother and how she had lived her life. Still, Jonathan couldn't imagine how Gabrielle was enduring all the pain of so many revelations and losses all at once.

The police and courts had swiftly and easily closed each case because of the accuracy and consistency of witness accounts and the wealth of evidence and almost two months of quiet and seclusion had passed for Jeremiah and Gabrielle.

After finishing his shower, Jonathan decided to call to see how everything was going, which he did infrequently so as not to intrude on Jeremiah's mourning. His chest began to ache again with the news that Gabrielle had left just that morning and Jeremiah had no idea where she had gone. He did tell him about what she had said was her reason for going. Jonathan asked Jeremiah if there was anything he needed and he reassured him he was doing well and would make sure Gabrielle called him, making the mistake, at first, of saying "if she returned" and quickly changing it to "when."

Jonathan tried to refocus his attention on the day ahead and was determined to be through early enough to meet Morgan by five o'clock as they planned. She had been taking care of some legal matters for Gabrielle, including her legal name change to Gabrielle Lyliana Benedict.

Morgan had also obtained a legal birth certificate, social security card, and passport which had been very involved. This marked the first time Gabrielle would have authentic identification in her life and it would be a matter of great relief for her.

A week prior to learning Gabrielle was gone, Jeremiah had called Jonathan to convey he felt it was time for Gabrielle to return to Cape Cod and move ahead with her life, something Nathaniel would have wanted very much. Jonathan planned to take a ride to Lake George on the weekend, to declare his love to her and, with Jeremiah's support, discuss the situation and persuade Gabrielle to allow him to bring her home. When Jonathan told Morgan he was going to Lake George, she had asked him to carry some papers to Gabrielle for her signature. He decided not to tell her, just yet, that Gabrielle had disappeared again and intended to keep his appointment with her as if all nothing had changed.

Morgan had enough to handle right now without added concerns. She and Jonathan had gone together on the previous weekend to Boston to spend a couple of days with Jesse before they both returned to their work. He had been flown from the hospital in New York to a Boston hospital, which had an excellent rehabilitation center, so he would be closer to everyone. This was the other reason for the extended leave Jonathan had taken. He had passed much of his recovery time in Boston in order to be with Jesse as much as possible, since he had such a small family. Jesse's parents were there, of course, and were spending as much time as possible with him. In addition, Jonathan's entire family had set up a visitation schedule, taking turns being with Jesse so he always had some support and company and to keep his spirits up. Jesse was very appreciative of their generosity and good humor, which contributed greatly to his recovery.

The first bullet meant for Gabrielle, which Jesse had taken as a result of putting himself between Gideon and her, had gone into the top of his head, through his neck and into his spinal column, leaving him in a coma for two weeks and paralyzed from his lower chest down when he finally awoke. Luckily, although there were some speech and slight memory problems when he first regained consciousness, he had no residual speech or cognitive difficulties, was able to breathe on his own. He had the complete use of his hands and arms, which would allow him to return to his profession with careful modifications to his office.

Jonathan, with his builder and Emory's help had been overseeing preparations for Jesse's return to Chatham and plans were going well. He had a ramp installed in the house, doorways widened and remodeled a bathroom to include a special shower that would accommodate a lift. A guest bedroom suite on the first floor had been turned into Jesse's room and Jonathan had also worked with the builder on planning changes Jesse designed to his office and treatment rooms. They all wanted Jesse's life to be as "normal" as they could possibly make it.

Chapter 23

Jesse and Jonathan

Jonathan finished dressing and was just sitting down to breakfast when the phone rang. It was Jesse, who was speaking very excitedly. "Hey! Stop the presses! And any further work on the ramps and changes! I have some feeling in my legs. It began in the middle of the night. The doctors were skeptical, when I told them this morning, and, even though they examined me and feel they see no indications of return, I really think there's something going on. They agreed to run a few tests later today and I'm supposed to rest until the results are in and then, hopefully, go to physical therapy to see if I can stand, at least that's my plan. I'm excited but am trying to stay calm and realize it may be very limited."

Jonathan was overwhelmed by Jesse's hopeful voice and almost broke down, his emotions getting the better of him for a moment because he was fairly certain he was hearing Jesse's denial of what doctors might actually be saying. He wanted so much to encourage him but, as a physician, he struggled with knowing what was probably a more accurate interpretation of his symptoms and prognosis. He said nothing for a few moments and then, friend winning over the doctor, replied "Jess, that's the best possible news. You haven't told this to Morgan, yet have you?"

"No. And don't you tell her, please, Jonathan. I know you're seeing her tonight for dinner but I want to surprise her when she comes up this weekend. Hopefully, by then, we'll know a little more about the extent of it. Jonathan, I'm so sorry you had all that work done to the house..."

"Don't you dare think about that of all things right now! It's just handicap accessible now which is never a bad thing. You may still need it for a while, Jess," an attempt at a return to something closer to reality and, then, he softened it with "and, anyway, we are all going to be old someday. I won't say a word to Morgan. I'd cancel but the reason I'm meeting Morgan tonight is to pick up some papers she needs Brie to sign." Jonathan didn't mention learning Gabrielle had gone away again to some undisclosed location either and wished he hadn't mentioned her at all.

"How is Brie?"

"Not sure. Jeremiah was concerned but I'm planning on seeing her this weekend to convince her it's time to return home. He feels she should too." This had been Jonathan's plan before learning she was gone so it wasn't entirely a lie.

"It would be really great, finally, to have her home. How are Cassy and Addae doing?"

"Addae is recovering well from his leg wound, although he's still on crutches until the cast comes off, and they seem to be falling in love. He had been torn about whether he really wanted to return to Africa because he made a commitment to his grandparents. Now the two of them are planning on travelling to Kinshasa together and Cassy doing some cultural anthropology research there while Addae helps transition the clinic. It seems to be moving too fast but I never remember seeing Cassy happier so I'm trying to believe it's all good. It's just so strange how things turn out, isn't it Jess? Who would have guessed that my oldest friend and my sister would meet again and become a couple?"

Jesse chuckled and, for Jonathan, it felt familiar and like the start of a return to normalcy to share laughter again.

"I've got to get to the hospital. Do exactly what the doctors tell you, Jess. Don't be so anxious to test your legs you risk re-injuring yourself. I know it's easy to say but be patient a little longer. We'll get you home soon, buddy!"

"Don't worry. I'm excited to see what I can do but am not going to take any chances which could risk being back at square one. I'll call you as I find out more."

"Okay, good. Make sure you tell Carolyn to interrupt me if there's important news."

"Will do. Take care. Geez! I'm such an idiot sometimes. I was so excited to tell you about my news I didn't even ask how you're feeling. You sounded a little upset when you answered the phone. Is everything okay?"

"Everything is fine. Just still feeling some tiredness from time to time and I'm preoccupied with what to expect when I return to the office today. I'll definitely speak with you later. Bye, Jess."

"Bye. Take care of yourself, my friend. You're still recovering too, you know."

In truth, Jonathan was preoccupied with trying to figure out the reason for Gabrielle's leaving, yet again, and where she might have gone. He really wasn't ready to start solving puzzles again and, in fact, was feeling very resentful she had decided, even after all they had been through, that disappearing without an explanation was remotely understandable or appropriate. He felt exhausted and absent of the energy to deal with it all at the moment.

As Jonathan hung up the telephone and looked out of the window at a flash of red, he noticed a cardinal couple on the ground by the feeders. The male was dancing around the female and bringing her little gifts, seeds, tiny rocks and twigs. The female would accept the gifts but then move away a little. Still the male persisted. After one huge breath in and one out, Jonathan said aloud, "Okay little guys I got it. Thanks."

His first day back was even busier and more chaotic than he had anticipated, with patients greeting him and expressing gratitude he had survived the much-publicized ordeal and was able to return to his practice. Linda was the most surprising of everyone, as the seemingly tough-skinned nurse dissolved into tears at the sight of him and again several times during the day.

Jonathan did manage to meet Morgan at five. She thought he looked completely exhausted and asked if something was wrong. Again, he used the excuse of continued periods of tiredness since the surgery, probably because of a change in lung capacity. He found it very hard not to tell her about Gabrielle's leaving or to prepare her for Jesse's news so he suggested they have a quick drink instead of going out to dinner. Jonathan felt badly about not spending the time with Morgan, who must be struggling with how to handle the changes and uncertainties brought about by Jesse's injuries. She was devoted to Jesse and planned to be a part of his life, whatever the outcome, but Jesse was stubbornly insisting Morgan should not feel obligated to remain in the relationship if he was permanently confined to a wheelchair.

While Jonathan was overseeing the renovations at his home and Jesse's office, Morgan was working with her brother to make changes on her side of the house to accommodate Jesse's needs. They hadn't needed to widen doorways, had already installed an elevator in the joint foyer and a ramp outside in keeping with the architecture of the house and modified the bathroom of a guest suite as part of the original plan. The only change needed was to make the bathroom in Morgan's master suite accessible to Jesse too.

Instead of a cocktail, Morgan ordered an appetizer and iced tea and Jonathan decided to do the same as they both realized they were really hungry. Jonathan continued the conversation about the renovations, "I'm surprised those accommodations already existed in your house. I had to make quite a few architectural changes."

In answer, Morgan shared the story of an experience, early in her law career, which inspired her and her brother to create a more accessible home where anyone could be invited. "I was placed in charge of scheduling a seminar, choosing the venue and making the dinner arrangements. I hadn't been informed one of the attorneys on the invitation list was wheelchair bound, a young woman who had been in a diving accident. My choice of a beautiful old inn and restaurant was based on feedback from a few of the attorneys in the firm who had eaten there and found the food first rate and described the atmosphere as enchanting. I was greeting guests at the first-floor entrance, which did have a ramp into the main dining area of the restaurant, and realized, the moment the young woman introduced herself, there had been an unforgivable oversight. The private dining room reserved for the occasion was on the second floor, up a long staircase. She was, clearly and rightfully, a bit angry, especially since she had, apparently, called the restaurant to be sure it was handicap accessible and was told it was. She accepted the offer of several of the stronger men in the group to carry her up the stairs in her chair and, as they began the ascent, handled it with grace and humor. Once the young woman was settled at a table, I sat with her for a moment and quietly accepted full responsibility for the mistake, apologizing for any discomfort she had experienced as a result. She assured me she was just fine and I didn't need to feel so badly about it but I never forgot that awful moment and was recently reminded of it with Jesse's injury."

Now Jonathan felt even more selfish about opting for a drink instead of dinner, knowing Morgan was lonely and sad. But he noticed she looked very tired and decided it would be better if they both went home early.

What Jonathan had no way of knowing was the relief Morgan felt when he postponed having dinner with her. She had been trying to think of an excuse not to meet him but felt guilty, with all he had been going through and the importance of getting the paperwork to Gabrielle. Afraid of revealing something she was struggling with and sure either she would have broken down and told him or he might have guessed, she was very grateful not to have to stay. She hadn't even told her Aunt Sarah or brother after learning, just three days earlier, she was expecting Jesse's baby. There had been little sleep while she went from sweet elation at the thought of carrying the child of this man she adored so, to plummeting despair at the unfortunate timing and his painful declaration that she shouldn't feel obligated to be with him under the circumstances. She had wept almost constantly the last two days and postponed her work appointments as she considered alternatives and felt as paralyzed as Jesse with indecision.

When Jonathan returned home, he called Cara and Emory to see how they were doing. Emory had been recuperating from the bullet which cut across his cheek, fracturing several facial bones, and into his shoulder as he dove, with arms outstretched, to protect Gabrielle.

Luckily, he was fully recovered, except for a scar on his face, because the baby was overdue by more than a week and Cara was to go into the hospital within the next few days to be induced, if she didn't go into labor on her own.

Cara answered the phone and laughed when she heard Jonathan's voice, "You must be clairvoyant. I just decided, five minutes ago, I'm definitely and finally in labor and we're expecting to leave for the hospital soon."

She asked about Gabrielle and Jesse and, again, Jonathan said all was well and didn't tell her Jesse thought he had a return of feeling in his legs or that Gabrielle was gone again. He just said he hoped they would be able to bring Jesse home soon and Cara was glad to hear something positive and decided she would focus on those thoughts during labor. Just as she said the word labor, she had a really strong contraction and said she probably should be going. Jonathan asked for a call when the baby was born no matter the hour and Cara promised. He also offered to come to the hospital if she needed him but she could hear how tired he sounded after his first day back and insisted he stay right where he was and they'd let him know.

Jonathan made a salad, poured himself some wine and settled in the living room after turning on the radio to a public station which was playing classical music. He was leafing through the newspaper and thinking about Cara and Emory when *"Water Music"* began to play. He didn't really notice it at first until "Lentamente" began and then, like a gentle wave he experienced a complete awareness of Gabrielle, of what she was thinking and exactly where she was. He understood her intention and that knowledge instantly cheered him.

Tomorrow, after his last patient, he would find Brie and bring her home. He decided not to tell anyone where he was going on Friday. This journey was a stepping stone on Gabrielle's pathway to healing and he needed to go alone to find her this time.

Chapter 24

Gabrielle and Jonathan

Jonathan slept soundly and was awakened, Friday morning, at five o'clock, by a call from Emory. Alana, (precious one in Latin), Grace Whitaker was perfectly healthy and incredibly beautiful, according to her proud and excited father, and Cara was doing very well. Jonathan was delighted to hear Emory's happy news and, combined with Jesse's possible return home and feeling he knew where to find Gabrielle this weekend, he felt there was definitely a shift in everyone's lives in a very positive direction for the first time in months, since Gabrielle left last November really.

He told Emory he would stop by shortly, when he arrived at the hospital for rounds.

A couple of weeks earlier, Cassy helped him choose the gifts they would give Cara and Emory from both of them when the baby arrived. She had wrapped them too, creating an extraordinarily beautiful bundle tied up in yards of ribbon. As soon as he finished speaking to Emory, he made a mental note to put the presents with his bag so he would remember them when he left for the hospital.

When Jonathan entered Cara's hospital room, she smiled broadly at him and he was struck by how lovely she looked. She was someone who adored being a mother and it showed in her radiance. Looking at her, one would never guess she had given birth only a few hours earlier.

"Alana Grace is, indeed, as beautiful as Emory declared her to be and so tiny," Jonathan told Cara. Holding her reminded Jonathan of the first time he held Cassy. Early on, he had decided against including obstetrics in his family practice but sometimes, when he held a newborn baby, he wished he'd made a different choice, despite the increasingly impossible cost of liability insurance.

He sat with Cara for a few minutes while Emory went to get something to eat and to meet up with their new nanny who was bringing the boys by the hospital for a quick visit before taking them to school. While she opened the gifts, which included something for her and Emory and small things for each of the boys, she shared her feelings.

Emory had never gone with Cara for prenatal care doctor visits or stayed with her for the delivery of any of their other children. A last-minute decision to accompany her to an appointment with the obstetrician, after his recovery from his injuries and surgery, changed everything. Cara was very surprised and pleased, "During the appointment, we viewed an ultrasound of our baby daughter and listened to her heartbeat. He'd never done this or heard any of the boy's heartbeats and said he regretted always leaving me alone for all of it and not participating in the pregnancies or births. This time he was determined to be with me for the entire birthing process and he was a wonderful partner." Cara was sure this change had to do with what he had experienced during the shooting. Every so often she would see him looking at the scar on his face and he would suddenly express his love and thankfulness for being back with his family. He seemed transformed by the miracle of it all, barely able to take his eyes off the baby or Cara. "It made all the months of carrying the baby, hours of labor and natural delivery so meaningful and joyful and I feel the birth of a new closeness between us and with the boys."

Jonathan touched her hand gently, "I can't tell you how happy I am for you both. You deserve this, Cara, more than anyone I know."

Just as he needed to leave for rounds, Emory returned with the boys, who were anxious to see their mother and to have a first look at their little sister. Jonathan slipped out quietly to allow them time together.

The day went as well as it had started and Jonathan was on the road by five o'clock.

As he drove, he put on *"Water Music"* and thought, again, about the significance of it on the day he and Gabrielle spent picnicking at Footbridge Beach, in Ogunquit. They discovered they each had been having recurring dreams which were related to the music, for about a year. Just at that point, Gabrielle became somewhat withdrawn and noticeably uncomfortable and ended the conversation by suggesting they write down their dreams to share at another time. She also said they should fold them up and place them somewhere until a later date. Jonathan thought this a rather unusual request, as though she were suspicious of something or didn't trust him but had said nothing and did as she suggested. She had taken a small jar she used for paint thinner, washed it out and placed the papers in it.

A couple of days after their return to Chatham, Gabrielle casually mentioned she had left the jar on Marginal Way. At first, he felt upset about it but, then, when they returned to their usual schedules and routines, and there was no indication she was interested in pursuing a relationship, he had just forgotten it, a useless vessel drifting in the ocean somewhere far away and unreachable as his feelings for her.

Now Jonathan left to find Brie on this night when the sky was so clear stars filled every view and a nearly-full moon accompanied them. He was sure his purpose for joining her on Marginal Way again was to share the final part of her journey home.

On his way to Ogunquit, Jonathan had stopped by the hospital to see Jesse. The return of feeling he was so sure he was feeling in his legs had remained unchanged all day and Jonathan observed no movement. After a day of testing, the doctors had all agreed there was no change. They did feel Jesse could progress to the next level of rehabilitation, a course of strengthening exercises but non-weight bearing, since his scans indicated he was healing well but not completely.

Jonathan reminded him how well he had progressed and tried to reassure him by suggesting, perhaps they should ask when his doctors would consider giving him a referral to a facility near Chatham, if they felt there was one which had adequate accommodations for Jesse's needs.

Jesse was pleased with the suggestion and said he would speak with the doctors about a more definitive plan in the morning.

To distract him and change the subject, Jonathan decided to tell him where he was headed and why. Jesse quickly forgot all about his own concerns and reacted angrily, at first, unable to imagine why Gabrielle was putting Jonathan through this unnecessary pain again. Jonathan reassured him, "I know where she's gone this time and it's for something positive."

It was getting late so he gave Jesse a hug and said he would stop by with Brie, on Sunday, on their way back to the Cape. Jesse smiled at the conviction in Jonathan's voice when he casually mentioned Gabrielle would be with him.

Jonathan didn't arrive in Ogunquit until far too late to walk Marginal Way, so he picked up some dinner and checked into the same guest-house suite at the inn where they had stayed the previous June. On the chance Brie was staying in the inn as well, he inquired whether a Gabrielle Benedict had checked in. Momentary disappointment when he was told she hadn't called for a reservation didn't linger and, unlike the many other times he had searched for her, he felt no urgency or desperation.

He slept well again and rose early enough to watch the sunrise, as they had together in June, then, showered, had breakfast in the center of town and was at the beginning of the trail by eight o'clock.

He walked slowly, enjoying the crisp sea air and the beautiful, spring day. As he approached the halfway point and came around a corner, he saw her sitting high on some rocks.

She was so breathtaking, her eyes closed, face tilted toward the early morning sun and her gleaming hair loose and flying in the wind just as it had when they were last there. Sensing Jonathan's presence, Gabrielle opened her eyes, lifted her hand to her forehead to shade them and, deliberately meeting his gaze, smiled and nodded slightly as if to say she knew he would come. Jonathan quickened his pace and she jumped down and they came together in a first kiss that lingered until they both were breathless. She continued to look in his eyes, something new.

They separated, finally, and she spoke first, "I can't find it, Jonathan. I searched all afternoon yesterday and can't find it." She didn't say what she had looked for, knowing he understood. "My memory of it is so...so lost."

He led her to one of the benches and they sat down with his arms wrapped around her. "Try to remember that day and what you did. I remember it was during the picnic at Footbridge Beach. We wrote down our dreams and you said you didn't want us to read them yet and so you put them into the jar and sealed it with tape."

"Yes, that's right. And, then, when I came here for my last meeting with my clients, I decided to hide it."

"So, why?" Jonathan just had to ask, since he hadn't felt comfortable enough to when she first told him what she had done.

"I...I was afraid...I...can't remember exactly but I think I thought...I have no idea," she finally gave up trying to explain and began laughing at his expression.

Jonathan laughed too and encircled her in his arms again. She closed her eyes and tried to remember, "There was a huge, gnarled pine tree, its trunk bent almost to the ground and then curving upward to twisted limbs. Standing under that tree and looking out across the water to the right, I faced a peninsula with a couple of houses on it. On the ground to the left of the pine tree were some small white stones and then a series of very large flat rocks piled one on the other, creating a cliff to the water below."

"Wow! That's incredibly detailed and descriptive, no doubt the artist in you. I remember the tree you described from one of the days you were meeting with your clients there and I think it might be closer to Perkin's Cove than we are right now."

Now Gabrielle could picture it clearly, "You're right. It is further along and I hid it in a little cave formed by the larger rocks and protected from sight and the direct splash of the waves. Why couldn't I remember this yesterday?"

They walked until they were facing the peninsula and both spotted the tree and stones at the same time. They were excited and climbed down onto the rocks, Gabrielle locating the hiding place immediately. She reached deep into the crevice and let out a little cry. The jar was still there just where she had left it, a lifetime ago it seemed now, and she hugged it to her as they returned to the trail. They decided to take it back to the inn, get some lunch and share the contents in Jonathan's suite while they ate.

It pleased Gabrielle enormously, when they returned to the inn and she realized Jonathan had taken the same guest house rooms they had shared in June.

Jonathan opened Gabrielle's dream note while she opened his and what they read, as they settled in the sitting room of his suite and opened their lunches, caused them both to stop eating and shake their heads in confusion.

The persistent dream Gabrielle had, for the last year or so, was of someone who was always behind her and out of sight, gently whispering in her ear; then, there was the impression of being touched lightly on her hair and face and then a pushing forward toward something she couldn't see or comprehend. She would try to turn around to see who it was that urged her on and felt this was someone she loved very much but, when she would finally manage to, there was only wind and a billowing white impression, much like the curtains in her studio. And there was always the haunting sound of 'Lentamente.'

"The dream ends with a feeling of being lost and wanting

something, although I have no idea what it is and I am always crying as I wake."

For Jonathan the recurrent dreams over the last year, involved a woman whom he does not know and cannot really see clearly, wearing a flowing white gown which blows in a wind he cannot feel. She takes his hand and is pulling at him. Then she goes on ahead, turning back toward him and beckoning him to come along. Sometimes she seems upset and there is an undeniable urgency and at other times she is laughing at his reluctance and questions. Each time, at some point, she raises her arms as if leading a symphony and *"Water Music"* fills his head and she begins to fade away, as if she is vapor, with her arms outstretched toward him and a huge tear lingering on one cheek as she disappears.

They lowered the papers at the exact same time and stared at each other in bewilderment.

Gabrielle spoke next, "A few days ago, for no obvious reason at all, Jeremiah mentioned that my mother and grandmother adored 'Water Music.' Apparently, she listened to it constantly when she was pregnant with me, and joked that, when I was born, instead of crying after my first breath, I would probably begin humming 'Lentamente.' He said he had no idea what made him think of it after all these years but, afterward, while I was painting in the garden and thinking about it, I knew, so clearly, I had to come here to find the jar and learn what your dreams had been."

They left the table and sat together in a quiet embrace for a very long time, allowing silence to dance among the unanswered questions. How was it possible to share such similar dreams? Was this, like the car and finding the letter from Nathaniel, connected to her mother or, perhaps, her grandmother Diana?

Why had Jonathan felt, from their first meeting, he knew Brie on a level he did not understand? These were very much like the questions he had pondered so often about energy and soul mates and connections. But he was a man of science, used to studies backed by data and statistics, and had difficulty with things theological, theoretical and unproven. Though he had no intention of spoiling Gabrielle's comfort with the thought her mother or grandmother was with her in some way, he wondered if experiences imprinted and were recorded in parts of the brain right from birth, creating memories we aren't consciously aware of but influencing who we become and how we behave.

Needing to put unknowns aside for a while, Jonathan suddenly pushed her away, just slightly, and changed the subject, "I looked for you here, just as you asked, week after week. Then, Jesse and I went to Greenwich Village because Cara remembered you had spoken of it as if you had been there very often, to Washington Square Park, and saw your father...I mean Gideon (this was the first time they had spoken of him) chasing you. Jesse went after him and I tried to find you but we weren't able to catch either of you."

"I know you did, Jonathan. Jeremiah told me about it and I was shocked and relieved too because it explained another strange incident. As I was running away, I thought I heard someone calling my name. At first, I thought it was my father and it scared me that he knew to call me Brie and might know about the Cape but, then, it sounded like your voice and I decided it was the wind reminding me of where I wanted to be, as though it was urging me to keep running and get away. And now I know you were there and saved me from him. Was it a mere coincidence you and Jesse came just at that moment?"

Jonathan ignored the implication of her question, still trying to let go of the unanswerable, "We wanted to find you so badly and searched the whole weekend feeling angry and upset about how desperately frightened you seemed. It was awful to see you that way and not be able to help. The only good coming from it was, as Jesse pointed out, at least we knew you were okay for the moment."

"Jonathan, I'm so sorry for all the pain I've caused you and for taking such a long time to sort out this strange tale of my life, the one I shared with Dulci and Emily. Emily and I consciously shared the chapters of that story but Dulci was...was like a forgotten scrap tossed aside, frayed and unwanted, and it's taken some time and help from Jeremiah and the doctor to patch things together, sort out all the strange details and decide how they could possibly exist cohesively. The deaths and dreadful injuries were impossible to accept, at first, and then there was *Don Quixote*, in my ceiling mural exactly like the sculptures, and the book my mother loved so much."

"Yes, the book. I reread it and was so frustrated at not understanding your request until Jesse found the letter from Nathaniel. And, of course, none of us had any idea of the significance of it to your mother and about Nathaniel's sculptures and your birth name." Jonathan took a breath, reached toward her to move a lock of hair out of her eyes.

"Even though I had no idea I would end up back with Nathaniel and Jeremiah at the time I left, I knew, if I never returned or was found dead, Nathaniel's letter would be the only clue to find out what had happened to me and all the things I hadn't told you."

Jonathan winced as she spoke of being found dead and took her hands and kissed them.

"The funny thing about the book is, I had no idea you would truly be searching for Dulcinea, you and Jesse, *Don Quixote* and Sancho Panza." She laughed at the idea and then her mood changed and she said through sudden tears, "I'm very sad about Jesse, Jonathan, I feel so wretched and sorry for him and for Morgan. Their lives are inexorably changed because of his unhesitating bravery in defense of me."

Jonathan explained what everyone had been doing to prepare for Jesse's return home and tried to reassure her, "Brie, you need to come with me to see Jesse so you'll know that he's really okay. It might take him a bit to become fully adjusted to it but he never utters one word of self-pity and you know his sense of humor and determination will carry him through this. He'll be the old Jesse once he can come home and he desperately needs to see you and be reassured that you're okay."

Gabrielle felt somewhat comforted and tried not to let guilt come over her and spoil how good it was, for the first time in months, to smile and feel this happiness. Then she realized, even with the moments of sadness which came upon her less often now, she had never felt this happy or carefree.

They remained together, each entrusting their hearts to the other, making love and talking in Jonathan's rooms. They didn't talk about her childhood or the events of that awful day, no need to relive what they both knew intimately now about her life. Instead, Gabrielle shared her mother with him, all she had learned about Lyliana and, in sharing, found a permanent and perfect place in her heart and intellect for her, which was as near as she could come to remembrance. Jonathan listened patiently, wanting to know and understand everything that was significant and sacred to her.

Breakfast was strange and wonderful, as both ate ravenously, staring at each other and laughing without apparent provocation, at least to others, and needing few words.

On Sunday morning, they decided they wanted to leave for the Cape but realized they would have to travel separately.

After returning to their rooms to pack, Jonathan suggested a visit to Footbridge Beach, which was where he first knew he was in love with her. The wind blew gently through her hair and she danced along the beach, just as she had when they lingered there in the moonlight, so long ago or so it seemed.

Suddenly she looked sad again, as if reminding herself she didn't deserve this happiness, "None of us will ever be the same, Jonathan."

"So, then, we will all never be the same together." Jonathan continued, encouraging and gentle, but determined not to let her become too melancholy or, worse, feel an overwhelming urge to run. "We're all a part of each other now, Brie, all of us who shared that day. We're a new family for you. You have all the colors now for a new perspective, Brie. All you have to do is decide which direction the light is coming from.

And, of course, you still have to experience meeting my family. Oh, and then there's the cherished old Blake-family tradition of a pint-of-ice-cream-and-two-spoons conversation we need to share."

Gabrielle touched his face, having no idea what he meant by the ice cream tradition but charmed by his expression as he said it. He took both her hands in his kissing each palm gently as they turned back toward the water.

The old Jonathan would probably have proposed at this moment but something had changed in him, something he was having difficulty naming. For now, it would be enough if she agreed to return to their home with him today. More importantly, he needed to be sure she could make the promise to him that, while she would be completely free to wander or travel as she liked, she would never just disappear again, the one element of trust he still needed reassurance about from her. Then they would truly be able to begin their life together.

Gabrielle was overcome by both the significance of this moment, standing together on the beach where they had fallen in love and by the expression on Jonathan's face. For a moment she thought he might propose to her, which she longed for and dreaded simultaneously. For now, she just wanted to feel the happiness she was overwhelmed with each time she looked at him and when they touched.

"Maybe...I mean...I think I should go back to Lake George first, Jonathan, and talk to Jeremiah. I did tell him I would be returning there."

Jonathan smiled and answered her immediately, "No need to, Brie. I called Jeremiah, before I left on Friday, to ease his concern about your whereabouts and tell him I would be meeting you this weekend to bring you home. He was very happy with the idea we would finally be together and offered to pack up your belongings and send them out to the Cape immediately. I suggested an alternative plan and was saving it for a surprise but will have to tell you now or be forced to watch you fly away again, oh lovely, winged proprietor of my heart. In anticipation of your concern about Jeremiah, I invited him to drive to Chatham to deliver your things in person and stay with us for a few weeks or months, whatever suited him.

He was especially excited about seeing our home and your studio and accepted my invitation with the understanding he intended to stay at an inn or hotel and not at the house with us. I promised we'd call and let him know when we found each other and were heading home to the Cape and he'll leave to join us there in a few days. I think it will be good for him to be away from Lake George for a while."

Gabrielle was smiling and could only manage, "You are the sweetest man. Thank you, Jonathan."

They stood at the water's edge, kissing and embracing for a little while longer, reluctant to let go of the moment.

Finally, Jonathan spoke, "So many people are waiting to spend time with you to reassure themselves you're doing well and I promised Jesse we would stop by the hospital on our way home. And then there's baby Alana. She'll be expecting those nursery murals you promised to create in her honor."

He took her hand and began to urge her toward the footbridge which led to the parking lot. As they turned away from the water, they were shocked by the number of sunbathers on the beach. They had been entirely unaware of anything except each other and laughed at themselves as they crossed the bridge, holding hands and swinging their arms like children.

As they reached the middle, Gabrielle spotted some early spring flowers among the dead weeds and climbed down to pick some. Jonathan, who had no idea what she was doing and was watching for her from where she had gone over the side, jumped when Gabrielle came up on the opposite side of the bridge, approaching him from behind. "Do you know what these are called?"

Startled, but relieved she hadn't disappeared again and greatly amused by her spontaneity, Jonathan laughed and answered emphatically, "No, I don't but I have the distinct feeling you are going to tell me, as she handed him the blue and white flowers on lacey leafed stems.

"Love-in-a-Mist," she answered triumphantly.

He smiled and playfully threaded them into her hair. Then, pulling her into his arms, he waltzed her round and round, over the rest of the bridge and across the parking lot toward the car, humming a piece from *"Water Music"* which, since their discussion of dreams, had a new and lovely significance and she threw her head back and laughed, dizzy and delighted.

The sky was becoming overcast and the wind had increased dramatically bringing a chill with it. Gabrielle didn't seem to notice and continued to laugh as she separated from him and began creating her own carefree dance. But Jonathan, feeling an unfamiliar urgency and uneasiness, abruptly ended the song, catching up to her and taking her hand. He kissed her quickly and then began to guide her toward their cars, speaking gently but with a determined tone, "Let's leave now, Brie. Let's go home."

*For neither good nor evil can last forever;
and so it follows that as evil has lasted a long time
good must now be close at hand*

- M<small>IGUEL DE</small> C<small>ERVANTES</small> – D<small>ON</small> Q<small>UIXOTE</small>

Postscript

May and June 1997

"Hello! Hello? Jonathan, it's Cassy. Can you hear me? Hello?"

"Cassy? I can just barely hear you. Are you and Addae okay? We've been watching the news and have been trying to get in touch with you. I'm so glad to hear your voice!"

"We are okay but I wanted to let you know Addae is trying to book a flight for us as soon as possible. We were coming in two weeks for the wedding but his grandparents are insisting we return to the United States immediately. They are afraid of something happening to us like when Gabrielle's grandparents were killed in 1960."

"Well, we share their concern and I'm glad you're heeding their advice. Are they coming with you?"

"No. This is their homeland and they aren't budging even though Addae and his parents have tried so hard to convince them to come. I just wanted to let you know we are heading home but have no idea what the next couple of days will be like because there are so many people trying to leave and a few complications we'll explain when we see you. I'll call you when we have a flight or when we get into New York if I can't before we leave."

"Thank you for calling, Munch. Safe trip! I love you."

"Goodbye, Jonathan. See you soon!" The difficult connection made it hard to discern her state of mind which probably was a gift for now.

Jonathan dialed his parents immediately to let the family know, after thirty-six anxious hours of trying to reach Cassy, they were safe and arranging their trip home. When they heard on the news that the Democratic Republic of the Congo forces, led by General Kabila, had overthrown Mobutu, who fled into exile, and were marching into Kinshasa, they became concerned about Addae and Cassy. Now they knew they were safe and would have to wait, possibly for a few days, to hear they were safely home.

Jonathan dialed Addae's parents to be sure they knew too and learned Cassy had called them briefly just after her conversation with him.

His last call was to Gabrielle, interrupting her conversation with Cara and Emory about the library ceiling. At Gabrielle's request, as soon as she returned home with Jeremiah, Emory had hired a painter to sand and paint over the inner circle, not wanting the gruesome reminder of a day they were all recovering from to remain in Cara and Emory's home. Although Gabrielle didn't feel ready to continue her work on the ceiling, she did think it was time to begin discussing whether the rest of the work should stay or if she should redesign the entire ceiling, a new beginning. The call from Jonathan was happy news and inspired a sudden idea for a design.

"What do you think of starting a completely new painting, a subtle background of a map of the part of Cape Cod and surrounding areas encompassing where we all live and then do paintings of each of our homes where they belong on it? We could include other significant places and landmarks as well and everyone can share in coming up with memories and ideas. We could call it 'Coming Home.'"

"Oh, Gabrielle, what a moving suggestion! I can't imagine having anything else now," Cara was smiling and clapping.

Emory said more seriously, "You have no idea how relieved I am to hear this new plan. I've been struggling for weeks with how to tell you I can't bear to look up at the ceiling at all, even with the middle removed, an awful thing to say to the artist, I know. It doesn't hold the charm for me it did before, I'm sorry to say, Gabrielle."

"You don't have to apologize, Emory. I couldn't imagine returning to it either. Please have the painters come back and remove every trace of it and prepare a new canvas. I'll begin taking pictures and exploring different map views since I'm free for a while." Gabrielle hugged them both goodbye and left, wanting to go home to Jonathan and share the relief of his news about Cassy and hers about the painting.

―

Wedding guests began arriving just as the sun decided to attend the ceremony. Escorted to their seats on the lawn facing a quieting ocean, each lady was handed an unlit sparkler and each gentleman a matchbook with the initials of the bride and groom. One of Cara and Emory's sons walked along each row of chairs with a basket of sunglasses offering them instead of the umbrellas they had ready in case the weather hadn't cooperated.

A string quartet performed "Spring" from Vivaldi's "The Four Seasons" as impetuous wind calmed to welcome breeze.

Cara, with Alana on one hip, was on the lawn behind the guests directing her youngest son how to hold the ring pillow and her oldest how to unroll the white carpet once all the guests were seated.

Up on the patio, Jonathan grabbed Gabrielle's arm dragging her into a secluded corner and scaring her. "It was not my intention to do this at this moment, but afterward, and not in this way but Jesse just sent me a message saying, if I didn't do it now, he would not give the signal for the wedding to begin because he wants to be the one to announce it at the reception and make a toast." He continued dropping to one knee, "And so, Gabrielle Lyliana Benedict, will you accept this ring, which Nathaniel said was your Grandmother Diana's, as my pledge to love you forever and agree to be my wife?"

Gabrielle gasped, "What?" Then, laughing at his expression, "I mean...yes...oh yes, Jonathan, of course I will."

The Justice of the Peace had just appeared under the decorated arch and Jesse steered his wheelchair, which was decorated with flowers, to his place at the end of the aisle.

Jonathan and Gabrielle ran down the steps of the porch, stopping so Gabrielle could straighten Morgan's train. As they stepped in front of the ring bearer, Jonathan realized he hadn't placed the engagement ring on Gabrielle's finger and they started their march down the aisle struggling to discreetly get it on. Jesse was looking directly at Jonathan who had forgotten to send the message back, with an answer, so he raised a thumbs up and smiled at him. When they reached the front, Jonathan took his place beside Jesse and Gabrielle waited at the left of the arch with Morgan's Aunt Sarah.

The quartet began Pachelbel's Canon and Morgan, in a simply elegant wedding gown with flowers in her hair, began her bridal march carrying their infant son, conceived days before the shooting, as her bouquet. Her brother, Alex, escorted her and gave her away while Gabrielle straightened Morgan's train and took her baby bouquet to hold. Morgan sat in a chair decorated to match Jesse's and bringing them to eye level. The ceremony ended in front of a Crayola sunset and guests waved their sparklers as Morgan and the baby sat on Jesse's lap and they moved up the aisle and across the lawn toward their home to Beethoven's "Ode to Joy."

Jonathan and Gabrielle were enjoying coffee and hot chocolate in the kitchen when Cassy and Addae joined them. All of them were still in their robes and looked equally exhausted. The reception had gone on well into the early morning hours, a well-deserved celebration filled with laughter and love.

After Jonathan made his Best Man toast to the bride and groom, Jesse announced Jonathan and Gabrielle's engagement as only Jesse could. When the laughter subsided, he made an eloquent toast to his bride and son. Finally, he raised his glass, "To all present and those remembered and to the majority of people in the World (forgotten in the celebrity of greed and violence), who struggle and serve, love and laugh and, in one heart, wish for peace with all mankind."

As they started to think about breakfast, Jonathan got right to the point about something bothering him. "So now that we're alone, Munch, want to discuss what is going on with you two and why you've been acting so strangely?"

They noticed an obvious tenseness when Addae and Cassy were around them. Jonathan was troubled about it but there had been no time to be alone because of all the shower, bachelor party, rehearsal dinner and wedding activities and the fact that Cassy and Addae were staying with his parents. Gabrielle looked at Jonathan with a slight grimace and offered them something to drink.

Cassy asked for tea and Addae went to pour himself some coffee. While they were all distracted with drinks, Cassy watched Addae, his muscular brown body, happy yet intense eyes, with lashes no man deserved, and easy smile never failing to catch her heart and breath. Those were his obvious attributes but, when he met her eyes and winked, the overwhelming gift of feeling loved and trusting him, unreservedly, filled her with gratitude. How she adored this man! Gathering her thoughts, Cassy replied, "Yes. We do want to talk to both of you about something very important."

So, they had been right to be concerned. Gabrielle, Jonathan and Addae waited for Cassy to continue as she tried to find the right words. She glanced at Addae, "Perhaps you should start."

"I don't know how much you know about the Republic of the Congo and Kinshasa but one of the issues my grandparents, Cassy and I have been addressing are the Street Children. Starting in the early-to-mid 90s, with the wars and deteriorating economy the population of abandoned and orphaned children living on the streets has become alarming. In the 1970s and 1980s there were efforts to take care of them and return them to parents or special facilities but there are no longer any programs funded by the government, only private organizations trying to help. There are now thousands of children living this way. This probably seems like a strange story or like a solicitation for funds or help but it isn't I promise. Cassy, do you want to take over at this point or should I keep going a while longer?"

"You're doing a great job. I'll jump in when I feel I need to."

"Okay. Three or four months ago Cassy and I started going out in the streets to gain trust and determine what was needed and how we could help. About a month into it, we came across a fairly large group of Street Children, more on the outskirts, who seemed to stay together and were just different in the way they treated and protected each other. We were concerned because some of them were very young and appeared terribly malnourished. When we tried to get closer to them, they would run away and would cry out a French phrase over and over again, 'Oú est la femme aux yuex bleus?'"

Fluent in French, Gabrielle understood it's meaning immediately – 'Where is the lady with the blue eyes?' and drew in a breath.

Cassy decided to take over, "We thought it was strange and started asking questions and learned from some vendors there was a woman who lived on the streets and took care of some of the children. They said there was something wrong with her because, although she was articulate, she often stared blankly when asked questions and had a number of scars on her face and head. She had a beautiful voice they said and earned money singing to get food for the children. It took a month but we found her. She was frightened by our attempts to talk to her and looked as thin and malnourished as some of the children.

It was probably not the kindest way to handle it but, because we were afraid of losing her again, Addae used his influence to have her picked up by ambulance and admitted to the hospital in a locked ward."

Gabrielle was sobbing and Cassy kneeled down in front of her and took her hands, "It was your mother, Gabrielle. We knew it the moment we saw her eyes. No one could imagine how she came to be back in Africa and she had no idea herself at first. She remembered being covered with branches and rocks and digging her way out. She also recalled wandering in some woods and being found by a group of hunters in Canada. Don't be mad at him, but we called on Jeremiah to give us information to use to treat her. He figured out that Brian must have transported what he thought was Lyliana's dead body in his car and buried her, in a shallow grave, somewhere before he settled with Emily, I mean you, in Canada.

Since she did not know her own name and had no recollection of her family history, she became a Jane Doe.

The hospital staff assumed, because she had a slight British accent and spoke fluent French, that she was Canadian. When no family came forward to identify her, she was adopted by a church whose members helped her establish a new life and identity.

While she seemed intellectually sound and was obviously educated and well-spoken, she had no memory of her life beyond Africa at thirteen or fourteen, except for occasional frightening flashes and dreams she didn't understand. She was chosen to go with one of the church's groups who were bringing food and healthcare supplies to the Republic of the Congo, presumably because of her apparent familiarity with the area. She seemed to feel it was her native land and appeared happy and content being there. At some point, she disappeared but they were required to return to Canada and she ended up where we found her, in the streets of Kinshasa.

We didn't tell you because we had to work with her to gradually introduce who she was and what had happened to her and restore her health. She was very fragile and asked for privacy, which, given the intrusive nature of treatment, we felt very strongly about honoring. Addae and I, along with a great team, worked with her every day for two months and Jeremiah's contribution was invaluable in reconstructing her life for her. We asked him not to say anything because we had no idea how long treatment would be and because of her request for privacy.

She's here Gabrielle. We brought her back with us, which is what caused the delays in getting out. But she wanted us to talk with you first so you would understand she probably won't know you and to be sure you won't feel hurt or disappointed. We have slowly shown her pictures and let her know who people are and what role they played in her life. She understands everything but that's not the same as remembering and she is very nervous. Jeremiah is with her and, while she didn't recognize him, there is some indication his presence is comforting to her.

Addae can explain the complex clinical component and what they found on tests and imaging later. She's been here for two weeks, waiting for the wedding to be over because she didn't want to distract from it, so you need to let us know when you feel ready to see her. And, just so you know, she and Addae and I have started founding an organization for the children. Jonathan said nothing and just held Gabrielle as she listened and sobbed, all the memories of what she thought was her mother's murder causing her to rock and moan.

"The reaction you're having right now is just what we anticipated and the reason we didn't just bring Lyliana right to you. We wanted to surprise you so badly but knew it would be too much of a shock for you and too upsetting for your mother to see. We had to do this gently and not be in a rush." Addae spoke honestly from a doctor's point of view.

Cassy brought her tissues and water and she and Jonathan looked at each other, recalling the awful scene in the garden more than a year ago. "This is really such a wonderful and happy gift no matter how difficult it might be in the beginning."

After a very few minutes, Gabrielle sat up and pressed the inside corners of her eyes with her index fingers to stop herself from crying and felt a calming energy run through her, "I'm ready. I've never had any memory of my mother, except flashes like in the garden, and she has none of me so I just realized we're starting in exactly the same place. I don't want to spend another moment without her in my life."

"Do you want to be alone or have us in the room with you?" Jonathan finally spoke.

"Cassy said she seemed comfortable with Jeremiah, so why don't we have him stay with us? Where are they?"

"They're at the hotel."

"Do you think she'd be comfortable coming here or should I go there?"

"I'll call and ask." Addae called. "Lyliana said she would like to come to your home so Jeremiah is bringing her in a little while."

Gabrielle jumped up to look in a mirror, forgetting, until she saw herself, they were still in their robes and none of them had eaten. Laughing, they all ran upstairs to quickly wash and dress as Jonathan said he would call out for a food delivery.

The moment Lyliana entered the house, she and Gabrielle ran to each other, holding hands and staring into identical eyes and faces, then tentative hugging and tears. Gabrielle led her out the back door to her studio. Jeremiah was crying and didn't see the need to follow them so he joined Jonathan, Cassy, and Addae as they all sat, anxiously, wishing they could know what mother and daughter were saying to each other.

Thirty long minutes had passed when the delivery driver rang the doorbell.

Then a sound they couldn't identify began, quietly at first, then louder, until they realized Lyliana and Gabrielle were singing the folksong Gabrielle often hummed or sang when she was painting, the Tom Paxton song "Whose Garden Was This?" singing together in perfect, natural harmony.

ACKNOWLEDGEMENTS

First, loving thanks to Robert, my husband and IT guru, who waited for each chapter, sometimes impatiently but always with enthusiasm and an invaluable eye for the smallest detail. To my *wombmate*, Carol Stockton, who turned images in my head into the book cover, with the inspiring art of her photography and technical skills, love and gratitude for sharing creative collaboration and laughter. To Nancy Shapiro, the first to read the draft, for embracing the characters and limitless words of "DGD" support. Thank you to my daughter, Kirsten, and son, Erik, for your love and encouragement. My thanks to family, friends, fellow book club members and strangers for early manuscript readings and honest critiques.

Thank you, George Frederic Handel, Antonio Vivaldi and the birds on the feeders for each exquisite note playing in my yard, on my iPad and in my head as I wrote.

I am grateful for Internet sources like Google, Wikipedia and Kindle for making some of my research expedient and convenient but want to acknowledge Public Libraries for Dewey Decimals, the feel of opening the cover and turning the pages of paper books, for book stacks and for the quiet echoes in history-rich scholarly places.

My favorite research was conducted while revisiting Ogunquit, Lake George, Woodstock and Cape Cod and each trip restored a sense of purpose and nourished me.

My gratitude to the Interior and Cover Design Teams of Palmetto Publishing for incorporating my ideas and numerous edits; and especially Stephanie Kenyon, Project Manager, for her patience, attention to detail, prompt responses and perceptive communications.

And special thanks to Ted Strayer, D.O., for caring for my health.

"Angel's eyes in the night sky" from *Water Music*, Collected Thoughts, Unpublished © 2003 by Judith McVety.